T0110454

DOWN HIS RIVER OF DREAMS

THE STORY OF THE
FIRST AMERICAN
BOY SCOUT

by
David L. Wiemer
Winter Haven, Florida

Illustrations
by

Daniel J. Wiemer
Red Wing, Minnesota

Order this book online at www.trafford.com
or email orders@trafford.com

Most Trafford titles are also available at major online book retailers.

Print information available on the last page.

ISBN: 978-1-4120-2200-2 (sc)

Trafford rev. 09/07/2018

North America & international
toll-free: 1 888 232 4444 (USA & Canada)
fax: 812 355 4082

ABOUT THE AUTHOR:

At age 13, in 1941, David L. Wiemer, of Troop 25 in Burlington, Iowa,
was his Scoutmaster's first Eagle
Scout. When he "retired" from Scouting, he had
earned 41 merit badges and had the Silver Palm
pinned to his Eagle Badge.

He served four years on active duty with the U.S.
Navy, on Guam and in the Korean waters.

His BS degree, from Iowa State in '55, was in
Landscape Architecture. His MS degree was from the University of
Illinois. He designed and built parks
and directed park operations. In 1990, after 35 years
of public service, he retired from the Rockford,
Illinois Park District. He now lives in Winter Haven, Florida.

In the distant past, in Illinois, Iowa and Missouri,
the author, walking construction sites, creek banks
and plowed fields, found many long-lost
arrowheads. When he rolled one of those old points
over in his palm, he always asked: "I wonder what
kind of story this one could tell?" Who knows?
Maybe the story of the First American Boy Scout was
one of them.

ABOUT THE ARTIST:

Dan Wiemer, the artist,
is the son of the author. He lives in
Red Wing, Minnesota. He grew up in Rockford,
Illinois, with a love of nature.

Dan studied art at Iowa State University, receiving
his BA Degree in 1986, specializing in graphic
design. Following graduation, he worked for a
Minneapolis design firm. Three years later he
began his freelance career. His studio and frame
shop are in his home.

Some of Dan's clients are:
Paul Masson Wines, the St. Paul Chamber
Orchestra, Pillsbury, Baker's Square Restaurants,
and Chippewa Water.

Dan does commercial illustration as well as fine
art. He contributed the cover and the black-and-
white illustrations within the book.
Water-color is his favorite medium.

ACKNOWLEDGMENTS:

To Wanda,
my wonderful and patient wife.
Thanks.

Also, to you, Daniel, my son, for
your superb art-work. It makes
the book come alive.
Thanks, Dan.

And, to my editor, Blair Ray, of
Winter Haven, Florida. You
are the best of the best.

CONTENTS

INTRODUCTION

This
is a story of a
Native American
who had to have answers
to his questions. To satisfy his
curiosity, he embarked on a jaunt
south, down his River of Dreams. His
experiences were beyond his wildest
expectations. He lived his dream. He
left Rockford, Illinois, as a boy, and many
moons later returned with the maturity of
a man. If you had lived in his time and heard
his stories, you would have doubted they
were true, although evidence
found many years later
would have cast away
all your doubts. Now
read and enjoy.

David L. Wiemer
Winter Haven, Florida

-FOREWORD-

"Unusual, yes, but why?" Professor Daniel Norman asked his archaeology students that summer session at Rockford College. The students who were gathered together in the classroom that August morning were also in search of answers, but the questions that needed answers were not even asked. The questions came from their "dig," their archaeological excavation, in Beattie Park, in downtown Rockford, Illinois.

It was a work session, a hands-on class, and the work had seen many cubic yards of dirt moved in the heat of the day. The excavation project started in mid-July. The students, all twelve of them, had labored long and hard for their class credit, and the five young women in the class had shown by example that they could work just as hard as the men of the crew. In fact, if the truth be known, they probably worked harder.

Dr. Norman wanted the dig to be meaningful and rewarding to the students. He also wanted it to be a scientific project of quality. He hoped the results would be of such magnitude that they would be worthy of a paper and a later presentation at the Twenty-fifth Central States Archaeological Symposium to be held in Chicago the following winter. A presentation at the meeting would be published in the proceedings. It would be one more credit to his professional involvement in the field of archaeology. Naturally, he wanted credit for himself, but, as with most archaeologists, he would be much happier if there were a discovery that would fill in one of the many voids in the history of early man in North America. A North American Rosetta Stone? That would perhaps, be improbable, but dream on. In any event this dig had to be pursued in a credible, scientific manner regardless of what it produced for the labor expended.

Professor Norman called on his friend Bob Carlson, a local surveyor, and persuaded him to tie in the dig to the Township and Section in which it was located. The professor told his students they would be excavating the large, conical Indian burial mound in Beattie Park, on the west bank of the Rock River, in downtown Rockford. Some of the other mounds in the park were larger, but they were effigy mounds, representing a lizard and a turtle, and there would probably be no burials or artifacts located within them. At least that had been the history of other such mounds across the country.

Referring to the Winnebago County Plat Book, Professor Norman knew his mound was located somewhere in the southeast quarter of Section 23, but he must locate his dig exactly. Science demanded it. Yes, archaeology is a science: it is the study of ancient life. Dr. Norman didn't know what would come from this mound in Beattie Park, but he did know good records must be kept. Of course the first record was the exact location of the mound.

Bob plumbed his transit directly over an "X" he had cut into the curb on the south side of the park some twenty-five years earlier. Looking through the scope, he shouted to Professor Norman, "Dan, move the range pole a little to your left. You want this dig to be right on the money, don't you?" Looking through the transit, he could see that the pole had to go another two inches or so. While he continued looking through the scope, Bob held out his right arm, then pushed his fingers out even further, motioning Professor Norman to move the pole just a little more to the professor's left. "Stop!" Bob shouted. "You're right on the line now. Next we'll use our steel tape and measure ninety-six feet on this line and we've got it." They measured down the line, and, with a little dirt removal, they hit Bob's old steel pin exactly on the mark.

Now Carlson set up his instrument directly over the pin that marked the center of Section 23. He remembered well driving in that pin so many years ago, replacing the original stone that had been lost when they built the Beattie mansion. The old house had been torn down about 25 years ago, just after the Beattie sisters bequeathed their land to the Park District. The land was about a block square, in downtown Rockford, and it contained the Indian mounds.

The professor drove a new pin into the ground at the exact point that Carlson had given him. The line from old pin to new pin would, be the baseline for the dig, and all measurements would be made from this new line. It would tie in the map of the dig to the section in which the students would be working. The bearing of the line from the center section pin to the new pin was exactly, South 45 degrees 0 minutes East, and the distance measured 120 feet. The line passed the mound on the south and stopped just short of a big white oak tree.

"Let's start digging," one of the boys said.

"No," Professor Norman said emphatically. "You know better than that. Let's just sit here on the grass for a moment and go over the steps of scientific archaeology."

They all sat down in the shade the oak canopy provided. Professor Norman then proceeded: "We now have our line and can orient our dig in relation to the compass, but what have we left out?"

Mary, the brightest girl in the class, responded, "We don't know the elevation of the mound, so we really can't draw a complete map of the site."

"Correct," said Professor Norman, "but how do we find out about elevations?" he asked, as he looked over the group of students.

One of the boys came up with a quick reply: "Have Mr. Carlson find it out for us; he's a surveyor."

"That's a good answer," the professor said, then added, "It's really quite a logical answer, too, and that's exactly what we'll do." Looking over the heads of the students, Professor Norman called: "Bob, would you come over here for a moment? We need some more of your professional advice."

Carlson walked away from his transit and over to where the students were sitting in the shade, seeking some relief from the morning heat that had already pushed the thermometer towards 90 degrees. "It's going to be a hot one today!" he thought. "What's on your mind now, Dan?" Carlson queried.

"Bob, in order to properly locate our dig, you've given us a line to go by; that's O.K., but now we need to find the exact elevation of our mound so we can draw an accurate contour map. Can you tell the students how one would go about doing that?"

"Why, that's easy," Carlson said. "First, there must be a standard of control, and the U. S. Government took care of that years ago. You see, the 'USGS,' the United States Coast and Geodetic Survey, established monuments across the country and they all have a known elevation above average sea level. I believe our closest monument is a brass cap located on the east steps of the old post office down on South Main Street. All the surveyors know where these monuments are located. What we do is run a level circuit and then set benchmarks of our own. We then record our elevations in our own field books for later use. I'm sure I can find an old one I've set that's fairly close by."

After flipping a few pages in his worn book, Carlson said, "Why, my closest benchmark is an 'X' I cut into the foundation of the Methodist Church, just across the street. I remember now. I chiseled that mark in that red sandstone almost thirty years ago. I believe I can see it now," he said, as he pointed over to the corner of the church. "I'll set an elevation, a datum point, for you here in the park. Having one close by will certainly make it easier for you to draw your map. I'll set it on the Navy Monument over there. Then you'll have one right next to your dig and you can use it as your reference point. How's that?"

"Good idea," said Professor Norman. "Bill, why don't you help Mr. Carlson with the rod and bring the elevation in? It'll just take a few minutes."

It was all quickly done, and now it was time to discuss the particulars of the dig. "We'll mark off two-yard squares to cover the mound and beyond," said Professor Norman. "We'll set our first grid line through the center of the mound perpendicular to our base line. Next we'll line up four squares on each side of it. We'll go parallel to the base line so we have exact squares. When we do this we'll set a pin at each point of intersection and at the perimeter points, too," said the professor. It took two holding the tape and one setting pins, and in about ten minutes it was done. The mound was almost eight feet high and the 36 squares covered the 42-foot-diameter mound with a little flat ground to spare.

"By the way, Bill, what elevation did Carlson give you as our datum?" Professor Norman asked.

"He said he'd make it easy, so he gave us a mark of 720.00 MSL. That's above 'Mean Sea Level'," Bill reported.

"O. K.," The professor said. "Now, let's take a reading on each of the grid corners so we can draw an accurate map of our mound as it now exists."

The students, using their level and their rod, took a reading on the ground at each red and white chaining pin. That was at each point of intersection as well as at each grid point around the perimeter. There were sixty-four locations. With a little subtraction from the known height of the level, they could now come up with the elevation at each point of the grid. Now their contour map would be easy to draw.

Professor Norman congratulated the students on their fine work and said, "When we're all through, we're going to replace the soil exactly as it is. The mound will look the same a year from now as it does today, even though we are now about to dismantle it completely."

4

Squares were assigned. Levels were set. Shovels were ready. The sifters were also ready, for not one piece of evidence should be missed. Every item in the mound had to be found and interpreted in context with every other item, both horizontally and vertically. Quality was to be of a high standard. The final class grades would depend on the exactness of each student's work. They would dig down on their squares, level, about six inches at a time. It would be slow work.

The digging began at about 11:00 AM that hot morning of July 14th.

Dr. Norman explained to the class that he had obtained permission to dig from the Park District, from the Illinois Department of Historic Preservation and from the U. S. Department of The Interior—Bureau of Indian Affairs. He also explained that this was originally Winnebago hunting territory but that the Winnebagos had been pushed out over a century-and-a-half ago. Some had been assimilated into the Sac and the Fox Nations west of the Mississippi and then settled on reservations in Indian Territory in Oklahoma. A small number of the Winnebago Nation, however, had been moved to a reservation in northeast Nebraska along the Missouri River. The professor told the class he had contacted the chief of these contemporary Winnebago Native Americans. They also wanted to know about their ancestors—how long ago they were buried and what kinds of cultural materials were buried with them. These Native Americans were also interested in their heritage. He said they had given their permission to dig. The only condition was to dig with respect and allow a ceremonial reburial of any human remains that might be found. Professor Norman had responded positively to that request but with a condition that the reburial take place only after any remains found had first been examined by qualified physical anthropologists. Everything was in order, he told the students.

They started the dig, proceeding carefully. Dr. Norman closed his eyes, acknowledging the Native American blood running through his veins. Professor Norman was one thirty-second Native American because five generations ago he had a Native American grandparent. He didn't know much about his ancestry, but he did know that his blood came from Illinois stock sometime in the late 1800's, well over a century ago. Somehow, over the years, that part of the professor's heritage had been lost. For all he knew, he could be part Winnebago! Yes, if a burial were discovered, it might even be of his lineage. However, because archaeology was his profession, the dig must go on. He decided the students did not need to know his very personal connection to this important project. Dr. Norman shook his head to clear it, returning to the moment.

Dr. Daniel Norman, Head of the Department of Anthropology at Rockford College, had all the necessary professional credentials. He oversaw his student's work, carefully directing them. He was almost fatherly to them, encouraging and instructing their slow digging and even slower sifting, for nothing must be missed. The students were assigned to their squares. Three of the squares, meeting the others at the corners, were cut into in order to view the sides of the cut. Dig, wheelbarrow, sift, wheelbarrow, then dump. It was monotonous work, but there were two strokes of good fortune. First, rain three days earlier made the digging a little easier, and second, the canopy of oak leaves shielding the site from the sun made the work more bearable on that hot July morning.

A few small flint chips and a small, white, flint arrowhead were found in the early sifting. Some charred animal bones were also recovered. Dr. Norman concluded they must have been carried in with the fill that had been used to build the mound those many centuries ago. The items, of course, were tagged, bagged, and saved; they would be studied later in the laboratory.

After each day of digging, the mound was covered with a plastic tarp held down with concrete blocks. At this point, as with any excavation, there are two potential enemies: One is vandalism and the other is rain. It was for that reason the students took turns watching the dig during the night to protect it. The site was very much exposed, being in downtown Rockford where all sorts of traffic went by. The site had to be protected, both from the rain and from any possible damage from unwanted intruders. Each student took his or her watch turn at night. The students were diligent and all went well.

On the tenth day of digging, with little having been found, the students struck pay dirt. After another six-inch lowering in a grid on the south side, one of the students discovered the top of a clay pot. Now progress would be slow. Fortunately, the pot had been made of good clay, tempered with ground clamshell, and fired fairly hot. Digging deeper around the pot, the students discovered that it had been crushed and had settled in on itself. It had probably been filled with food for the interred. Virtually hollow, the pot had simply succumbed to the weight of the overhead mound, broken, and been reduced to a fraction of its former shape. It was evidence, though, and care must be taken in its removal. All the pieces must be recovered so it could be reassembled. The material that had been inside, whatever it was, was put into a plastic bag, labeled, and set aside for future research. Its location was recorded on the site map the students were keeping.

"Now is the time to excavate slowly and carefully," Dr. Norman cautioned the students. "A pot is usually an indication that bones might be close by."

He barely had the words out of his mouth, when one of the girls gave a loud shout, "Hey, everybody, I found him!" Yes, she had discovered toe bones at the edge of her square.

Smaller tools were needed for this painstaking work: small steel spatulas and even smaller dentist's picks were used to cut into the soil around the bones. The work progressed up the legs of the Native American who had been buried those many centuries ago. Brushes cleaned excess soil from the bones, which shone a greasy white.

The professor then noticed something completely overlooked by the students. "Stop your work for a minute and all of you come over here," he said. "I want you to take a look at a feature that's hardly noticeable. Look carefully at the shinbone." He then pointed to a small ridge about one-third up the right tibia, and said, "At an earlier time in his life, this Indian broke his leg badly. It was a break clean through; as you can see, it healed remarkably well. Someone with medical knowledge must have set it and seen to its healing. Quite remarkable, don't you think? Let's take a picture of it just as it is in the ground." "Snap!" and the picture was taken.

"The bones are in pretty good condition," Professor Norman observed. "That's probably because the body had a thin layer of blue clay placed upon it at burial time and also because the body was deep enough in the mound to be below the frost line, even in the coldest of our Rockford winters." They were now down well over six feet.

"We must protect it as we go," cautioned the professor. "After we've cleaned the bones as clean as we can get them with our brushes, we'll remove them and wash them carefully with soap and water. Next, we'll rinse them and allow them to dry. Then we'll use the clear liquid preservative I brought along. Brush it on the bones and don't use it sparingly—cover everything. I was anticipating we might find something of value," he said reverently.

The excited students dug deeper and carefully brushed the soil away from the skeleton, applying the clear preservative to the bones after they were cleaned. All soil from the mound went through the sifter as the soil was removed. The sifter was producing some interesting items, too. More white flint chips were recovered. More pieces of baked clay and potsherds were being recovered from the soil near the rib cage. Some small charred fragments of organic origin were also found associated with the potsherds. A large quartz crystal and a cube of lead ore were also found adjacent to the waist of the skeleton. As they went deeper, they found a row of large white shell beads, all about the size of a quarter. It was a long row and there was a turquoise teardrop pendant at its center. The students also found a small lump of green copper ore. There were almost too many different items for one burial, but there they were. A large shark's tooth also puzzled them. All the artifacts were cleaned, photographed in place, removed, further cleaned, then tagged and bagged to be evaluated later.

The skeleton was prone on its back and oriented exactly north and south. What was unusual, Dr. Norman said, was that the head was to the south. As the students cleaned the soil from the old bones, working up the rib cage, they saw that the hands were crossed over the chest, folded, the left over the right. As the thin, stainless steel spatulas and the stiff brushes cleaned the soil from the ancient bones, they saw something white come into view under the fingers. The ancient Native American was holding a large, white shell in an almost reverent position. "Leave it where it is," cautioned the professor. "Clean up around it, but leave it where it is. Photographs must be taken to accurately record and document what we have discovered," Dr. Norman said this in a soft, empathetic voice that the students noticed was not like his regular voice at all.

After the photographs of the hands and the shell were taken, the bones were removed, cleaned, covered with preservative and allowed to dry. They were then put into respective plastic bags and labeled, left and right. The white shell was now in plain view. It was nearly rectangular, about five inches by two inches. Dr. Norman commented, "That's quite a large shell to have come from the Rock River, and pure white too . . . ." He said it rather questioningly.

The white shell was smooth and polished, and after the early cleaning, it shone with an iridescent glow, even in the dark shade of the oak trees. "We must preserve it well," said the professor, "for an old shell, when exposed to the elements, may tend to crumble."

The students cleaned the soil from along the edges, which raised the shell on a small pillar of dirt. Hardly a breath was taken. The students were quiet as the soil was carefully cut away from under the shell. Finally, with a nudge, it was free.

Professor Norman gently picked up the shell, turned it over, and washed it in the bucket of clean water. On closer examination he was surprised at what he saw. There were markings on the surface. "This is amazing," he said. "It's almost as if our Native American had left us a message. We must now preserve it and examine it more carefully later." Some of the clear preservative was brushed on the shell. After it was dry, it was carefully put into a plastic bag, then into the small, hinged, red plastic lock-box for safekeeping and for further study. It was mid-afternoon now, and the students were in their eleventh day of excavation. They had uncovered some unique and interesting ancient artifacts. They wondered if there would be more surprises. After the excitement of finding the shell had subsided, they went back to work with their picks, spatulas, and brushes and resumed cleaning the soil from the bones. They were removing the soil carefully. It was slow going. At the right waist of the skeleton, adjacent to the pelvis, a portion of a dark, smooth stone appeared. As the soil was carefully cleaned from the object, a smooth, black, circular stone about three inches across and three-quarters of an inch thick was exposed. "It's a discoidal," Professor Norman exclaimed.

"What's a discoidal?" one of the students asked.

Professor Norman answered, "It's an old gaming stone; you know, ancient north Americans had their games too. They rolled these small, flat, round stones across bare ground and had various competitions with them. This one is small, but they come in various sizes. Some are even indented on the sides." It was black hardstone and ground perfectly round, a true work of prehistoric art. The students never expected such surprises from this mound of earth that had rested on the west bank of the Rock River for who knows how many centuries. The discoidal, the "chunky" stone, was also put into the plastic lock-box.

"Let's continue with our work," said Dr. Norman hurriedly. "We still have a long way to go before it gets dark."

Next, at the right side of the pelvis, they found a little, black clay pot, no bigger than a closed fist, and it was full of soil. It would be checked later. It was placed with the other artifacts in the lock box. Then a white flint knife was found.

The rib bones were removed, cleaned, allowed to let dry, covered with preservative, then put into a plastic bag. The ribs had settled in against the backbone, but they were all easily removed and tagged. Then a rosy-white arrow point appeared. They cleaned it with brushes, just as it lay. Dr. Norman just stared at it. It was only an inch-and-a-half long and about three-quarters of an inch wide. It was perfect, with a notch at the center of the base and a notch on each side. "It's a three-notch Cahokia point," exclaimed one of the students. "That it is," said Dr. Norman. "Let's take a photo of it in place, then tag it and keep going," urged the professor.

"Wait a minute, what's a Cahokia?" one of the freshman students asked. Another answered quickly. "You know—it was a large Mississippian village located seven or eight miles east of Saint Louis, in the American Bottom. The high point of its culture was about 1050 AD. This particular type of arrow point was named after that culture because so many were found there."

"Very good, Kathy," said Dr. Norman. "But let's keep going."

They removed the skull, the backbones, the pelvis and finally the large leg bones. At his feet they found another pot containing many small bones. Now the space where the old Indian had lain was finally bare.

"Let's go another couple of inches deeper to make sure the old boy wasn't on top of something that we might have missed," admonished Dr. Norman. "Also, check the soil profile for any changes in color." So it was back to digging for the students.

"You, Tom and Mary, each dig further down along the side where the skeleton lay so we can see if there might be something more below." Although they were already ninety-two inches below the original top of the mound, they had to go deeper.

Professor Norman's instincts were right; below the left waist, in the blue clay, a group of beautiful, small, white, triangular arrow points came into view. They were all pointed in the same direction, slightly to the west of north, bunched together as if someone had carefully placed them there. After final cleaning, seventeen points were discovered. They were photographed in place, removed, labeled, and put into a plastic bag and then into the red security box. The blue clay was now gone. Original soil now covered the bottom of the pit where the Indian of old had been buried. The work was complete. The mound had been thoroughly excavated. Daily records had been kept, and photographs had been taken of all the important findings. Dr. Norman stressed how important that was, because now only a shallow hole existed; everything was excavated, gone, as if nothing had ever been there. However, a map, a diagram of all the finds existed, so all was not lost. Now the artifacts must be taken to the laboratory for cleaning and fine-tuning. Each item had to be interpreted in context with each other item.

On Friday, the class reassembled in Beattie Park. It was cleanup day. The wheelbarrows buzzed back and forth, full on the way to the new mound and empty on the trip back to the dirt pile. It didn't take the students long to return the dirt to its original location. The students, like the early Indians before them, trampled the soil in thin layers to compact it. They went by their contour map, and the mound looked virtually the same as it did when they had started their project, except that they had some soil left over. Professor Norman told his students, "Don't you know, you always come up with more dirt than you took out of a hole or from a mound? There's a logical reason, too, so ponder on it. It's also a pretty good test question, so you'd best find the answer to it." He then told the students to spread the remaining soil completely over the mound as evenly as they could, but with the most on the top. "We'll come back next week and sod the mound," he said, leaving them. It had been a long, hot day.

Much later on that July evening, in the coolness of his air-conditioned study, Professor Dan Norman sat in his recliner. He leaned back, closed his eyes, and slowly recalled the events of the last twelve days. He thought, "The students did a very respectable job and they must be rewarded."

In his chair that evening, the professor could come up with only one word. "Interesting, yes, mighty interesting. No," he thought, "perplexing might be a better word. I know what we found, but interpreting it will be quite a complicated task."

"Why?" he asked himself out loud. "Why the Cahokia points and such beautiful ones, too? Why an Arkansas quartz crystal? Why a shark's tooth? Why a little clay pot with four, three-inch-long, round teeth inside? What kind of teeth and why an oyster shell too? Why the little piece of green

11

copper ore and a cube of galena ore? Why the long string of white shell beads with the little triangular turquoise pendant? Why that neat little pile of triangular arrow points under the body, and why such a large and beautiful, incised shell amulet?" There were just too many questions that needed answers.

The answers to the professor's questions were slow in coming that evening. In fact, before they did come Dr. Norman dozed off.

Resting comfortably in his recliner, the professor had a wonderful dream of the Native American they had just excavated and the items they had found. The artifacts reminded him of his earlier experiences, when he was completing merit badges on his way to becoming an Eagle Scout, many years ago, in Boy Scout Troop 25, back in Burlington, Iowa.

He wondered about this early Native American—what story could this early "Boy Scout" tell?

-1-

On this bright, cool, crisp, spring morning, Little Red Feather made his usual monotonous trip to the flowing spring. It was his duty, early each morning, to fill the two large, brown, cord-marked clay pots with clean, clear water.

The boy's father, Flowing Spring, had placed boulders around the source of the water that always flowed from Mother Earth. This raised the water level of the spring and formed a small reservoir. It was easy for the boy to dip out the clean, cool water that sustained life for the family.

The water from the spring had a fresh taste and always quenched the Indian boy's early morning thirst. The boy's mother also cooked with the water. She made the early meal by placing small, hot stones from the fire into a large clay pot containing water about four fingers' deep.

She had long ago learned from her elders that by using sticks to place and replace small, hot stones in the pot, she could make the water hot enough to bubble. After she had accomplished the bubbling, she placed a large handful of ground acorn meal, mixed five-to-one with little brown seeds, into the hot water. When she added the meal, the bubbling stopped, so she added more hot stones to get it going again. After a little stirring, the thick, dark-yellow porridge was ready to eat. It was not much, but it was enough to provide the early morning nourishment needed by the boy, his father, his mother Blue Damsel Fly, his little sister Otter Tail, and his two younger brothers.

Little Red Feather looked up in search of the faint, distant honking that he could just barely hear. He saw a long line of high-flying geese going north. He was glad the long, cold winter was just about over. He would begin his twelfth year early this spring, at the time of the Green Moon, when the tree with the little pink flowers would be in bloom.

Before the coming summer ended, he would have to pass his test to become a man. The test would require strength, silence, endurance, and ingenuity. The usual test was to live alone in the forest or on the prairie for one full moon period. The time would be a complete moon cycle, from full moon through no moon, then back to full moon, as all of the men of the clan had done. Some had done it better than others, for he had listened to their tales. From these stories he had mentally recorded the best methods of providing food, clothing, shelter, tools, and weapons—all needed for survival. He knew he would survive the ordeal, pass his test, and become a man when it would be required.

He had learned his hunting skills from his father and from the other elders of his small nation. He listened more than he talked. All Indian boys knew their place. When in the presence of the elders, a boy spoke only when spoken to. Little Red Feather listened to the tales of exploration, of hunting, of surviving the cold winters, and of providing the necessities to feed the family, and sometimes other families of the clans of the nation. The time for his test would come soon. But, first, Mother Moon would have to be in the right position. At present, Little Red Feather would have to be content just being a boy.

After gathering the water and taking it to his mother that morning, he went back to the spring. He sat down on the high side and looked eastward, over the spring, where the morning Father Sun was peeking above the horizon. In the wet marsh beyond the spring, the little blue forget-me-nots were coming into flower. He liked them, for they were a guarantee that the Green Moon of spring would soon be here.

The constant flow of the water coming out of Mother Earth amazed Little Red Feather as it went smoothly over the boulders. It provided the necessary water for the little brook, which flowed southerly, down the broad, flat valley. He played in the sparkling water every chance he got. There he caught frogs and once in a while he even caught a small fish. Today he took a closer notice that the water flowed from higher ground to lower ground. "Yes," he mused, "It always does that, for it is impossible for water to flow uphill."

As he was watching the moving water, he was almost in a trance; however, he noticed a small spider on one of the boulders. He said, almost out loud, "Coming for a drink, eh?" as if he could talk to the little creature. Spiders provided nothing of value, but their round webs had always fascinated the boy. The orb webs were the guiding design of the medicine wheel, so, yes, he knew that the lowly spider actually had some value.

Little Red Feather picked up a curly brown leaf, a cast-off from last year from the large oak that sheltered the spring in summer. He coaxed the spider onto the leaf, and then held it up and looked closely at the little creature's patterned back and yellow bottom, eight legs, and a rear that could spin a thread so thin as to be unimaginable. He looked at the spider. The spider looked back. The spider seemed to say, "Put me down, I'm not of your world."

Little Red Feather placed the leaf, with the spider on it as a passenger, into the basin of the spring where the water flowed. Immediately, the leaf was caught up in the moving water, slipping through a cleft between the boulders it began its journey southward. Little Red Feather quickly got up and followed the leaf and its tiny passenger. Downstream the three went in the early morning: the leaf, the spider, and Little Red Feather.

The leaf, floating and spinning, soon was caught in an overhanging sedge plant that was growing half-in and half-out of the brook. Little Red

Feather grabbed a stick during the quick pursuit and with it he gently touched the leaf to give it a restart. The leaf, again free, was now moving downstream, pulled gently along by the current. He followed.

The narrow little brook of clear spring water cut its way southward down the broad valley. It flowed to lower ground for quite a distance, then it joined a larger brook and became a small creek.

When the leaf floated into the creek, it was caught up in a new current. It spun around to the left, the spider spinning with it. Soon it was out of sight, behind the overhanging willows.

"Let them go," Little Red Feather said to himself. "Yes, let them go with the water to wherever the water goes."

He backtracked up the brook, back to his spring, to his camp on the high ground where the giant oak in the future would provide shelter from the hot afternoon summer sun. He hurried, because it was time for the warm early morning meal his mother was preparing. He hoped he wasn't too late.

The family was just sitting down to eat as he arrived. His mother was portioning out the porridge, and he was just in time to get his share.

The day would go on as usual. After the morning meal he would go into the forest with his father in search of food. Flowing Spring worked daily with him to guide his son towards becoming a man. He showed the boy the best wood to use to make a bow. It was from the greenball tree. The wood was straight-grained and made the best bow of all the trees that grew in the forest. The wood was cut from this tree in the winter because the tree juices at that time had all gone back to the roots of the tree. The winter wood was much lighter and much stronger. When completely dry, the bow would have the best pull of any of the woods of the forest. Little Red Feather and his father traveled west to the open ground where the greenball tree grew sparsely at the edge of the forest. Today he would get the wood for his first bow.

With his white flint knife, Little Red Feather spent a long time separating a branch from the tree. Then he stripped the branch of its bark and thorns and cut it to length, from the ground to his chin. Since this was a practice bow, it would not be tapered on the large end to obtain the balance so necessary of a worthy bow. He cut deep notches in each end of his new bow stick. His father gave him a string of twisted sinew with a loop already tied in one end. Little Red Feather slipped the loop end of the bowstring onto one of the notches. Then, measuring carefully, he tied a loop in the other end of the string about ten fingers short of the other notch. He flexed the stick

16

with his leg and then slipped the remaining loop over the notch. It wasn't much to look at, but he was satisfied. He held it up, gave a little tug on the string, then released it.

"Twang!" Yes, he had made his first bow.

Little Red Feather's arrows were also like his father's. They were from the same tree as the bow—straight twigs, cleaned of thorns, stripped of bark, and allowed to dry. Straight half-feathers from the hawk's tail were fastened to the smaller, notched end of the twigs. The notch was carved so the string would fit it snugly, to propel the arrow when the fingers released the string. The boy's arrows had no arrowheads, for he was not yet a man and also because arrowheads were too valuable to be lost.

The Indian boy and his father hunted most of the morning, leaning quietly against the ancient oaks of the forest. It was spring, and the squirrels had to eat too. After a wait that seemed forever, a red squirrel came to the ground, smelled here and there, then started digging for a treasure that it had buried last fall. Being interested in his work and anxious to taste last year's acorn, the little squirrel forgot and let down his guard for just a moment. In that instant, the boy's father drew his arrow, leaned away from the tree. "Twang!" The squirrel was knocked back by the impact of the arrow. The tiny sharp point, followed by the shaft, had gone clear through the throat of the little squirrel.

The wounded squirrel sprang for a nearby oak and started a frenzied climb but was slowed by the arrow and the loss of blood. After it had climbed a little higher than Little Red Feather could reach, the squirrel stopped and hung suspended by one front claw. Finally, relaxing its death grip on the rough bark, it fell back to the ground. The boy gave his father a proud smile, then walked over and picked up the warm, dead squirrel, the arrow still in its throat. Eventually two more squirrels from the same oak grove were added to the take for the day. Little Red Feather had also practiced on two other squirrels, but that's all it was, just practice, for he had missed them both.

Next, the father took the boy to a thick elm grove. There were many trees that had died of old age, becoming logs on the forest floor. In the bark mold on the ground, on the shady north side of the logs, the father showed the boy where to find the rough-top mushrooms. After three wet, warm days, the father knew they would find some.

The boy filled his deerskin bag with mushrooms. His father told him to leave three of the best ones on the outside of the ring. "They will be seed for others to come in the future. If you take all of them, there will be none next year," Flowing Spring told him. "We must plan for next year."

That evening Blue Damsel Fly prepared the mushrooms in clear, bubbling water, as she had fixed the morning meal. After skinning the three squirrels, she cooked them, first on a stick over the fire, then on a hot rock at the edge of the fire, adding the little hearts and livers of the squirrels to the mushroom pot. The flavor was tantalizing. The family ate well that evening. Then they settled into their lodge made from branches stuck into the ground, bent together at the top, and then covered with deerskins. They lay down on their soft deerskin robes, and after a few stories of the hunt, they went to sleep, all except Little Red Feather. He couldn't sleep.

He slid carefully and quietly from under the cover of the small lodge. Mother Moon was just rising in the east. He walked softly to the spring and sat on a flat boulder, a sort of worktable, which was adjacent to the spring. For a long time he just watched Mother Moon and her reflection in the reservoir of dark, shining water, reflecting on the events of the day and brushing away a few mosquitoes.

"I wonder," he thought, "just how far my spider floated down the creek? How far will the leaf float?"

He sat in the still of the night, looking at the bright, silvery Mother Moon. He watched her rise to twice the height she was when he had come to the spring.

Wondering about the spider, he returned quietly to the shelter of the overhead skins that would protect him from the dew and the pesky mosquitoes. Once inside the lodge, he lay down again. He was awake for a short time, still looking at the moon through a little gap in the door flap. It seemed he couldn't get the image of the leaf and the spider out of his head. Shortly though, the busy day's fatigue overtook him and he was fast asleep.

That night Little Red Feather dreamed of the leaf and the spider. He knew the brook emptied into the creek, but he wondered where the creek went. He knew it flowed downward, for all water flows downward, looking for the low spot to fill up. He dreamt on and on.

In the morning Little Red Feather, remembering his restless night, vowed to follow the creek and find out where it goes.

Little Red Feather rose early, even before Father Sun was up. He gathered the water, as he was accustomed to doing. Although he was tired from his restless night, today he had a mission.

First, he told his father what he wished to do. His father was glad his son hadn't gone off on his own without at least telling him because his father had information that would be of great value for such a trip. He told his son that he, too, had made the trip downwater many times, and Little Red Feather's trip would be eventful and enlightening. Such a journey to the Rocky River and back would take most of the day. In fact, it might take longer if the boy explored along the way.

"Go, but do not tarry, for the day will grow dark before you want it to. Go," said his father, remembering the first time he had gone down the creek and the surprises the trip had brought him. Little Red Feather also told his mother that he had to find out where the creek goes. He hoped he would be back to the camp at the spring before Father Sun was overhead, but he didn't know.

Father Sun was climbing higher in the east, so Little Red Feather knew he should start soon. He packed his deerskin bag with jerky, ground acorn meal and brown seeds, and dried watercress from the brook. He was off, giving his mother and his father a final wave as he moved quickly away from camp. Now they were out of sight and he was on his own. He was anxious, but he would be cautious of the unknown.

Little Red Feather followed the brook to the creek and turned left, just as the spider on the leaf had done. He made the best time he could, but he had to break a trail through the willow thicket, the brambles, and the cattails. Sometimes he sought the high ground in order to bypass some of the thicker growth. That made for easier going; however, he didn't want to lose sight of the creek that continued flowing to the east, towards the rising sun.

After a long eastward travel, the creek veered to the south. The valley became broad and there was no high ground, so Little Red Feather trudged on through the thicket. Soon the creek was flowing straight south. On the other side of the creek was a grove of giant oaks. In their high branches the squirrels were chattering at this intruder who had penetrated their solitude, but they knew they were safe on their side of the creek.

Little Red Feather paid them no attention, steadily traveling toward his goal. Onward he went. Father Sun was now halfway to overhead.

Little Red Feather was tired. He sat down on a fallen log and picked some thorns from his left leg. Awhile back he had become entangled in a blackberry patch. In pushing forward to get through the tangle, he had encountered those sharp, hooked thorns. After he had removed them, most of the irritation was gone, and he would forget the incident. He slowly followed the creek in a southerly direction.

He always kept to the left bank of the creek. Now his actions rewarded him; another small creek entered his creek on the far side. He would not have to wade. The creek, now wider, had become less clear because of this new flow of muddy water. Two creeks were now one larger creek; however, it was not the answer he had been seeking. He did sit down at this confluence to rest, however. He had been traveling without letup for quite a long time.

"More water into the flow, and all going downhill, but to where?" he wondered. He closed his eyes and listened. High in the air, a woodpecker hammered at a dead limb, probably making a spring nest, thought the boy. A large frog down over the bank gave a "hooonk, hooonk." He opened his eyes, peered over the edge of the bank, and looked at the plump green frog. A quick jump, and the frog was gone. The creek continued noisily flowing, gurgling at him. It seemed to say, "It's time to move on if you want answers to your questions. It's time to move on before the day runs out."

He got up quickly. As he did, a small fish jumped in the stream. Then all was quiet. He followed the lazy current of the creek as it widened. When the new creek had entered his creek, it pushed the flow towards the east, meandering through several "S" curves. Now this new and larger creek was flowing downhill through a deep cut in the thick, black soil. The bank on the opposite shore soon began to rise, becoming much higher than the bank on his side of the creek. He soon discovered the reason for the high bank: a yellowish-brown limestone outcrop rose almost perpendicular to the flowing water. The resistance of the stone bank had redirected the water to a more easterly direction. Little Red Feather hesitated for a moment and looked on with astonishment, for he had never seen such powerful force against the water.

All of a sudden his nose tingled, and he sensed the slight smell of smoke. Further downstream, on the top of the high bluff, he saw a curl of white smoke rising through the oaks. Next he saw some movement. Not wanting to give himself away, he hid behind a large, dark willow tree and stood perfectly still. From his vantage point, he watched to see what was going on. "Who are those people?" he questioned out loud, but softly to himself. "I wonder if I should know them?"

Movement again brought his attention to the top of the limestone bluff. Looking carefully, he saw a young girl. A long braid of black hair swung to-

and-fro as she descended the narrow pathway at the edge of the limestone leading down to the creek. He followed her movements but then lost sight of her as she went behind some bushes that were growing out of the rocks. Just as quickly, though, she reappeared and soon was at the level of the creek. The girl knelt on a flat slab of limestone. She had two clay pots with her, and after carefully placing them on the stone, she began filling one from the quiet backwater. The boy knew the water was not as clear as the water of his spring. The girl would have to let this water sit until tomorrow, when it would be clear and fit to drink.

After the girl had filled the two pots, she carefully adjusted them, one in the crook of each arm. She folded her fingers together so she could carry them more easily. Standing, she turned and started her climb back up the path that led to the top of the bluff. Now she was out of sight. Little Red Feather waited and watched. She was gone. Then, out of the corner of his eye, he saw a small blacksnake slither over and around some limbs that, during high water, had been washed down into the creek. The snake had finished sunning itself, and now it, too, was gone.

No other motion came from the high bluff, so Little Red Feather left the shelter of his protective willow, continuing downwater, but higher up on the bank on his side of the creek. He used the willows as a buffer between himself and the unknown, up on the bluff, on the other side of the creek.

As he kept moving, the limestone bluff was soon behind him and out of sight. He was still cautious, however, and stayed on the higher ground as he followed the creek. He looked ahead and saw that the forested bluff across the creek had turned back to the right and then vanished in the distance. Downwater, and to the east, was an even higher bluff that looked like it would be a barrier to his creek. It stretched to the right and to the left as far as he could see. He continued trudging downwater. Soon he heard the sound of rushing water coming from his left.

He broke through the line of willows and arrived on a gravel bar that extended out into the water. Walking to the end of the bar, he looked in both directions. He had come to a river. His father had told him he would have surprises, and this was certainly another one of them. The river was moving from left to right, the water moving rapidly downstream. "What now?" he wondered.

He leaned on the staff he had been carrying and then sat down on a dry log that had washed up on the gravel. Had he found his answer? He didn't know, but he didn't think so. He did know, however, that he was very tired and hungry.

Slipping the strap of the deerskin bag from his shoulder, he let the bag drop to the gravel, bent over, opened the bag and took out some deer jerky and greens. He had waited almost too long to eat, for he had an ache in the hollow of his stomach. After mixing some water with the greens and eating them with the jerky, he felt much better. He rose from his crouched position and looked downstream, where the water flowed swiftly away from him. He picked up a smooth, dry stick from the gravel bar and threw it into the flowing water. It moved quickly. "Downwater," Little Red Feather said to himself. "It's still seeking lower ground."

He reflected while standing in the sunshine on the rocks of the gravel-bar at the end of his creek: "My spring, my brook, my creek, then the larger creek, and now the river. I wonder where the river goes?" He picked up a flat rock from the gravel at his feet, threw it, and watched as it skipped downwater.

The sun was warm as he stood on the gravel bar that spring morning. His shadow was as small as it would get. "Father Sun is high," he said to himself. He mentally retraced his steps of the morning, estimating the time already spent on this day of new experiences. He didn't want to cross the creek today or even follow the river downwater. He knew he would be back to this place on another day.

Little Red Feather looked upriver and saw rough, white water as the river rushed along. It intrigued the boy, and without hesitating, he started following the river edge, upstream. He knew he had come south and east and he also knew that north and west would lead him back to the family campsite. So north he went, along the west bank of his newly found river.

Little Red Feather soon discovered that the white, rushing water was only the river flowing over rough limestone rapids. The river had cut its way through some of the same buff-colored limestone he had seen at the place where the girl had gathered her water. He walked out into the river, for it was very shallow, wisely taking off his moccasins first. His toes helped keep him from slipping on the smooth, mossy limestone underfoot. He maintained his balance by holding his arms out and using his staff. He had walked out into the river, perhaps ten paces before he thought better of it. He quickly returned to the safety of dry land. It was an interesting experience; it seemed he could walk on water

But enough of this child's play. He returned to the shore and continued walking upriver. It was easy going along the edge of the water because of the fine sand that had been deposited there. Little Red Feather walked upwater for quite a distance, occasionally climbing over a few downed trees and some large driftwood logs.

Coming to a bend in the river, he could see a great distance upwater. It seemed like the river went on forever. Within his view, on the same side of the river, he noticed a rise in the riverbank. On this raised area was a grove of oak trees just coming into leaf. He decided he would go at least that far before turning back.

As he came closer to the grove, he could see that a portion of the high ground was covered with a patch of green grass, a short-grass prairie, already dotted with the white and yellow flowers of spring. The oaks were still on the other side. As he approached the prairie, he had a queasy feeling in the pit of his stomach, one that he couldn't quite figure out. He suddenly knew that he was on Hallowed Ground. He had no business here. He climbed a small, white-and- brown-barked sycamore tree for a better look. From that height, he saw several small mounds in the open area all covered with short grass. He counted five, round-top mounds. His father had told him stories of the mounds and their reason for being, and he knew he should leave this place now.

He slid down from his perch in the tree and looked downstream, south. Closing his eyes, he thought for a moment, mentally drawing a picture, retracing his steps of the day. "What if I were to return home, to my spring, by another way?" he said to himself. "It will probably be shorter. Yes, I will do it," he resolved.

Father Sun was well past the high point of His travel across the sky. Little Red Feather faced west, then held out his right arm at the diagonal, and said, "This way should take me home."

He was a boy who knew the forest—a real scout. He knew that in the uplands grew the oaks, hickories, and maples. He also knew it would be faster traveling across the forest floor than going back along the watercourse and through the thickets and the cattails and briars. He set out in the direction he had pointed.

Little Red Feather skirted the hallowed ground and made his way northwest. It was easy traveling, but it was new territory, so he was cautious, looking, listening, and smelling the forest as he moved quickly over last year's leaves and the new small, white, woodland flowers of spring. He was very cautious because he didn't want to get into any trouble. He was also tired, but he knew he must move forward. The forest was a wise choice; there was much less undergrowth, and he made good time.

On the way he was quiet, his footsteps making very little noise. Once, in a small clearing, he came upon a pair of red foxes nosing one another. He watched them for a moment. The foxes quickly scattered when they saw Little Red Feather.

He was also alert to the position of Father Sun and realized that perhaps He would go down in the west before Little Red Feather could get back to his camp at the spring. He was racing against time. He didn't want to spend a night in the forest alone. He quickened his pace and continued.

Plodding on, a small brook soon came into view; it flowed in a southerly direction. He remembered that earlier that morning he had crossed a small brook. "It must be the same one," he said to himself. In one giant leap he was across the small flow of water and it was behind him.

There was a break in the forest ahead because he could see the trees thinning out. In the distance, down the hill and to his left, he could see the creek that he had traversed that morning. Between the boy and the creek was a wet prairie, teeming with color. "The flowers of spring," he said to himself. There were white, yellow, red, blue, and purple—all the colors he had ever seen, and all in tune with one another. "We can thank both Father Sun and Mother Earth for giving us such beauty," he said to himself. "I recognize this place." Yes, he was now on familiar ground. The boy and his father had visited this prairie several times, seeking the underwater roots of the arrowhead plant and the painted turtles that his mother used in her wonderful stew. He knew his way home from here by the landmarks.

He had taken this overland route with his father last spring. It certainly was the quickest way home and also the shortest. His guides would be the oak and hickory grove on the highest rise, then the burnt tree which lightning had struck some years ago. Next, there would be a small patch of very tall grass where the bluestem and turkeyfoot grew together. Finally, he would cross another brook, climb a small rise, and come to his spring.

Father Sun, ahead of him, was almost to the horizon, turning the feathery white clouds gradually pink and then purple as He sank lower. Soon the red ball of Father Sun would be gone, below the western horizon, and he would have missed the evening meal at the family camp by the spring. The day was almost gone, and Little Red Feather was tired.

He paused for a moment, taking the last piece of pemmican from his bag and putting it in his mouth. The taste of it immediately relieved his hunger. He would not chew it. He would just let his mouth soften it, savoring it for as long as he could. He knew that would be all he would have to eat until morning. "It will be enough," he said to himself. "I've been hungry before. I can hold on till morning."

As Little Red Feather trudged down the path through the emerging yellow-green cattails of the low, wet ground east of the spring, Otter Tail, his little sister, gave a shout. She had been waiting and watching for him, although she didn't think he would come from the east. She had hoped he would get back home this day. If he hadn't made it home, she would have drawn and carried the water from the spring in the morning. She was small for her nine summers, but she could have done it. Otter Tail was glad her brother was safely back to the campsite. And, yes, tomorrow Little Red Feather will get the water, as usual.

Little Red Feather raised his right arm, palm out, and gave the "friendly meeting" sign as he approached the spring where his family had gathered to meet him. "What shall I tell them?" he wondered. "Where shall I start?"

Red streaks of twilight graced the sky. The fire was gray and quiet, although now and then a few yellow-orange embers were crackling and flaring up. He had indeed missed the evening meal, but he was too tired to care.

"Tell us about your journey," his little sister requested.

He told his story as a storyteller would tell it, not leaving out a single detail. He was still rambling on as the family crawled into the shelter of the lodge. Mother Moon shone through the east opening of the lodge, brightening the boy's face as he continued. He was only halfway through his story when he began to slow down. He was so tired he could not finish. He closed his eyes, and after a few incoherent words, simply slipped off in a deep sleep. Little Red Feather never moved until morning.

"Where did I leave off last night?" he asked his father.

"Just when you arrived at the bluff," said Flowing Spring.

"Oh, then I didn't get to the really important part yet," he said eagerly.

He told them of the smoke, of the limestone bluff, the girl collecting water, the little blacksnake and the camp he imagined must have been on the high bluff above the limestone wall. His father was pleased that Little Red Feather had discovered the bluff people by himself. Little Red Feather wondered if he had been too cautious, but his father said, "That was good, for I have often been in similar situations. One can't be too careful.

"Always practice caution because the cost of blundering can sometimes be fatal. You may have only one chance. Remember the squirrels?" his father asked.

His father told the boy that the bluff people were friendly; in fact, they were distant uncles and cousins on his grandfather's side. "Well," the boy said, "I'll probably go that way again, so next time I'll know what to expect and how to act. Next time I'll meet the people of the bluff and give them the sign for: 'hello, I'm your friend, you are part of my family and I come in peace'."

Little Red Feather told his father that the creek flowed into the River with Rocks.

"Do you know where the river goes?" the boy asked. His father, with his arm extended all the way, the sign for "far away," told him it flowed to the south, but he did not know how far or where it went. Little Red Feather told his father of his walk upriver, of "walking on the water," of the Hallowed Ground and of his journey through the forest.

Flowing Spring was proud that Little Red Feather had used his imagination to come home by a different route. He had figured out that a trail in a straight line, like the bee flies to the bee tree, would be the shorter and faster way home.

. . . .

The spring gathering, the Powwow of the local clans, would soon begin. The meeting always convened during the Green Moon when the geese, ducks, and of course the large flocks of passenger pigeons, and all of the other smaller birds were returning to their nesting grounds. By then, the small, pink-flower tree had shed its withered blooms and was producing leaves.

The clans met at Council Oaks, a grove of giant white oak trees. From Little Red Feather's family campsite at the spring, the oak grove was in the direction where the winter sun rises. The old oaks had been there for as long as the boy's father could remember. The various families and clans of the Rocky River Nation had been coming to the Powwow there every year since the eagles had spent that fateful day in the tops of the mighty oaks, and that was many springs ago. The white and black feathers on the top of the ancient staff attested to the fact that something important had happened on that dark day so long ago.

The story went, that Father Sun disappeared and dark clouds covered Mother Earth. The sky had grown even darker and appeared green in the middle of that morning. At the same time the wind began to blow, and the rain came down in torrents. The thunder was louder and the lightning was brighter than anyone could remember. Stories of that great storm were told at the beginning of each Powwow. They set the scene, the reason for the meeting, and were always told by the senior elder, as though the event had happened only yesterday.

Just before the storm struck, a pair of eagles took refuge in the top of one of the giant oak trees. These mighty birds, in full adult plumage, had also sought protection from the fierce wind. They could not make headway, nor could they even glide on the downdrafts, because of the severe gusting.

The leaders of the two local clans were also meeting in the oak grove that very morning, and they too sought protection from the storm within that grove of towering giants.

When the wind was at its worst and the day was at its darkest, there was the brightest flash of lightning ever seen, followed by the loudest clap of thunder ever heard, and immediately came the splintering of bright yellow wood and a puff of smoke.

The two leaders, knocked to the ground, shook themselves, looked at each other, and then threw their hands in the air, thankful they were still alive.

In the next moment of stillness, two majestic birds fell between the seated men. Both birds were male, singed and smelling. The great eagles had died instantly, and in all their magnificence, had been delivered to the two leaders. The eagle, the symbol of strength, had been handed to them, for they had survived the ordeal.

In the wet darkness of the day, they looked at the symbols and knew they now had the power of the eagle. They lifted the eagles gently. The Great Spirit had given them the power by his action. They counted the twelve perfect tail feathers of each bird and carefully removed them. "These will be our call to meeting each spring," they said, almost in unison. The two elders then gathered some of the oak splinters that had exploded from the tree when the lightning went to ground. One large sliver was taller than either man, almost as big around as the heads of the dead eagles lying on the ground. To the top of this staff, they attached the eagle tail feathers. They severed the eagle's legs at their knee joints, making the claws grip the staff and binding them in place just below the feathers. "Yes, this will be our gathering totem," they agreed. "We will meet here each spring and give thanks that we are among the living. We will exchange gifts. We will help one another. Yes, we will gather here like the eagles — and henceforth will be called the Eagle Clan. We will pass this legacy, this staff, to our children, that they may, in turn, pass it on to their children." They took the eagle's wing feathers to fletch arrows.

This event had occurred many, many moons ago.

Now it was time for the spring gathering and time to add another notch to the "staff of time." The old oak staff had seen sixty notches added since the day it had been bedecked with the tail feathers and the legs and talons of the great eagles. It had long since been smoothed with rough rocks and rubbed with bear fat to prolong its life. It was a magnificent totem.

The staff of the Eagle Clan stood upright in the ground in the center of the clearing, a symbol of the strong family relationships that had evolved from the meetings of the sons and grandsons of the two who had met in council on that fateful day so many springs ago.

The meeting today would present an opportunity for learning without the risk of experience, thought the boy's father. He gathered Tail Feather, Wing Feather, and his son, Little Red Feather; the four of them sat under the scarred oak whose top had been torn apart those sixty springs ago. The burnt oak had grown even stronger in the healing process.

The father asked his son to speak, for he knew the boy had something to say.

"I'm a dreamer," the boy said. "My dream is of the water going down the river, but I don't know where it goes. I must follow the river to see for myself where it goes. Do you know where it goes?" Little Red Feather asked the two elders.

Tail Feather, who was the older, told the boy that he had been down the river to the sandstone bluffs, but no further. He said he had stood on the tall, smooth rock and from that high vantage point had looked downwater, but he had not gone downwater. He had no reason to, so he had returned to his campsite.

"How was your trip to the sandstone bluffs?" the boy asked.

"It was quiet, but fulfilling," Tail Feather replied. "I saw many animals, and I caught a large, smooth-skinned, whiskered fish, which I cooked. Its white meat was delicious. I also found many clams on the river bottom. I split them open, cooked them in bubbling water and even ate some raw. They were very good. My trip downwater only lasted six days, three down and three back, but that was enough for me, being all alone and in a hurry."

"Were you afraid?" asked Little Red Feather.

"No, but I was concerned and thinking about home all the time I was away," responded Tail Feather.

Thinking out loud, the boy said, "If I were to go downwater to find out where the water goes, I wonder how far I would have to go? I wonder how long I would be gone?"

"Who knows?" questioned Wing Feather. "I certainly don't."

"I do want to find out," said the boy, with a gleam in his eye and a smile on his lips. He related to the two elders from the bluff the story of his one-day trip from his spring to the Rocky River, wondering again how many days it would take him to find out where the water from his spring flows.

Both Tail Feather and Wing Feather told the boy he would have many experiences if he traveled down the river. He would have to find food along the way. He would probably meet other people—but would they be friendly? He would have to protect himself from wolves and bears. What if he got sick or hurt himself? There were too many unknowns. Why embark on such a journey? But if he chose to go, he must bring back proof of his journey.

They knew the boy was serious about his dream and felt bound to make this journey, so they related stories they knew of the long trips that they and others had taken. The two elders and his father recalled many stories providing advice and insight on how to meet the unexpected on such a trip downwater. They related their own experiences—how they had survived the heat, the cold, the hunger, the wild animals, the floods, and the accidents, and how Mother Earth had provided for their needs. They advised the boy about what he should take along on his journey, insisting that taking trade goods along would be imperative.

The four sat in the shade under the giant oak. The three elders told stories all afternoon. Little Red Feather listened intently, knowing he could profit by the experiences of his elders. He asked an occasional question to seek greater insight, but, mostly, he listened, absorbed, and learned.

Several days after the Powwow, Little Red Feather and his father sat down to talk about the events of that meeting. "Father, what gifts did you receive?"

"Well, after I had given my gifts to Tail Feather, Wing Feather, and the other elders, they, in return were exceptionally kind, giving me this pouch. Look, it's a hunting kit."

The leather pouch was just large enough to hold the items necessary for arrow-making. It was sewn with gut and wound with a cross-stitch pattern, one that the boy had never seen. A flap closed by a small, white, shell button was sewn in place with the same fine gut thread.

The father turned it over, and on the back there were four more buttons sewn in a diamond pattern. A diamond pattern was burned into the skin, which went from button to button. The bag was sturdy, made of smooth, scraped deerskin.

The father unbuttoned the flap and pulled out three of the finest bowstrings the boy had ever seen. They were rolled up in a small coil that fit the pouch exactly. Made of the sinew of the deer's leg, they had been stretched tight before being allowed to dry. Three strands of sinew to each string had been back-twisted and woven together with great uniformity to make a bowstring of great strength. The finishing touch, however, was that they had been rubbed with bee's wax. The father told his son this made them soft, flexible, and long lasting. There were also pieces of sinew in the pouch for tying arrow points to shafts; they would have to be wet and stretched first. There were also some short pieces of hawk feather for fletching. The pouch also contained ten small, white, perfectly matched, triangular arrow points. They were beautiful. White cutting blades to shape and notch arrow shafts were also included. The father told his son he would share the contents of the wonderful kit with him when the need arose. This brought a gleam of anticipation to Little Red Feather's eyes.

"What did you give as a gift?" the father asked his son.

"Father, I had nothing to give," said the boy. "There were very few gifts given or even received by the children. I did tell the story of my one-day journey downwater. I guess, in a way, that was my gift."

"I wish I had really gone downwater—down the river, I mean, so I could complete my story," he added.

They talked the greater part of the morning. Flowing Spring told stories of his own adventures, more than the boy could even imagine. Some of the events had happened when Flowing Spring was a boy, also yearning to wander, to see what was over the next hill, to see what he could find and bring home.

Flowing Spring's test to become a man was different from the ordinary test. He was provided with food, covers of deerskin, and weapons to protect himself. His was a test of distance and endurance. He was to follow the setting Father Sun, from full moon to no moon, then return home by the next full moon with proof that he had actually fulfilled the task.

"I know you made it, Father," the boy said excitedly, "but what did you bring back as proof?" The father told the boy that he had traveled far—over many brooks, creeks, streams, and hills, across broad valleys, and through thick forests. He had traveled towards the setting sun until the night of no moon, when he came upon a small river. In that river valley he had met a clan of people "not unlike us," he said. "They had plenty of food and meat. They accepted me as a visitor, a traveler, and a friend. Some of their words were the same as ours, but often we had to talk in sign," said the father. He had invited those friendly people to the valley of the Rocky River and to the spring Powwow of the clans, but they had yet to come.

"As a gift, the people of the far west river gave me some hard, heavy, shiny, rock cubes, and these I brought home as proof that I had completed my task," said Flowing Spring. "The people of the far west river valley called them 'galena rocks.' Our people had never before seen such beautiful, shiny objects, so heavy too, for their small size. I prize them very highly," said the father.

"Do you still have them, Father?" questioned Little Red Feather.

"Yes, but I've put them away for safekeeping. I'll show them to you tonight. I only have three left. I gave many away as gifts at some of our Powwows. I also gave one to your grandfather, and he carried it with him on his way to the Great Beyond," replied his father. "I placed it in his right hand when we laid him in his resting place in Mother Earth."

They finally got around to the subject of the trip the boy wanted to take. He knew he would have the consent of his father. He knew it would be given when he finally asked for it. He did not want to ask yet. He wanted to learn more about how to take care of himself on such a long trip.

He asked questions all morning: "Will I see any strange animals? How far will I have to go? How long will it take? How will I communicate with others who don't speak our language? Will I be able to find enough food along the way? Can you teach me to swim? Can I float downwater on a raft? How can I obtain a raft? How far can I float in a day, or in a moon's time? What if I get caught in a great snow?" Question after question he asked. His father was wise and was able to answer most of the boy's questions.

Little Red Feather's mother could also give him insights with her knowledge of plants used for food, of cooking, and of fire, so he spent many afternoons with her.

Blue Damsel Fly, explained that feeding the family was mostly a matter of planning, and of course, the availability of food. The boy's mother was also thankful that he had asked her for information and for advice. She freely shared her knowledge with her son on those quiet afternoons, sitting on the flat rock near the spring.

She told him that, in the time of the Green Moon, when longer and warmer days came, the plants awoke from their long winter sleep and began to grow again. After the flowers, came the fruits of the bushes and trees, which would provide life-giving nourishment. Seeds were also important. They were collected and stored for later use. She told him that the large seeds of the low ground plants such as squash and pumpkin were long lasting if kept dry. Maize seeds were important too. They would keep a long time. She told him she still had some seeds from the last growing season, and that when he went downriver, he could take some along. The nuts of the walnut, the oak, the burr and hickory trees should not to be overlooked, for they too kept well, and could be used late into the winter and on into the spring to provide quick nourishment.

His mother also told him that the birds, the fish, and the smaller animals of the forest provided eggs and meat. Blue Damsel Fly told him that it was the boy's father's responsibility to hunt for the larger animals. "He brings them home and together we skin, dress, and cook them."

She explained the value of the deer. Some of the red meat was used immediately, and some was pounded, flavored, and dried as pemmican for future use. The insides were eaten first because they spoiled easily and had to be used quickly. The hide was especially valuable. After removal, cleaning, and scraping, it was tanned with deer brains, water, sand, and burnt oak leaves, and worked until it was soft, ideal for clothing. The deer hide was also used for shelters, stretched tight over a light, bent sapling framework and also to make the skin canoe for short river trips. The bones of the deer were even boiled to get at the rich marrow inside. The deer horns were used as tools for digging and for arrow-point making. Some clans also used them as food for their dogs. The boy listened as his mother told him of her experiences of providing for the family.

"Even the quick, little white-tail rabbit is important," his mother said.

Now he was seated on one of the flat boulders near the fire ring, listening intently as his mother related her experiences and advice. "The rabbit's skin has kept us warm on winter days; it takes many skins to make winter clothes. The garments must be loose with the fur on the inside for best warmth," she told her son. "Your father keeps us well supplied with rabbits from his snares and from his quick arrow. The rabbit is best when caught in the winter when the fur is longest; then it does not drop out. We also use strips of rabbit meat for pemmican. But best of all, red rabbit meat cut into small pieces and roasted over the fire—well, what could taste better?" asked his mother. "Mother Earth has provided well for us," Little Red Feather's mother said. "There is always more than enough to eat."

The mother stressed that fire would be most important on his journey; he must take along a fire-making kit. "When you go, I'll wrap one up for you and tie it very securely so it will stay dry." The boy's mother's responsibility was also to make sure the fire was tended. If it went out, she had to start it anew. She banked it at night so that in the morning there would still be hot coals under the gray ash. With these few coals and some dry sticks, she would restart the fire. She gathered the wood for the fire as the generations of women before her had also gathered the wood for the fires that provided for the well being of the many families of the Nation. In the winter, she also built the reflector of rocks behind the fire so the heat would not be lost, but directed towards the sleeping family in the lodge during the White Moon, the season of snow and ice.

As his mother kept talking, the boy's mind wandered. Then and there, he realized just how important were his mother's tasks. She had many responsibilities on her shoulders.

He quickly returned to reality as his mother said, "I have to go now and finish the evening meal."

Talking to his father and his mother, Little Red Feather had learned many important lessons. He wondered why he had not had these conversations before. He realized his mother and father were the two most important people in his life. He had also learned some of the most important lessons of his life. What if he were not making a trip downwater; would he have had these same discussions? He knew his life was now much richer.

Little Red Feather went over the stories and the information and advice his parents had given him. He was especially appreciative that his father had let him handle the small, but heavy, shiny cubes, the ones he had brought back from the river, far to the west.

Down His River of Dreams ...

As Little Red Feather lay under his deerskin cover that night, he recalled over and over the events of the past several days. Before he knew it, he was breathing heavily and was sleeping deeply.

That night he had another very vivid and realistic dream of his journey downwater—his trip to come. Yes, Little Red Feather was getting eager to go and concerned that he make all necessary preparations.

"Be prepared," he kept saying to himself. "Yes, that must be my motto on my journey down the water."

. . . .

Several days later Little Red Feather was back at the spring looking easterly towards the red, rising Father Sun. "It's going to be a fine day today," he said to himself in the early morning as he listened to the birds calling one another from high in the tree tops.

He sat on the bare ground with his legs crossed beneath him, looking at the shapes of the clouds that were turning from dark gray to deep red. He listened acutely to the spring water as it flowed over the boulders, running so quietly that he could just barely hear the trickle on the smooth rocks. He began daydreaming, fantasizing the shapes of the early morning clouds into bears, wolves, rabbits, and other animals of the forest.

He was not aware that his little sister had also come to the spring and sat down beside him. They sat there together that quiet morning, watching the eastern sky lighten, as the red Father Sun rose above the trees of the far horizon.

The boy's sister spoke first. "I can see the time getting short between now and when you'll be leaving on your journey downwater."

He jumped, not realizing that she was next to him. "Oh, yes," he said. "Time is getting short, and I'm making a mental list of all the things that I must take along. I must not forget anything that will make my trip easier. Father and Mother said they would help. I'll decide soon when to leave."

They sat quietly together, Little Red Feather and Otter Tail, his little sister. She was three summers younger than her brother, but she had an understanding that his trip would be a dangerous one. "You will be gone a long time," she said.

"I don't know for sure. All I can do is dream about it. I try to dream good dreams, for I want good things to happen to me on my journey. If I dreamt bad dreams, then I think that bad things would surely happen to me.

34

I am eager to leave, and, yes, it will no doubt be soon," the boy said to his sister.

By now Father Sun had come into full view. The red clouds had gone through several shades of pink and now were pure white. Still, the boy gazed eastward as if in a trance.

His sister broke the silence again. "You really are a dreamer, aren't you? You won't be satisfied until you're on your way downwater. Older Brother, I'm going to call you 'Dreamer,' because that name fits you exactly. You dream about the journey you hope to take. You dream in the night and also in the day. I can hardly talk to you because you're so preoccupied."

"I don't *hope* to take this journey, I'm *going* to take it. There are a few other lessons that I have to learn first, but I'll know when I'm ready. Yes, it will be soon. If you want me to, when I finally decide to go, I'll tell you first. How does that sound?" He continued, "The nights are still too cold and I don't want to leave our campfire just yet. The white water crystals of morning are still on the dry stems of the tall grass until the sun melts them. It will be warmer soon and then I'll go." He continued, "Dreamer? It's a strange name, but it does fit me. I'll wear it because it will only last for a short while. After I complete my 'man task,' I'll be given a new name anyway. 'Dreamer,' hmmm?

"When I leave on my journey, you know, you'll have to carry the morning water," the boy said to his sister. "If Mother wants a lot and it's too heavy, you'll just have to make two trips."

"Yes, I'll do it," she said, knowing that a smaller amount would be needed, because her older brother would be gone. She was glad that the spring was so close to the campsite because, during the day as each one of the family got thirsty, they simply went to the spring, scooped up some water with their hands, drank it and satisfied their thirst. That made less water to carry.

"We are so lucky to have such a clear, cold, pure source of water so close by," said Otter Tail. "Yes, Father picked a good campsite."

"Luck had nothing to do with the choice of our campsite," said the boy. "Father had been here before. As a boy, when he traveled across the brook on his way to the Powwow, he noticed how clear the water was. He followed the brook until he came to the spring. He claimed the area of the spring from Mother Earth. She said she would share it with him, so he cleaned out the brambles and the brush. He and Mother claimed it when they were mated. I don't know about you, but I'm happy here," said Dreamer.

"Oh, yes," said the little sister. "This is a wonderful place to live. I do wish we had more families with us though, for sometimes I get lonely."

"When it's time for each of us to get our own mates, then there will be more of us. I do miss Grandfather, though. His sickness and passing two winters ago left an empty space," the boy said.

"At least we do get visitors once in awhile, to break the quiet," said his sister.

After a little while, Dreamer asked his sister, "Do you have any advice for me?"

"Be careful," was all she could come up with after such a quick question from her older brother. "I want to see you again. I want to hear the stories of your journey downwater. I know you'll have some wonderful experiences. Why, you'll have some that you can't even imagine you'll have," said the little sister. "And, I hope they are all good."

He thought, "She's concerned for me. I do appreciate that."

"Dreamer," she said, "I wish you a careful and successful journey with many wonderful experiences along the way. But above all, do be careful," she cautioned him again. They walked back to the campsite together, arms around each other, hoping that by now the morning meal was ready.

. . . .

Immediately after the morning meal, Dreamer was on his way across country. Customarily, on this first day after the full moon, all the boys of the clan got together at one of the clan sites to play games. Today they would be at the site of Beaver Tail's clan, at the edge of the forest, just up the hill from the wet prairie.

If all the boys came, there would be at least ten or twelve of them. They would tell stories, have games of skill, and perhaps practice an actual hunt to see who could outdo the other. Whatever the kill, if there was one, the lucky boy would take it home so his family could have it for a meal.

It was always fun when all the boys were together. Today they each brought their chunky stones. Those who didn't have one had to borrow one from an older brother or from his father. Since the boys had few possessions, they just played the games for the fun of being a winner. There were no high stakes in their games.

They paired off and practiced rolling their stones on the smooth-dirt chunky court. A short stick had been placed upright about 20 paces beyond the start line.

The game began in earnest, with each pair rolling stones toward the stick, trying to get closest. With each pair, one of the rollers was eliminated. In the next round, half again were eliminated.

Dreamer's perfectly-round, smooth, black chunky stone had been handed down to him from his grandfather. It was quite heavy, but he could roll it better than most of the boys could roll theirs. That morning he won each one of his matches and was now in the final match, rolling against his friend, Little Beaver Tail.

He rolled his stone straight down the court. It curved in toward the stick and stopped, leaning upright against the little post. He jumped for joy. He knew Little Beaver Tail could not be so good; he just knew he couldn't.

Little Beaver glanced out of the corner of his eye towards Dreamer. He knew he had seen the best throw of the day, and he mulled over his strategy as to how he could beat it. Could he throw his stone a little harder and knock Dreamer's away from the post? If he did, he might even leave his own leaning against the post. He would try, but he knew his chance of winning this match was slim.

Little Beaver Tail bent over behind the starting line, swung his arm back, then came forward a little faster than usual, and aimed at the post. Unless he hit the post or Little Red Feather's stone, he would be far past his goal, and he would lose the match. As bad luck would have it, he missed and rolled right on by. He had missed his target by only a few fingers' width, but he missed it.

Today Dreamer won the chunky game. He got pats on the back from all the other boys. Reluctantly, Little Beaver Tail put his arm across the shoulder of his friend, Dreamer, and congratulated him on his "lucky" throw and his win of the match.

Beaver Tail then suggested that they sit together on the log next to the chunky court. They sat a little apart, looking at each other, then Little Beaver Tail became quite intent. His voice lowered into a very serious tone, and he said, "About your journey, your plan to go down the river, don't you know it's dangerous? Don't go down the river. You will never return. The water goes into a hole in the ground. My father told me so and I believe him. He says the water goes into the ground, into a big hole, just like the water comes out of the ground; like it does at the spring at your camp. I know you won't come back; you won't survive if you go down the river. Please don't go. I beg you, please don't go."

Dreamer scowled and brushed his long black hair over his shoulder. He thought for a long moment and said, "If I don't try, I'll never know where the water goes. I'll have to see it to believe it. I'll be careful. If the water does go into a hole, I'll probably hear the roar before I see the hole. You know I might not even be on the river when I come to the horror that you speak of. I'm going to start my journey by walking. I'll walk down the path next to the river. Later I'll probably be on the river, floating on a log, or a raft, or maybe I'll even be in a canoe if I can find one along the way. I'll just take my chances, but I'll watch out for the hole that you say is there."

With that serious talk out of the way, they joined the other boys throwing stones. It seemed that no one wanted to win the stone-throwing contest. Next was the arrow- shooting contest. Bundles of dried grass were tied up to look like rabbits. They were even the size of a rabbit. Four of these "rabbits" were placed alongside the pathway, into the wet prairie. The boys would walk the path, and when they came upon one of the grass rabbits, they would shoot an arrow at it. The arrows were blunt, without flint points on them, since flint points were too valuable for them to play with. They would have to wait a few years for the good points.

The grass rabbit hunting over, Little Beaver Tail and Dreamer went back to the log next to the chunky court and sat down on it again.

"I heard your warning," continued Dreamer

"Well, does that mean you're not going?" his friend asked.

"Oh, no, I am going, but I will be very careful and watch for any dangers along the way," Dreamer laughed.

Since the Father Sun was now high in the sky, Dreamer decided to head west along the well-worn path to his home by the spring. He thought over what Little Beaver Tail had told him: "A hole in the ground? There couldn't be. Or, could there really be such a danger? Well, I'll just have to see for myself," he thought with concern.

. . . .

Preparation for adult life did not allow a growing boy much chance to enjoy a carefree childhood. Many demands were placed on him; at an early age, he was taken seriously. Because of the "Code," he was responsible for his actions, giving him a secure and authoritative feeling. He went with his father on hunting sojourns. He observed his father's activities at the Council when he could only listen. He also saw how his father respected the elders and the women of the clan. He learned by observation. Dreamer quickly grew into adulthood. Actual age meant little compared with actions and responsibilities.

From his father's teachings, he learned to track animals and to hunt them with the spring-trap, the fall-trap, the sharp-stick-trap, and also with the bow and arrow. He could barely pull the string of his father's bow to his nose, but he could hold the arrow steady until it was time for the "twang." His aim was nearly always true. Knowing his destiny, he learned many things to prepare for the journey he knew he must take.

Tonight he was to learn some of the secrets of the sky. His father had chosen a night of no moon and a clear sky because then the stars shone their brightest.

After a short sleep, the two left the comfort of their soft deerskin covers, slipped from the lodge, and walked together to the spring. To the north of the spring there were no trees to hide the sky. The stars were as bright as the boy had ever seen them because the rain of the day had also cleansed the night sky.

His father broke the silence, as deep as the sky was dark: "So you're a dreamer? At least, that's what Little Sister is now calling you. How do you come by such a name?"

The silence continued, and they could hear the movement of the leaves high in the oak trees, the distant chirp of the frogs that made the trees their home, and the quiet gurgle of the water as it flowed from the spring. "Until I fulfill my yearning and find the answers to my questions, all I can be is a dreamer," the boy finally answered. "I can almost find the answers when I sit down and focus on nothing and think of what might be. In my dreams I find beautiful answers to the unknown. I dream of having wonderful experiences on my journey." He looked up at the dim silhouette of his father and answered, "Yes, I guess 'Dreamer' fits me pretty well."

"Very well then, 'Dreamer' it is," said his father. "That shall be your name until you complete your journey down the water. Then, perhaps your dream will have been realized. If you want or deserve a new name upon your return, we'll discuss it then. For now, you are just 'Dreamer'."

Both stood silently, becoming a part of the darkness of the night. Then Flowing Spring spoke, "The stars are our guiding talismans. If you understand them, they will be your friends and bring you good luck. You must learn about the stars and Mother Moon before you leave on your journey down water." Flowing Spring remembered his own father teaching him the lessons of the stars many years ago. He, too, had needed the knowledge on the journeys of his youth.

"We will be here most of the night," said Dreamer's father. "If you are to learn, you must pay attention—you must stay awake.

"You can draw pictures with the stars, just like you can imagine pictures in the shapes of the clouds in the daytime. There is a difference though," said the father, "the clouds are scared, frightened by the wind, and they take on new shapes very quickly. The stars are not like that. They remain almost fixed. Let's set up some wooden poles and I'll show you what I mean."

The father had known what he must teach his son, so he had prepared two wooden poles, one shorter than the other. The longer pole he forced into the soft soil near the spring in a true, upright position. The pole was taller than the boy, so that Dreamer had to look up to see the top of it. Flowing Spring now took the shorter pole, and, with some sighting, also thrust it into the ground in an upright position. It was a long arm's length away and directly south of the taller pole. The father had carefully lined up the tops of the two poles on a particular star. He told the boy to bend down and get behind the shorter pole and sight up over the taller pole to see the star.

"The 'Pole Star' never moves. It is a constant star, and the tail end of a star picture that the early Wise Men called 'Little Bear.' The end of the tail always remains in the same location. It is a guide star," the father continued. "You must always remember where to find the pole star in the night sky because knowing directions in your travel will be essential. Time will not matter much, but the right direction will matter.

"Listen carefully, for what I'm going to tell you is not easy to understand," warned his father. "Some say the pole star is also the last star on the handle of a 'little dipper'; you know—a gourd dipper—one that can hold water. At least, that's the picture I see. Well, this little dipper rotates around the end of its handle, since the pole star always stays in the same location.

"Now, there is also a picture of another dipper, a 'big dipper,' and it is up and to the left." As he said this, his father pointed. Placing the boy before him he held his hand and pointed to the location in the sky where he wanted his son to look.

Sure enough, there was another dipper, much larger than the one with the pole star at the end of the handle. The boy stood in front of his father and studied the two dippers. He had seen them before but had not realized what he had seen. His father told him that the two stars on the outside of the bowl of the big dipper always pointed to the pole star and that he must always remember this when he looked into the night sky for guidance. "It's a good way to find the pole star."

The father turned his son around. He stooped down so he could peer into his face and said, "You already know that Father Sun rises in the east and sets in the west, but you have not lived long enough to track Him in the winter and the summer and remember His travels. This you will learn later. Tonight your quick lesson is about objects in the night sky.

"Now let's talk about the big star we call Mother Moon. You already know that our shortest time measurement is the day, from one sunrise to the next. Our next time we tell by the light of Mother Moon, from one full moon to the next full moon; as I have been watching and counting, she averages about twenty-eight of our days.

Long ago a wise man counted the days from the longest summer day until the next longest summer day had returned. He, too, used a pole, but he watched the sun's shadow at the top of the pole, and he pegged it as it moved across the ground. He found there were 365 days from summer to summer, or from winter to winter. He was a very wise man, and his teachings have been handed down from father to son, just as we are doing on this dark night.

"Father Sun is mysterious, but He is regular," said Flowing Spring. "We don't know how He got there or how He manages to stay suspended in the sky. We're all just glad that He doesn't fall like the stones we throw into the air. Father Sun provides warmth for us.

"Now, think. Where is He at midday in the winter?" asked the father. The boy looked south, away from the pole star, and he pointed halfway up towards the southern horizon. "Correct," said the father. "Now, where is He in the summer?" The boy pointed almost overhead. The father, who had kept track of such events in his lifetime, now asked the boy how long it had taken Father Sun to go from low to high. The boy had a perplexed look on his face, but since it was dark, the father didn't see his expression. "Well," the father said, "What is the answer to my question?"

"But, Father," the boy said. "This is all new to me, and I don't know the answer."

"Think," the father gently prompted the boy. "How many moons from one high sun overhead until the same sun comes back to the same spot high overhead again?"

"Well, about twelve or thirteen; we all know that," said Dreamer. "Oh, that means that about half should be the answer."

"Correct," said the father, with an air of satisfaction.

Flowing Spring picked up a third pole he had brought to the spring. He placed it in the ground at the location of the short pole and said, "Suppose we're at this point" Now, moving the pole in a sweeping motion, but keeping one end on the ground, he said, "If we point it first at the winter sunrise, then at the high winter sun and then at the winter sunset, it moves like this. Then, if we point it at the summer sunrise, then the highest sun of summer, then to the summer sunset, it would be here." He moved the upper end of the pole while leaving the lower end firmly on the ground at the base of the short pole.

He continued with the lesson. "Father Sun gives us light and heat. He shines much longer in the summer than He does in the winter. You can see that by the movement of the stick, can't you?" the father questioned. "In the winter there is much darkness, and it is colder and there is snow and ice."

"Yes, Father," the boy said, half understanding what his father was getting at. "The high sun shines longer and makes our Mother Earth warmer," said Dreamer.

"Yes, the sun makes the seasons," replied the father. "When it's cold, the plants rest, but when the high Father Sun comes, the plants grow. The oak tree gets leaves, then flowers, then has acorns which ripen, then the cold comes and the leaves die and fall off. It's the cycle of the seasons, and it all has to do with Father Sun shining on Mother Earth. We name our moons after the seasons, like the Green Moon of Spring, the Hot Moon of Summer, or the Brown Moon of Autumn and, of course, the White Moon—the Cold Moon—of Winter."

That all made sense to the boy, but it was night, and it was dark, so why talk about Father Sun now?

Flowing Spring continued, "The stars will guide you at night, like Father Sun guides you in the daytime. Watch carefully and you will see the stars move slowly as the night progresses. They will all turn around the pole star. Those that are above the pole star will turn towards the setting Father Sun, and those below will move up, towards the rising Father Sun. The pole star will remain in the same place.

"Now that we've been here quite a while, line up again with the tops of the two poles and look again. See, as I told you, the pole star has not moved." Sure enough, it had not moved. However, the boy could see that the other stars had moved ever so slightly, just as his father had said they would. Some had disappeared beyond the horizon, and new ones had appeared at the opposite horizon.

The father, said, "Look at the big dipper again. If you come out every night at the same time, you will find that it moves too. It goes around the pole star and makes a complete circle.

"Our wise men call this big dipper the 'Big Bear,' because more stars help make the picture of a bear. It is hard for me to see the bear, so I just call it a dipper, like our long-handled gourd. The dipper also goes halfway around each night. This I discovered once when I couldn't sleep. It made me to wonder, so the next night I went without sleep. I watched the dipper go around to the other side of the pole star, and that's how I learned that the stars go half-way around the sky each night. I guess they must move back to their original positions as the day passes," said the father, "although in the daytime we can't see them.

"It's not easy to learn so much in one evening, but since you will be going downriver soon, you must learn as much as you can as fast as you can," said the father. "You must ask questions."

Dreamer didn't know what to ask; he was silent beside his father.

After a long, quiet moment, Flowing Spring continued. "There are several other bright stars in the night sky, but they move around altogether differently. One has a reddish tint and the other is white. Sometimes they are morning stars; sometimes they are evening stars. Sometimes you can even see them in the daytime. This is especially true of the evening star. To do this you would line it up as the sun goes down each day, then on the following day you would look earlier and higher and you would see it. Do this often enough and earlier each day and you can actually see the star at mid-day. Sometime we'll track the star so we can see it during the day," said the father, "for seeing is believing, even though it is difficult to understand. We'll use our poles again when we do it."

Just then a shooting star streaked from left to right, high overhead, in the dark sky. "Well, another one of our people has gone to the Great Beyond," said the boy's father. "There he can hunt and never go back to camp empty-handed. I wonder where he lived? I remember when your grandfather went to the Great Beyond. I had just gone out the entryway of our lodge into the dark night when I saw his star go streaking across the dark sky. That was only two winters ago, but the time has passed quickly. I hope my star is a long time away," said the father.

"Mine, too," said Dreamer, "because I have so many things I must do before it happens."

"Now, let's talk about Mother Moon, the biggest star in all of the night sky, the one star that's always changing. She shines in the night like Father Sun shines in the day. When she is full and bright, we can see features on her, like the bumps on a toad. She is not like Father Sun. She seems cold. She must be much closer to us than Father Sun or the other stars. I believe that Father Sun shines on Mother Moon when she is full and He does not shine on her at all when she is dark. This I believe because when Mother Moon is full in the east, Father Sun has just gone down in the west. When there is no moon, maybe He is just shining on her back side. I just don't know. I believe that Father Sun and Mother Moon are balls in the sky.

"Mother Moon is mysterious," continued Flowing Spring. "One day, I remember, She completely blocked Father Sun from shining. We were all afraid. We thought we had lost Father Sun , but after a few moments, He reappeared on the other side. The daytime Mother Moon had gone between Mother Earth and Father Sun, and it was almost dark. It was a peculiar experience. As the crescent sun shone through the tree leaves, one could see many little baby crescent suns reflected all over the ground.

"Did I tell you that we can break moon time into quarters? We can keep track of the halfway time between full Mother Moon and no moon. When she is exactly one-half bright, that is the quarter moon. Remember that. It's easy to remember because it's a about a seven-day period, one quarter of a full moon time.

"We have days, quarter moons, full moons, and sun years. That's how you will have to keep track of time on your journey downriver. It is hard to teach about the stars and Father Sun. One can learn more by watching. You will have to train yourself to observe them. Observe, learn, and remember. While you are on your trip downriver, you will have plenty of time to observe, since you will be alone. Are you sure you don't want another boy to go with you, someone you could talk to and someone who could help you if you need help?"

"No, Father, I have to do this alone. If I had someone else along, then I would have to help him too, and that might just slow me down," said Dreamer. "You have given me much advice and many lessons. I have

44

listened to the elders at the spring Powwow. I listened. I learned. Now I believe I am ready to go. I wanted to wait until Mother Moon was full, but now I believe I am ready to go."

"Well, why not leave tomorrow? It's late, but you will get enough sleep if we return to the lodge now. Your mother and I will see that you have what you need for your long journey. We have been gathering things together all during this last moon. You name the things that you want to take, and we'll gather them together. We all want to help you," said his father with great reluctance, because he knew he would miss his son very much after he was gone. "Son, my 'Dreamer,' it is time for your test to become a man.

"When we were at the Spring Powwow, I informed the other elders of the journey you were dreaming about. They were all in accord that if you completed your journey, you would indeed be a man, for no other boy has ever had to pass so great a test. They agreed that if you returned home, you would be given a place of honor among all the clans of the Rocky River Nation. Then you would be a 'Great One,' sharp-eyed and wise, like the owl, the eagle of the night, who can see the slightest movement below. I know you are already wiser than all of the other boys of your age.

"I, like my father before me, will give you my best greenball bow, my best arrows and quiver, and even my prized arrow kit, the one I received as a gift. After you are gone, I will have time to make new bows and arrows— yes, I'll have plenty of time.

"Your mother has been preparing and saving food for you to take along. She too knew you would be wanting to leave soon." The father and the boy took one more look over the poles at the pole star. The boy could see that the other stars had moved slightly towards the horizon and in the direction that his father had told him they would move. "The pole star is our guide. It will always be there to serve you," said the father. "Remember this first star lesson. You must learn other star lessons from others wiser than I. You must learn and become a teacher. If we are ever to live better, each next generation must know more, and have fewer burdens than the generation that has just passed. We must all work together to make life less difficult. But, enough now, it's time to get some sleep," said Flowing Spring, his friend, his teacher, and, as always, his father.

Back at the lodge Dreamer crawled under his deerskin cover. It was late, but he shook his little sister awake and told her of his plan to start on his journey down his River of Dreams in the morning.

Half awake, her murmur came out, "O.K. Tomorrow."

Down His River of Dreams ...

. . . .

It was now morning. Dreamer's father had spent a very restless night thinking about the problems and dangers his son might encounter on his journey down the river. Since he was an early riser, his father was already on his haunches beside the spring when Dreamer came to draw the morning water.

He looked up at his son, as only a father concerned about his son's well being can look. Dreamer sensed his father's serious mood, so he dropped to the ground beside him.

They sat together for quite a long time, neither speaking. The only sound to be heard was the rapid "tat-tat-tat," of a far-away woodpecker, working intently on a dead limb, and the soft gurgling of the water spilling over the boulders at the nearby spring. There was no wind, and daylight was beckoning through the gray clouds in the east. Father Sun would soon be casting His rays through those morning clouds at the two silent figures at the spring.

Finally, Dreamer spoke: "Father, some people see things and they question. I dream of things that I have not seen, and I believe I can find the answers."

There was a long silence.

As they stood facing each other, the father took his son by the shoulders, looked squarely into his eyes, and said, "Son, that's what makes you different. You think for yourself. Yes, you really are a 'Dreamer.' Some want to see what is beyond the next bend in the river. I believe you are one of them. Go, and may the Great Father Sun above protect you."

After a slight pause, he added, "Go where your dream takes you. Live your dream each day as you go down the river. It will be quite an undertaking, your trip down the river to find out where the water goes. Who knows what is beyond the last bend of the river? Do not depend entirely upon yourself. Listen to the animals and the birds, for the Great Spirit speaks through them. They will warn you of trouble. Listen to their wisdom. They live today because they listened and heeded the warnings."

Quiet prevailed as Father Sun began casting His warm rays on the two standing together. "I wish I were going with you, but I know that cannot be. The journey will be yours alone; I will await your return. My journey was many years ago, to the unknown lands towards the setting sun. You have already heard my stories. When you return, I'm sure you will have even greater stories of your own to tell.

"Do not take a scene or situation as a matter of fact, but see it as a story with a beginning and an end. Study the clouds and see how they move. Listen to Father Wind as he blows the trees and notice how the birds have to fly a little left in order to go a little right. Listen to how birds and other animals communicate, and watch to see how the insects work to find food. Watch and listen and you will learn.

"Now, regarding learning: you can learn by listening to teachers, those who will tell you what is over the next hill or what is around the next bend of the river because they have been there; or you can learn by watching others who are more skilled than you are and then copying their actions; or, finally, you can learn by your own trial and error.

"I hope your trials are small and your errors few. When you leave our camp by the spring and go down your River of Dreams, you will face many uncertainties.

"As with most opportunities in life, you will probably never get the chance to do it over, so, plan your journey with thought. I've done my best to give you my good advice," the father told his son that morning. "Use caution in everything you do. Beware of the wolves at night, because it is in the dark when they gather in packs; they can then take prey much larger than themselves. Beware of friendly people whom you meet along the way, or at first use great caution, until they have proven their good intentions. Be careful along the way. Never leave your back open to harm, and always be ready for trouble. If you see trouble in the distance, then you are the fortunate one, with the advantage on your side. Then you can usually skirt the problem and never know how bad it might have been. Use caution in your every action, no matter how small your move might be. Most times it will be best to go slowly. Scan the broad horizon.

"My Dreamer, you have an intense curiosity about things," said the father. "I can't give you much more advice than what I have already given you. I can't pick you up if you should fall along the way. I want you back safe and sound. If you are not back within a reasonable time, I'll come looking for you.

"I want to go over our code one final time.

The father slowly ticked off the items of the code on his fingers:

1. Listen to your elders, for they are wiser than you are.

2. Know that you don't know it all. There is too much for one to know everything, so benefit from the experiences of others.

3. Think in terms of success and have faith in your actions.

4. Do what has meaning to you.

5. Try it if you think you can because most everything is possible.

6. Stalk with the wind in your face and use all your senses—look, listen, smell, touch, and even taste if you have to.

7. Know where your belongings are at all times, for sometime you might have to find them in the dark.

8. Watch your back and sleep with one eye open and one ear listening.

9. Always get a good night's sleep, for you don't know what tomorrow will bring.

10. Assign yourself a goal each day.

11. Promote fair play and treat others as you would want them to treat you; share with others who have less than you.

12. Evaluate yourself at the end of each day. Ask yourself, If I could have done it in a different way, how much better off would I be?

Dreamer listened. He nodded his head each time his father counted off an item as he went through the list.

The bond between father and son on that early morning was like the bond between a mother and her unborn child. After his final words of advice and caution, his father turned and walked, head down, towards the shelter. He lifted the door flap and in a moment was gone, the flap settling down behind him as if it had never been opened.

Dreamer was now alone in the still of that early morning, with the rising Father Sun warming his face. The trickle of the spring water over the guardian boulders and the soft cooing of a pair of doves were the only faint sounds to be heard. The woodpecker in the far-distant dead tree must have found his worm, for he was now quiet.

. . . .

Little Sister began to stir under the soft, well-worn deerskin. She stretched as she woke, and one foot came out from under the covers. She lay still for a moment, felt the chill of the morning on her foot, then pulled it back to the warmth of the covers. She rolled over, seeking her mother's back against her own little back. She rolled into emptiness, so she raised herself on her left elbow. Everyone was gone. She was the only one left in the lodge that had protected the family from the chill and the dew of the night. She dressed quickly.

There was a hustle and bustle around the campfire that morning. Father Sun was already up in the east, two hands above the horizon. The fire had been restarted and was glowing with a bright orange flame. The pots of water were sitting on the hearthstone, ready for the hot stones to make them bubble.

The day was a beautiful, clear, blue-blue day. Not a cloud was to be seen. A slight breeze from the northwest gave a chill to the air, so Dreamer, his mother and his father all had their outside clothing on. Dreamer had picked a fine day to leave on his journey.

Little Sister noticed that something seemed a little out of the ordinary. Two of her father's bows, a quiver of arrows, the arrow kit, and her brother's deerskin pack were stacked together next to the spring. She got up quickly, not wanting to miss anything, and hurried to the fire, pulling on her buckskin jacket as she went.

Little Sister went directly to Dreamer with a perplexed look on her face. Had she lost his confidence? She said to her brother, "Dreamer, you said you were going to tell me first when you decided to be off on your journey." There was a tear next to the bridge of her little nose. A sad look was on her face, and she spoke with a lump in her throat. She felt he had wanted to leave before she even knew about it.

"But, Little Sister, when I came to the covers late last night, I woke you and told you tomorrow would be my leaving day. You said, 'Tomorrow—O.K.,' don't you remember?"

"You told me no such thing," she said emphatically.

"You must have been in deep sleep when I told you. This morning I'm off on my journey. You can see what has been put together already. This morning I will be on my way."

Little Sister looked at the pile of deerskin clothes, the two small bags of food, the deerskin pack, the bows and arrows, the arrow kit, and the soft deerskin night covers. She also saw some patches of soft leather and several breechcloths. Leggings made of rabbit skin and ropes, made of waxed and twisted deer sinew were also on the pile. His mother had not forgotten the fire-making kit, which sat at the edge of the pile, neatly wrapped and tied together in its waterproof pouch.

The boy's mother had made a special vest for him, and he tried it on. It was a little loose, but the fine otter fur against his skin felt good. He knew if it were any tighter, it would not be a warm garment. He would turn it with the fur outside when the warmth was not required. It had four otter tails hanging from under the left arm, two at the front and two at the back. The arm holes were just loose enough to give him room to use his arms. On the front of the vest his mother had sewn a long flap on each side. These pockets would hold necessities during the trip. The boy felt honored that his mother had made such a special vest for him. Otters were hard to catch, for they were sly and quick. He also knew he had his father to thank for the vest, for he knew it had taken many otters to make such a large and beautiful garment, perhaps as many as eight. Blue Damsel Fly had matched them carefully and sewn them together. She had also sewn two extra pairs of moccasins for her son. Deerskin cords went from the top of the arch to tie them around the ankle. His mother had put double soles on them and tied the tops and bottoms together high along the edge so they would last longer. The soles were made from the tough skin on the back of a deer's neck. On the topside she had made a design of the sun with water beneath it. On each moccasin she had also sewn four beautifully matched, small, white shell buttons as a decoration, knowing that, if he needed to, Dreamer might use the buttons for trading purposes.

As for trade goods, his father opened the pouch that held his three galena cubes and gave his son two of them. Flowing Spring also gave his son all but two of the white flint arrow points from his Powwow gift pouch. His son would need them on his journey and he could make more for himself.

Flowing Spring had talked to the elders of the bluff people, convincing them to provide Dreamer with some soft, heavy, brown-green stones to use for trading purposes. He explained to his son that they were very scarce and desirable stones that could be bent into different shapes by pounding. They had originally come from the land further north. His father knew the people downriver also prized these stones. "There will be some conditions attached to receiving the stones," the father told Dreamer. "Seek out Wing Feather when you reach the bluff. He is the one with whom I made the pact. He will give you the stones."

Little sister came to where Flowing Spring and Dreamer were talking. She felt it was her turn to have some time with her brother. Otter Tail said, "I'm still feeling bad you didn't tell me first that you were going to leave today." She and Dreamer sat together on the cool rocks next to the spring.

Dreamer repeated, "I thought you were awake and understood what I had said."

"She shrugged and said, "Here, I want you to take this 'good luck' with you." She handed him a cleverly woven fetish of grass, sticks, and hair. It had a continuous, twisted, coiled rope of grass and eight small sticks radiating out of the center, all tied together with her black hair. The grass had been dyed black and yellow, and the sticks had been stripped of their bark. The whole coil was about the size of the boy's palm. As Dreamer looked closely at the wheel, he noticed that the coloring and the weaving had a resemblance to a spider in its web. He thanked his little sister as he gave his interpretation of the fetish.

"You're right," said Little Sister, pleased. "It's because the spider started you thinking about the trip you will be taking down water; this time you will be the spider."

He said under his breath, "Yes, I'll just be a little spider on a leaf going downwater." Now he spoke more loudly, "I may be the spider on this trip, but I'll have more control.

Father, I will be careful; I'll return with the proof that I made the trip to wherever the water goes, no matter how long it takes."

Dreamer looked over the pile of food, clothes and other odds and ends he would take along. The pile had grown quite large. "Will I be able to carry all this? His backpack would hold many of the smaller items and most of the food and extra clothes. The bows and quiver of arrows he would take but, he decided he didn't need two bows, so he handed Flowing Spring one of the bows. "Father, you keep your best bow. The one I will take along is equally good, and the pull is easier for me."

The father accepted the bow but took the five small red feathers from the top end and tied them to the bottom end of the bow his son would be taking. "The red feathers will bring you good luck and good hunting, and you will need both on your trip down your River of Dreams." he said.

The father further cautioned Dreamer, "When you meet other people, or when you are in their camps or villages, always meet them in a friendly manner. All people respect friendship—but always be cautious."

The boy's mother prepared the meal a little later than usual for she wanted her son to partake of his morning nourishment just before he left. The family was quiet for a long time as the six of them ate in silence. Dreamer's mother was the first to speak.

"You know, you will have to spend a lot of the time on your journey just finding food. Then you will have to spend time preparing it. This journey will not compare with your one-day trip down to the Rocky River and back. When you meet hardships, or go hungry, remember your home, the spring, the campfire, and our stick lodge covered with deerskin, which gave you the protection from the dew, the rain, the cold and the snow. On many stretches of your journey you will probably have to make a trail for yourself because there will be none. We all wish you the speed of the Great Spirit—and his protection." The mother turned her head away from the boy; a tear in her eye, a tear of love and concern, not of sorrow.

Flowing Spring had returned from the lodge, where he had been thinking. Now, back at the spring, he put his hands on Dreamer's shoulders.

"My Dreamer, you are going off into the unknown. You will be among strange surroundings, and you'll meet strange people. I hope you will have wonderful experiences. Don't think all will go well, for when you least expect it, you will have a test that will be greater than any that you have had before. Be careful; that's all I can tell you."

Dreamer listened and thought, but did not speak as his mother and father gave these last cautions before the final farewell.

Dreamer was also quiet when his little sister spoke: "Yes, I want you to be careful too and come home and tell me stories of your journey down your River of Dreams. I'll be waiting for you."

All the farewells complete, Dreamer went to where his backpack and other necessities lay. First he put on the double-thick moccasins his mother had made for him, binding the thongs around his rabbit skin leggings. The fur was on the outside now because it was beginning to warm up. He knew he would shed the leggings soon and put them back in his pack for safekeeping. He pulled the backpack over his shoulders and shifted it until it felt comfortable. Slipping the arrow kit over his left shoulder, he swung the quiver and unstrung bow over his head and onto his right shoulder. He carefully placed his white flint knife with the deer antler handle into the leather sheath on the thong that held up his breechcloth. Concealed in the sheath, the sharp blade wouldn't cut into his skin.

Finally, his father gave him the clan totem to take along. It was protected in a deerskin cover to keep the eagle feathers clean.

2

Dreamer was ready to go. Father Sun was working His way halfway overhead, but Dreamer was in no hurry. He knew he would spend many days and nights on the journey. His goal today was to go only as far as the camp of the bluff people.

The farewells over, his belongings packed, he walked to the spring, turned right and walked down the path beside the brook. Before going out of sight behind the willows, he turned and waved a final farewell to his family.

They waved back.

He was on his way at last.

As he disappeared, his little brothers questioned their parents, "Do you think he'll ever come back?"

Dreamer, loaded down with all his belongings, continued down the path beside the brook away from his campsite. He didn't look back.

When he came to the creek, he turned left, continuing on to the grove of oaks where, earlier, the red squirrels had scolded him. The little animals were gone today. Downstream, the other creek met his creek and it became larger.

This was familiar territory. Downwater he continued, on to the sandstone bluff. He walked out onto the gravel next to the water. Here he waited and watched, looking for activity on top of the bluff. He scanned the path where only two moons ago he had seen the young girl, with the long braid of black hair, as she came down to the stream to fill her water pots. He stood still next to the creek for a very long time. Father Sun was just past overhead. Dreamer had made fairly good time.

He heard a bark and a shout from the top of the bluff. Several boys of the clan and their dogs had seen Dreamer waiting at the water's edge for some recognition. Three or four adults were now in plain view, motioning Dreamer to come over to their side of the creek, to climb up the bluff and be recognized.

He took off his moccasins, secured his backpack and waded across the creek. The creek was shallow at first, but became deep enough to cover his knees. Climbing out of the water on the far side, he was now on the flat rock on which he had seen the young girl kneel to gather her water. He climbed the narrow path that led to the top of the bluff. It was steep, so he had to be careful.

After he reached the top and had taken a few steps, a little coyote-like dog, brown and gray in color, came within two lengths of him. Dreamer stopped, but the dog still growled a warning. Standing quiet Dreamer didn't know what to expect. The dog was called off by one of the children. Wing Feather then came forward, making the sign for, "I'm a friend and I come in peace." Dreamer responded with the same sign, realizing that he should have signed first because he was the intruder.

Dreamer knew the bluff people were part of the greater Rocky River Winnebago Nation. Since they all spoke the same language, he understood when two of the elders welcomed him to their camp. He looked around, taking in every detail. This is a clan of at least four families, maybe five, he thought, and that included Wing Feather and Tail Feather.

Then he saw the girl who had gathered water, the one he remembered as so beautiful. Yes, it was the same girl he had watched when he had concealed himself behind the big black willow on the opposite stream bank. She was shy at first and stood behind her mother. He also recognized her from the Spring Powwow held only a half-moon ago. He hadn't known it then, but now she was introduced as the daughter of Wing Feather. Her name was Bright Spirit.

He knew the elders from the day at the Powwow when the four of them, he, his father, Tail Feather, and Wing Feather, sat all afternoon under the Council Oak. Wing Feather had not told him then of his beautiful daughter. Wing Feather knew he would come by the bluff camp for the brown-green stones. Now that he was here Dreamer admired her. He was not yet a man, though, so he could only look. Several times he caught himself staring.

Wing Feather confirmed that the boy's journey would be his test of manhood. All the elders at the Powwow had voted, and no broken sticks were in the basket that day. They all agreed, but only if he would complete the journey, return, and enlighten all of the clans of the Nation about what he had found down his River of Dreams.

Now it was time to discuss the heavy, brown-green stones. To his surprise, Dreamer found that the only condition attached to receiving the stones was that he return to the place from which he started. This was quite a condition—for it had a hidden meaning. If he didn't return, he wouldn't be a man. He knew he must return.

Wing Feather handed him six of the stones. Dreamer was surprised there were so many, so heavy, and yet so small. Would they be a burden on his journey? No matter, somewhere along the way, he knew he would use them to good advantage. He thanked Wing Feather.

Returning from his journey was an awesome responsibility. "The elders must have much faith that I can complete my journey and bring back information about the lands downwater," he said quietly to Wing Feather.

"Yes, they do," was the short answer.

Even though he was now in a hurry to be on his way, he stayed for the evening meal. He decided he would spend his first night with the bluff people.

Bright Spirit talked to him shyly as they sat around the campfire. She wanted to know why he had taken on such a dangerous and awesome task, being so young. He told her of the spider, the leaf, and his dream. He told her it was something he had to do. "I have faith that I can do it," he told her. "I believe in myself and must take this chance to prove I can do it. My father, Flowing Spring, has taught me many ways to survive on my journey, no matter how long it may be. All the elders at the last Powwow shared ideas that I can use along the way.

"I am confident I will return. I'm not fearless though, for I know I will have many trials, and perhaps, even make some mistakes.

"I do want to see you when I return," said Dreamer, looking straight into her big, brown eyes.

Wing Feather then said from the darkness, "Come to the warm covers. Come—for it is time to rest. Tomorrow you will want to be fresh and ready. Tomorrow you will begin your journey downwater—your test to become a man. It's time for sleep."

Together, Bright Spirit and Dreamer went to her father's lodge. They raised the doorway flap and went inside. Dreamer went to the men's side. All that was left was a place next to the outside wall, where the poles had been forced into the ground. It was a bit uncomfortable, but he lay down on his side and pulled his deerskin cover over his shoulders. Soon he was fast asleep. It had been a long day. There was no dreaming this night.

. . . .

Dreamer woke early and went outside the small lodge. He was careful not to disturb any of the sleeping people who had accepted him into their camp. A light fog in the valley below the bluff was gradually disappearing. He hoped it would be a good day.

The eastern sky was getting brighter, but Father Sun was still below the horizon. Dreamer sat quietly on a log next to the fire ring. He held his hands close to the heat in the small mound of ash.

Wing Feather's wife, Warm Feather, came from the lodge. Letting the entrance flap fall back into place, she went over to the pile of wood, selecting four medium-sized logs about as big around as her arm, she brought them to the fire ring and gently placed them on the warm ash. Soon orange flames were licking at the dry wood. The blaze radiated heat, and Dreamer again held out his hands toward the fire. The heat felt good.

Warm Feather spoke, "Dreamer, you will no doubt want to be on your journey before Father Sun is high in the sky, won't you?"

Warm Feather continued, "I'll fix you some porridge and add some ground brown seeds to give you nourishment on your journey down the Rocky River."

Even though Warm Feather and Dreamer had been speaking in hushed tones, the rest of the Bluff Clan were now rising. The eight adults and ten children included Bright Spirit. She was especially charged this morning because she would wave farewell to Dreamer, as he would begin his journey downwater. Many times she had looked down the river from the gravel point where the creek meets the river. A long way down, the Rocky River turned left and went out of sight. Bright Spirit spoke: "Dreamer, you must hurry back so you can tell us where the water goes."

After the morning meal Dreamer put on his moccasins and shouldered his pack and slipped his other belongings into their proper places. He remembered especially to replace his flint knife in its sheath, in the deerskin sash that held his breechcloth tight around his small, sinewy body.

The great oaks growing on the bluff obscured Father Sun, finally rising in the east. Wing Feather told Dreamer he could follow the creek by walking downwater along the top of the bluff; the well-worn path would make the going easier.

Dreamer checked his backpack where he had placed the six, heavy, brown-green stones, the small pieces of float copper given to him by Wing Feather. They were wrapped tightly in a small, triangular piece of deerskin and tied into a neat little bundle. He placed his hand down around the package and gently lifted it. It was heavy, so he knew the prized stones as well as his two galena stones were safely tucked away.

He thanked Wing Feather, Tail Feather and Warm Feather. Then, with a look toward Bright Spirit he said, "I'll see you when I get back." He was hoping she would still be here when he returned because he liked what he saw. They gave each other's hand a slight squeeze...Oh!

The path curved to the right skirting a small sacred mound Wing Feather had told the boy about. He had also told Dreamer to keep to the path to go around it. Passing the mound quietly, a short walk took the boy to the River with Rocks. He looked upstream and saw the river splashing with white ripples over the rocks. He recognized the gravel bar at the mouth of the creek, but this time he was on high on the right side of the big creek.

3

In order to get started this morning, Dreamer must do one thing, if only to reinforce his sense of direction. He picked up a small piece of dry wood and threw it into the mouth of the creek. It floated eastward. Upon entering the Rocky River, the floating stick took a gradual turn to the right, to the south, and continued downwater.

Pausing briefly to adjust to his surroundings and seeing all was in order, Dreamer followed the well-worn path. It was close to the river, on top of the bank, fairly high above the water, and stretching as far as he could see. "This will be easy," he said to himself, and he was on his way.

It was easy going. Even though the hill next to the river rose to twice the height of Wing Feather's bluff, there was still a pathway, which led southward.

The path apparently had not been used for some time, because small fallen limbs blocked it and slowed his progress. He felt he didn't have to be too careful here because he was still close to home. He picked up most of the small branches, pitching them far back into the brush or over the bank. Some of the small limbs he simply grabbed, lifted them, walked under them and replaced them across the path. The spider webs blocking the path he brushed aside. There were too many of them to worry about. It would be a give-away, their not being there, that someone or something had used the path recently. But he really didn't care; alone, this morning, close to home, he felt safe.

He continued on, going downstream along the west bank. Sometimes he was at the water's edge, and sometimes he was on the first terrace looking down into the river. He walked steadily, stopping only to drink from a spring feeding a small brook he had to cross. He had to cross one just about every time he felt thirsty.

Now he stopped under a large oak tree on a flat area about twice his height above the river. He could see quite a way upwater and perhaps twice as far downstream. The river in his downwater view was making a bend to the left again. Would the river ever let him see its end?

Dreamer, now tired, put his pack on the ground. Untying the flap, he reached inside and found something he had not packed. It was a small package, just large enough to fit inside unnoticed. It was tied with another twisted sinew bowstring, similar to the ones in the kit that his father had given him. Unwrapping the package, he found some deer pemmican and some freshly cut watercress.

"Bright Spirit must have packed this, or perhaps her whole family had a hand in it," he said to himself. He was right. The family of Wing Feather had each contributed to their little send-off for Dreamer. He nodded with appreciation as he downed the meat and greens, saving the small piece of deerskin and the bowstring, tucking them into his backpack.

After shouldering up, he was on his way again. He wondered how far he would go on this second day of his journey and hoped it would be far enough downwater that he wouldn't want to quit and go back to his camp by the spring.

With Father Sun directly overhead, Dreamer came to another small river about half the width of his Rocky River. Up this little river he saw two otters sliding down the bank into the water, then climbing out, and sliding back in again, playing tag. The otters' antics had dislodged some of last year's willow and maple leaves from along the bank. They floated downstream towards the Rocky River. "I'll call this little river the Leaf River," said Dreamer. "Those leaves remind me of the little spider that I sent down the brook on a leaf well over a moon ago. I wonder if he made it this far, or maybe even beyond?"

Turning, Dreamer saw two oaks growing together, not more than two arms' length apart. Although it was still early, he said to himself, "I've gone far enough today." With that decision made, he turned and looked for some downed logs to stack on the windward side of the two oaks.

He tugged several small logs to his campsite and leaned a log against each tree, next, placing a small log about chest-high across the top of the two diagonals. On the windward side he then stacked logs vertically, leaning them against the top log. He planned to crawl in under this leaning stack of logs later when he went to sleep. Wanting protection from the falling dew, he covered the outside of the logs with last year's dead grass. Then he put a couple of additional logs on top to hold the grass in place.

"Yes, it will do. Even if it rains, it will do," he said out loud. He looked around to see who might have heard him. It was quiet. He was alone. Dreamer sat a long time, his back to the tree, looking at the river. Later he decided to eat some of his dry food for the evening meal. After portioning out a small amount, he ate it very slowly. He leaned back again against the large white oak that faced his shelter, running the events of the past two days through his mind. It had been a busy time.

Looking down the Rocky River, Dreamer saw that Father Sun was setting exactly over the middle of the river. "Strange," he thought. Then he remembered all the twists and turns he had taken that day as he followed the river.

"Now the river flows west," he thought. He leaned back against the oak through twilight time and on into the dusk, staring. He was tired.

His eyes closed. Then his head jerked, and he was awake again. It really was time for sleep, so he unrolled the deerskin cover that had been tied on top of his pack. He slid in under his protective log shelter, lay on the cover, and then rolled over, pulling the excess deerskin completely up over him, and soon he was fast asleep.

Dreamer had never traveled so far in one day. No dreams came this night.

He awoke the next morning to the "Caw, Caw, Caw" of six black crows, high in the tall branches of the soft maple trees across the river. Could they be warning him of danger?

Slowly, he slid out from under his shelter and looked around. "Nothing that I should worry about," he thought. "Perhaps it's only something that they should be afraid of, or maybe they just woke up too, and felt like they had to stretch their voices. Well, at least I'm awake, and up—even though it is early. Wing Feather said the high sandstone bluffs would be three days' travel from his camp, so, I'd better be on my way." He packed his belonging and was on his way again.

He had to go upstream on the Leaf River for only a short way before he found a tree down, spanning the river. He crossed on the tree very carefully. Back to the Rocky River, on his left, he continued downwater.

He passed a, small, wet, boggy prairie that went off to his right into a little valley full of white daisies, several different kinds of tall grass, blue flag, and yellow marsh marigolds. He would like to have explored it, but he knew there would be others like it along the way. He decided he should push on towards his goal. "The high sandstone bluffs shouldn't be too far ahead," he thought, as on he trudged.

Sometimes he was at the river's edge and sometimes he was on the first floodplain terrace, but he was never out of sight of the river.

Dreamer crossed two small streams this day, one when Father Sun was halfway up to overhead, the second a little after mid-day. He held his moccasins high and dry over his head as he steadied his pack to cross the streams. By then Dreamer was hungry. He ate as soon as he had crossed the second stream.

The Rocky River next took a bend to the right. In the distance he saw tall, green, pine trees They were high on the bank across the river. They were the tallest evergreens he had ever seen. There were so many that they made the distant hills look black. Scattered among the pines were smaller, white-and-black canoe bark trees. Dreamer had only heard of this tree because there were none where he lived by the spring. It was said they only grew farther to the north. Now he knew different.

On his side of the river, down past several bends, Dreamer saw some very high, brown bluffs. He wanted to keep going because he could now see his goal, but he was tired. "It'll keep till tomorrow," he thought.

He prepared his campsite in haste, rolled in underneath his deerskin cover, and was fast asleep on this, his third night out.

. . . .

This day was much like the first. Dreamer kept to the path on the bank at the river's edge. Sometimes he had to go around marshy areas, especially where a small creek flowed into the Rocky River. The path took him around these wet spots quite nicely. Many had used it, and he could see footprints upon footprints in the mud. Occasionally, he would meet another person coming up the river. He had no idea where they were going, and he didn't want to know either. Most of them just nodded and gave the "I come in peace" sign, which he returned. The women he met didn't look him in the eye, they just turned their heads and kept going.

Late in the day he met three hunters whom he had first seen on a high point of land at the very edge of the river, down at the next bend. He caught sight of them every once in awhile as they came to an opening in the trees. One of them was carrying a small limp deer over his shoulder. Another carried two bows and quivers, evidently his own and those of the deer carrier

Dreamer sat on a log at the edge of the path and waited for them as they slowly made their way up the path on the west bank of the Rocky River. When they saw him, they were quite close. The forward lookout, the one with the notched arrow in his bow, stopped. The one carrying the deer almost bumped into him. The lookout apparently decided that a boy sitting on a log with his hands folded on his lap was really no threat, so the three continued on.

When they were abreast of Dreamer, they stopped. The one carrying the deer leaned sideways, and the deer slid to the ground. Needing a rest from the heavy burden, he also sat down on Dreamer's log.

"Good hunting," signed Dreamer, as he nodded his head.

They nodded their heads, too.

Dreamer, not knowing whether they would understand him or not, said, "I'm sure your clan will be glad to see you bring back enough food to last for a quarter-moon."

They acknowledged his message with more nodding.

"You hungry?" the one carrying the deer questioned, signing and pointing to Dreamer, then pointing to his own mouth.

"Yes," Dreamer nodded.

"We can share," the hunter said. Removing his flint knife from his belt, his hand went to the bottom of the deer's neck, where he had already made a cut. He further opened the cut and stripped some of the red meat from the still supple animal. It was time for the evening meal; Dreamer could feel it in his stomach.

While one stranger was cutting out some meat, another had his fire kit out and was spinning his spindle into the dry wood of the plate. He held the plate down with his left foot. Soon smoke was rising. He dropped the spindle, carefully scooped up the hot coal, placed it into his tinder of cedar shavings, then after he blew a few times, a flame appeared.

In the meantime, Dreamer had been gathering some dry sticks. Together, the two built a small fire.

The fire was not large, but it didn't have to be. They each held their own meat over the fire. Raw deer was a delicacy, but cooked venison was easier to chew, and tasted better, especially when rubbed with some of the strangers' flavoring herbs.

Right there, next to the path, sitting on the log, the four of them ate their evening meal. Dreamer thanked them and told them where he was going.

They looked at one another puzzled, as if to ask, "Why make such a trip?"

The three indicated that their clan lived in the pine forest not too far away. Their camp had been short of food, so the three had gone on a hunting trip in the river bottoms and had killed this yearling deer. Later tonight the whole clan would be eating venison, thanks to their skill and accuracy.

Before they departed, they gave Dreamer several strips of deer meat. This time the second hunter took his turn in carrying the limp deer. Now Father Sun was almost down in the west.

"How fortunate for me those hunters came along," Dreamer thought. They have completed their task; I have a task to do and I'd better get on with it." Dreamer picked up his things and continued down the path from which the hunters had come.

Dreamer was thankful he had met the three friendly hunters. His stomach was full. He was again on his way, but Father Sun was now far down in the west. Had he spent too much time with the hunters? Would he make it to the sandstone bluff today? The day was running out.

After walking around the next river bend, Dreamer again looked downwater. On the right, and not too far away, he saw his goal: the huge sandstone bluffs. They looked threatening. The river had cut into them over many years and at the riverside there was an almost vertical drop. He was anxious to get there and climb the bluffs. These certainly were the bluffs from which Wing Feather had said the view was awesome and inspiring.

Dreamer hurried downstream. The going was quite easy because of the path along the top of the riverbank was well worn by the animals of the area and the local people alike. Dreamer recognized many of the small animals' prints. The path led around the backside of the sandstone bluff, but Dreamer took a side path leading up toward the top of the bluff. It leveled off, and then climbed again. He noticed small cedar trees growing out of the cracks in the sandstone rocks.

At last, he came to the promontory. It truly was an awesome view, and just as inspiring as Wing Feather had said it would be. Dreamer was tired, so he sat down on a small outcrop of sandstone, a perfect seat. For a long time he was content just to sit; even though Father Sun was almost gone. He would spend tonight high up on this great rock.

Dreamer noticed that others had used this campsite. In this high, flat area, there was a ring of rocks that had held previous campfires. He could see flint chips lying on the ground; some flint-shaper had also worked here. Dreamer decided to use the same fire ring. He could tell it had not been used since the last rain, seven or eight days ago. Again, he felt safe.

He gathered wood from the valley behind the great rock. On the third trip up the rock, he saw a little whitetail rabbit watching him from under a low currant bush.

He continued on to the top and carefully put his armload of wood down. Picking up his orangewood bow and two arrows, he made his way back down the path to where he had seen the rabbit. As he had hoped, the little white-tail was still sitting in the same spot, his nose and whiskers working up and down, as though nothing had happened, or was even about to happen. He used an oak tree as cover and crept closer to the little animal. Every move must be slow.

With the bow and one arrow in his left hand, Dreamer took the other arrow and set its notch into the bowstring. He laid the arrow down over his hand on the bow and moved slowly around the tree, not wanting to frighten the rabbit.

Slowly, with the bow taut and in position, and using the third aiming mark, he let go of the arrow. "Twang-zip-thud!" He had learned his bow and arrow lesson well. He now had tomorrow's meal lying on the ground only sixteen paces away, but still kicking. With his flint knife he made a quick cut at the neck to quiet the rabbit.

Back on top of the bluff, with the fire-making kit his mother had given him, he started a fire. He used dry grass as tinder, and blew and blew on the little red coal he had moved onto the dry tinder. First there was smoke, and then a little flame appeared. He carefully placed the burning grass next to a small bundle of dry twigs and soon a small fire was burning. His mother would have been proud of him. Then, after warming it, he finished the remainder of the deer meat.

He would keep the fire going through the night to provide some warmth as he slept. His campsite was already in the shade since Father Sun was now down in the west, behind the high oaks and the green pines. Now he could feel the chill of the night air on his face.

Dreamer sat with his back to the great sandstone rock and his bare feet to the fire. Directly across the fire ring was a rise in the rock that sloped straight upwards. It was a flat surface with a small horizontal crack, but it was sound and looked as if it would never break. He picked up a large flint chip from the ground and went over to the vertical rock. He made a few scratches, and before he knew it, he had drawn what looked like a feather. Then he scratched some lines into the rock, which retraced his route over the last four days. His drawing on the wall began at Wing Feather's camp on the creek and wound its way down the Rocky River.

It was a map, but it was also more. It was a timeline that showed the Rocky River he had traveled, the streams he had crossed, and the springs where he had quenched his thirst. He placed an "X" where he had spent his first night with the bluff people. His next "X" was at the Leaf River. He then marked another "X" where he had spent his third night on the river. He drew the evergreens between the third and fourth mark. Now his "X" would be right here where he would spend his fourth night high on the great sandstone bluff.

Where would he spend his next night? He went over the route again with the flint chip and dug it deeper into the sandstone.

"How can I remember it all?" Then it came to him. His little flint knife was sharp enough to make a slight cut into one of the deerskin patches his mother had given him. He started a crude map on one of the larger pieces of deerskin, rubbing a burnt stick into the cut. Now he had a record scratched into the deerskin. He started at the top; he could add to his map as his journey progressed. He was pleased. Dreamer banked the fire with several more logs.

Looking eastward, he saw the shadows creeping in over the tops of the tall pines growing on the hills in the distance. He had arrived at the sandstone bluff with no real problems, and he had a full stomach, thanks to the three friendly Indians he had met on the path, and he had a warm fire and a good place to spend the night. He also had his meal for tomorrow.

How would he take care of his rabbit kill? He certainly didn't want anything to get it during the night. Larger animals prowled at night looking for food. He tied an extra bowstring from his pack to one of the legs of the rabbit, and then dangled the rabbit over the ledge of sandstone on the riverside. He hooked the eye end of his bowstring to a stub on a small cedar tree. Tomorrow's meal was secure for the night. He felt comfortable and turned back to the fire.

Dreamer laid on several more logs. His deerskin cover was already spread out and ready, so he slipped beneath it.

As he lay there watching the small, crackling, orange fire, he thought about his journey. His dream of finding out what was downwater was becoming a reality. The first leg of his journey was complete. From here on, everything would be new. "What experiences will I have?" he questioned himself. I can hardly wait until morning, so I can . . . , " and he was fast asleep.

. . . .

Morning came quickly. The clouds in the eastern sky again went from gray to light gray to red. Father Sun peeked through the dark-green pine trees. Darkness was gone.

Dreamer stirred, rolled over under his deerskin cover, and was up on an elbow very quickly because a small rock had dented his back. He was quite stiff from his sandstone bed, so he stretched out as long as he could. "Why didn't I find that little rock last night?" he wondered.

Looking carefully, he surveyed his surroundings. Without moving his head, his eyes took it all in. He finally decided he was all alone, so he sat up, but continued to check for any signs of danger. He remembered the cautions his father had given him five mornings ago.

He pulled up his rabbit kill of the night before. The little fellow was rather plump after all but quite stiff. He removed the bowstring, carefully wound it around his hand and put it away in the side of his pack.

"I guess I should have dressed him out last night; though, being stiff, he'll be easier to clean up. At least I can hold on to him better."

With his flint knife, Dreamer went to work on his rabbit. In no time at all, he had stripped off the furry skin. Next he cut off the head and feet and left them with the skin. He then pitched the fur ball into the river. If he'd been at home, he would have given it to his mother.

Next he removed the insides, throwing them into the river, too, thinking they would be good food for the fish. He was surprised that he had quite a lot of good, red meat. In order to keep it clean, he placed it on a small piece of deerskin.

Now Dreamer stirred the fire. Under the gray ash there was still life—a bed of hot orange coals. He placed several of the unused logs on the fire that had reawakened.

He cut the red meat into strips and placed them on the charred, black rock on the downwind side of the fire. He could have used a forked stick, but, since he wanted to check and pack his belongings and be on his way as soon as possible, he decided to cook his meat the easy way. He turned it once; it was brown and dry.

He ate some of his cooked rabbit and also some of the watercress he had saved from the spring water of yesterday, then he wrapped most of his rabbit in a piece of deerskin, and placed it in his pack. Next, he tied the cover on the top of his pack and picked up his bow and quiver of arrows. He slung his pack onto his back, and was ready to go.

Last, he scattered the fire. Glancing around once more, he saw the map scratched into the sandstone wall.

Now he was off, down the path — leaving the great rock behind.

About mid-day, after traveling down the broad valley, Dreamer came upon some new sandstone bluffs that blocked the flow of the river and sent it back toward the direction from which it had just come.

"Strange, this reversal of directions," he said to himself. He followed it back anyway, but then it turned again. He continued following the river as it made this grand loop.

Towards evening he came to some rough water such as he had seen on his one-day trip to the river not too long ago. That was the day he had walked on water, the day he had discovered the Hallowed Grounds. He could probably walk on water here, too. He didn't chance it, though. He kept to the path, following the river as it went downstream.

After eating his cooked rabbit, this night he again slept under the stars with his deerskin cover over him. It kept the mosquitoes of the early evening and the dew of the late night off him. As he looked back with his mind's eye, he thought, "I made pretty good time today."

The river valley was now quite wide, so he decided to keep to the upland forest as he followed his river. He trudged on until he was tired. Father Sun was now going down in the west. He was restless that evening. That night, before he turned in, Dreamer added a few more lines to his deerskin map.

. . . .

The morning dawned dark and gloomy. The fog would take its time to lift, but this didn't bother Dreamer as he gathered his belongings. He had now spent twelve days and nights on the river. He had seen new lands and new people, some of whom he hadn't wanted to see him, so he skirted them widely and quietly.

Today the valley was broad, and the bluffs were taller. He skirted the sloughs in the flatlands, as he was climbing higher and higher into the bluffs.

He always kept the Rocky River in sight. The oaks and hickories made a forest with less undergrowth. Now was easy going. He had traveled far by the time Father Sun was high overhead,.

As he came to a point where the bluff rounded off to the right, he suddenly saw a great, wide river. It seemed more than ten times the width of his little Rocky River. His father had told him there would be more surprises; the Father of Waters, the Great Mississippi, was certainly one. It flowed from right to left, and he was on the wrong side of his Rocky River. He was now 13 days from home.

There were two cottonwood trees, one on each side of the Rocky River, and there were eagle's nests in them. He would be very quiet. He would sleep near the large log up on the beach.

He would spend the night right here at the confluence, looking down the great river, contemplating his actions of tomorrow and reflecting on the adventures of his trip so far.

The trip had been easy so far. He had made good time walking the worn paths along the bank of his Rocky River. The small brooks and streams he had crossed with very little effort. But he could see that tomorrow would be different.

First he would have to cross his Rocky River. It had now become very muddy. He could see it quite well as it bent to the left and entered the Great Father of Waters. "Ohhh . . . , " he moaned, "tomorrow may be quite a day."

Dreamer found two small trees, not too far apart, forked in the same direction, about shoulder- high. He placed a stout, dead limb horizontally in the two forks. Then, after leaning a few short sticks on the horizontal limb, he stretched his deerskin blanket across the sticks. After placing a few more sticks on top, he now had a shelter in which to spend the night. He built a small fire to drift smoke over him as he slept to protect him from mosquitoes.

The Great Father Sun was lowering Himself toward the distant horizon. Dreamer watched Him play tricks with His many colors upon the ever-changing clouds. Red, orange, magenta, then dark maroon to dark blue, and finally a break in the distant clouds near the trees on the distant horizon allowed a streak of sunlight to shine through. Again Father Sun was red-orange as He disappeared behind the trees far across the river.

It was twilight now. The Great Father Sun was below the tree line. Darkness would soon be upon him.

Dreamer didn't want a big fire this night for fear that the light might give away his presence. He didn't want to disturb the eagles either. Anyway, the breeze in from the river would also help keep the pesky mosquitoes away. Sleeping would be no effort tonight.

Even the distant howling of wolves didn't bother him. He knew there were more wolves on the far bank of the Great River than on his side. Only one or two returned the call from his side of the river, and they were quite a distance away and on the other side of his Rocky River. He had no worry there.

He sat up for awhile. It was quite dark when he finally lay down. Tomorrow would be a big day, a day of decisions, and he had better be ready for it, and for them.

. . . .

The cool morning fog drifted across the water like dense clouds that had come down to Mother Earth. It continued like white smoke from a dying campfire.

As Father Sun rose higher in the east, the sky was slowly getting lighter, and Dreamer could now see beyond the trees and across the rippling water. The fog was slowly lifting; finally he could see the sandy shore across his Rocky River. He must follow the current of the great river, but how would he do it? Looking around to solve his puzzle, he saw several driftwood logs, just the size he could handle. "They can float down the Father of all Waters, and I can float with them—on them." He started building himself a raft by lining up seven logs, side by side, at the water's edge. One of them had a limb sticking out. He would place that spar straight up; it would be a good place to hang his pack and his bow and quiver of arrows. There they would be high and dry, out of the splashing water. He would also tie his eagle feather totem on it because he wanted to keep it dry, too. Then he went back to the undergrowth and cut many lengths of greenbrier vine. Three small vines braided together made a rope. He made many strands of the greenbrier rope. Further up on the slope, he also found some new growth grapevine and brought it back to where he was building his raft.

To make his raft sturdy, he put some smaller pieces of driftwood across the ends of his logs. Then, he tied it all together with his newly made rope.

He needed one final addition to the raft, a drag with which to steer the raft. He would use that long narrow pole further down the bank. He fastened it in place on the backside of the raft with some more of his rope. Now, was he ready to go?

"If I leave any of my belongings behind, I'll never be able to come back and pick them up. Once I've started down the Father of Waters, I'll have to keep going. I hope I can steer my raft—or will I just have to go with the current?" he wondered.

He hung his belongings on the spar, pushed the raft down over the

rocks, and was in the water and underway. His raft worked well and was so solid that it functioned perfectly. Dreamer was quite satisfied. Drifting with the current he could steer his raft.

"Perhaps I should stay close to the shore. That way, if I have any trouble I can wade out of it. I'll use the extra dry log if I have to. I can hang onto it and kick and paddle my way to safety."

He was on the river and making good time, counting the trees going by as he drifted quietly passed them. He soon learned that he could steer his raft by moving the trailing, long, narrow pole in the direction he wanted to go. Though the steering pole was about as thick as his arm, it was light enough to lift out of the water. Yes, he could actually steer his craft.

Dreamer made good time when the wind was from behind. He knew those were his best days, and he counted on them.

When he was on the shore, Dreamer hunted for food, gathering birds' eggs, frogs, turtles, snakes, last year's nuts, berries, roots and greens. He stocked up on food to carry along on his raft journey down the Father of Waters. Drinking water was no problem; he drank from the river, although he preferred a clean, cool spring, as he had at home. Food was more of a problem.

As a lone traveler, he had observed the cautions given by Wing Feather and Tail Feather. They had told him to be wary of strangers. They told him of others of the clan who had been away by themselves and never made it back home. They warned him that certain clans made it a practice to steal the very young and raise them as their own. They also told him that a lone individual could be captured quite easily by a band of warriors out looking for a "prize" to bring home.

For this danger, the elders had decided to let him take the totem on his journey downwater. They said it was a "holy staff," and it had magical powers because it bore the talons and the tail feathers of the majestic eagle, the mother of all birds and the protector of all life on earth. Since it was so all-powerful, it would protect him from all dangers. He was glad to take it along. It was tied to the upright spar in order to keep it high and dry.

He knew the staff's protective qualities were real, for on several occasions he had seen strangers approach his craft, only to turn away when they got close enough to see the large white and black feathers flying in the breeze. Dreamer intended to protect the totem with his life.

The river was getting larger and wider. His Rocky River and other streams and rivers that flowed into the Father of Waters made it grow. This

Down His River of Dreams ...

Father of Waters had many "children." He wondered if all the streams that fed the Father were similar to his Rocky River. When he came upon the larger ones, he knew there were stories to be told, if only rivers could talk. Perhaps he would meet another dreamer coming down that river from the land of the setting Father Sun, a dreamer like himself. However, he met no one.

His Great Father of Waters flowed downstream in mighty, large curves. By the time he passed one point, he would see another point on the opposite shore, and he would direct his little craft towards it. The Great River constantly turned and turned again. Sometimes it was forced around a high bluff where Dreamer might beach his craft, securing it with vines and pushing poles into the bottom of the river.

He took his possessions with him when he climbed to the top of a high bluff. Almost always it was covered with trees. From his high vantage point, he would look down the river and see the never-ending forest and the Great Father of Waters threading its way through the low land, going on and on. There were many islands on the insides of the curves. Sometimes he would take the broad, outside curve, and sometimes he would take the narrow chute, out of the wind. When he cleared the chute, he would look back on the other side of the island to see where he might have come from had he taken the long way around.

It was on the sandy islands that Dreamer liked to spend his nights. He felt more protected there, especially on the chute side. The river shore adjacent to the chute was usually marshy and muddy, and he felt that in itself was a deterrent to any stranger who might try to creep up on him. He was right, too, for one time he tried to camp on the shore side of the chute, and as he got off his raft; he sank in mud up to his knees. This scared him; however, he was reassured knowing others would have the same problem.

Floating down Father River was no easy task and it took careful attention. He had to be on the lookout for water snakes, especially the poisonous ones. He had handled snakes, but having been bitten once, he was wary of them. A snake could be food, if he was hungry enough. He also watched out for bad ripples on the water, which usually indicated sunken logs or rock outcroppings that could upset his raft. Quicksand, overhanging branches, and of course, other people who might harm him were also concerns. So far, his journey had been without any bad luck, and for that he was thankful.

Late in his seventh day on the Great Father of Waters, Dreamer saw a small camp at the mouth of a creek on the right shoreline, farther downwater. Since he had been keeping close to the right bank of the river, he was close to the camp and could see about twenty people gathered around a campfire, most of them children. They were preparing the evening meal.

It was time for Dreamer to eat and, perhaps find some fresh, clear, clean water. A rest was also due, so Dreamer steered his log raft for the rocky shore, toward the people.

The people of the Black Hawk Clan were friendly, especially the children. They wondered about a stranger coming in from the river, floating on a raft of logs. They had seen Dreamer long before he saw them.

Chief Hawk Eye lived at the mouth of a narrow clear-water creek. He was the Chief of the Hawk Clans of the area. He saw to it that his clan shared their fish and spring greens. Hawk Eye apologized for the skimpy meal. He said the nuts and seeds had all been exhausted before the last winter snow had disappeared. Maybe they would have venison tomorrow.

Dreamer spent the night with them. After the meal, they all sat around the campfire. Combining his language and sign, Dreamer told them of his quest, down his River of Dreams.

None of the elders knew where the water went, so they had no answer to his question. They did understand what he was telling them—where he had come from, and where he was going.

Their question to him was, "Why?"

It was hard to explain something to them when they couldn't understand all of his words; although they understood the man task part. They thought Dreamer was on a dangerous mission, and they told him so—in words and signs. The negative comments didn't deter Dreamer from his task; in fact they challenged him.

As they talked on into the night, darkness fell, and it was becoming more difficult to see the hand signs. One positive exchange, however, did take place.

Dreamer discovered that Chief Hawk Eye made his arrowheads from the white flint of Hawk Eye Creek. He said it chipped even and true and made the finest points. Chief Hawk Eye understood that Dreamer had some trade goods with him—pieces of brown-green, native copper ore and he very much wanted a piece.

Dreamer, after quite a bit of haggling, gave Hawk Eye one of his smaller pieces of copper ore in exchange for ten pieces of the white Hawk Eye flint.

The flints were the size of his palm; in fact they were "pre-formed," and each one fit nicely in the palm of his hand.

Dreamer thought he got the best of the deal, but Chief Hawk Eye knew he came out on top. They were both satisfied with the exchange—as it should be.

Now it was time to turn in. Dreamer was given a place next to the fire. When he went to sleep, his pack and his bow and quiver of arrows were within his folded arms. He stuck his totem upright into the ground and supported it with a pile of small rocks. It would protect him.

. . . .

It was Hawk Eye's mate, White Daisy, who woke him as she was adding a couple of logs to get the morning fire started. Birds' eggs cooked in hot water would be the morning meal

Now that the meal was finished, it was time for Dreamer to go. The children of the Hawk Clan helped him push his raft off the rocks. They were in the water, pushing with their hands, and Dreamer, with his long pole, was also pushing away from the shore. Finally, off the last rock, the current took control of the raft, and it was moving downstream. The children waved as he departed. The others waved goodbye from along the shore.

Dreamer guided the small craft a little further out into the river, where the current finally pulled it along with ease.

The broad valley, extending far away to his left, was covered with willows, maples and an occasional cottonwood. On his right, after he passed another creek, he saw a high bluff. He wondered why Chief Hawk Eye had not built his camp there, for it had the security of a steep bluff on the riverside and only needed watching from the back side. From it one could see upriver to the first bend. He thought it would be a great place for a campsite. But, with the fresh water of Hawk Eye Creek, it was easy to see why the chief had chosen the location he did. "I suppose I'll also find other clans with camps on clear-water creeks as I go down my River of Dreams," he thought.

When Father Sun was highest, Dreamer came to a large, muddy stream on the right. On the gravel bar where this new stream met his Father of Waters was a mother skunk, the stinky animal, teaching her three little skunks how to find food. Skunks liked fish, and if they could find dead ones, that was all the better. Now, next to the water's edge, one of them was reaching out with a tiny paw to secure a fish. They looked up at Dreamer as he went by their Skunk River.

The Great Father of Waters was getting wider, and the curves were getting longer. Dreamer decided he had better stay close to the shore, for he felt safe there because he couldn't swim. Maybe someday he would learn. Because he couldn't swim, he kept a smooth, light piece of driftwood loose on the raft, wedged between the spar and the second log, easy to get at, in case his raft overturned. He thought this might happen if it hit a submerged log or a floating tree. He wanted a guarantee he could make it to shore. He was following the code that his father had reviewed with him the day he left camp back at the spring. He knew he should be prepared for anything.

The Great River made wide turns as it flowed downstream. Dreamer had a second thought, "Why should I spend so much time staying close to the shore? I can make much better time by going from point to point." Changing his plan he straightened out the curves, as he navigated the great river.

Many large streams emptied into his Father of Waters, making his river larger—greater than he had ever thought it could be.

He made it carefully through a channel at the white rapids three days after leaving the camp of the Black Hawk Clan. Now, drifting west, he came to another muddy river much like his Rocky River from back home. This river also made his river muddier. He thought, "The rains must have washed off Mother Earth, and in cleaning her, just dumped the muddy water into the streams to get rid of it." He passed many of these rivers and streams, all pouring water into the Father of Waters, some from the right and some from the left, some large, some small; so many children!

Dreamer had spent many nights on different gravel bars these rivers and streams had washed down as they wore away their banks. Some of the gravel points even had large trees on them, their roots washed clean of soil, trees now dead and breaking up. They provided the firewood Dreamer needed to make the fire that cooked his food and kept him warm at night. The smoke from his fire also kept the pesky black mosquitoes away. His night fires served him well.

Waking up, Dreamer rubbed his eyes. When he took his hands down, the great flock of birds that had spent the night in the cottonwoods were now high on the bank across the river, toward the rising sun. He knew they were having their morning meal from all the fluttering activity and their quick moves, which he could detect even from his distant location. It was time for his morning meal, too. What was there to eat? He had used up all the food he had been carrying, the food that had been given to him as he left the camp of the Black Hawk Clan. Now he would have to find some.

He followed the path, stepped over a fallen tree, and went through a couple of spider webs covered with dew. Then, as he jumped a small stream, he scared a bird from its nest. The nest was built of grass and located in a thorny bush, just arm- high and easy to reach.

He put his hand in the nest and pulled out three, small, blue eggs, still

warm from the mother bird's protective feathers. "There will be more eggs and more birds," he said apologetically. "Thank you, Mother Bird."

Birds' eggs were best when cooked in very hot water, but there was no time for this, so he cracked the eggs together and let the liquid run out into his hand. He looked at it for a moment, then raised his cupped hand to his mouth and took in his morning nourishment. He ate a few black and red berries and went back to his raft. On the way he found some burr-nuts and he took them along. No game today, so he was still hungry, but it was time

to be underway.

He passed more streams on the right and on the left. Then his own Father of Waters took a sharp bend, turning back on itself; still going downstream. Again on the left a very large new river met his Father of Waters. (Today it is known as the Illinois River.) It was the largest river he had encountered on his journey down his River of Dreams. He kept going though, his raft serving him well.

Coming around the next bend in his mighty river, he saw high on the limestone bluff, on his left, a picture of a big bird painted on the face of the rock. It was facing right, but looking in the opposite direction. The large red and black bird had a hooked beak, long wings and four feet with large talons. It was painted on a smooth, vertical face, high up on the bluff.

"How could someone have painted this bird?" He asked himself. There were trees on top of the bluff, so he decided the painter had used vine ropes to lower himself down to work on the picture. It was under a small overhang and had survived the elements fairly well. Dreamer knew the colors had to be renewed every once in awhile because the hot afternoon Father Sun would be hard on it. The rain would try to wash it off, too.

I wonder what kind of stains he used to make the picture? Mulberry, elderberry, and black tar that seeps out of some of the cracks in the bluff? He must have used them all," he thought.

I'd best honor this 'Great Bird' as I go by." He held up his Eagle Totem as high as he could. "I honor you, Big Bird on a High Rock," he said aloud.

He thought, "Wouldn't it be a good idea if we had 'our eagle' on one of our rock bluffs back home? No, we can't do it. We don't have a place for it. Our rock bluffs are crumbly, not nearly as nice as this."

Soon the "Piasa" Bird was out of sight, behind him, back over his left shoulder. Now he looked ahead.

. . . .

There was another big river on the right. It was a wide river pouring great amounts of muddy water into his Father of Waters. It was also turbulent and carrying all kinds of trees, driftwood and debris with it

"I'm very glad I'm on this side of The Father of Waters," thought Dreamer. "There must have been bad rain storms far up this new river because it is carrying everything with it. This new muddy river must be one of the biggest children of my Father of Waters."

He watched the debris pour forth from this new muddy river. He knew he must stay close to the shore because he didn't want to get tangled up in any of the trees and limbs that were floating in the water. He stayed very close to the east bank of his Father of Waters.

Dreamer pushed his steering pole towards the bank even more. He glided safely down his side of the Great Father of Waters.

It was now mid-day, and he felt a little hunger pang. Having traveled now for many days, his food supply was quite low. He was concerned, and he knew he would have to put into shore soon and find some food. There was always an abundance of food to be found in and around the water. Whatever he saw first he would take, whether it was frogs, turtles, snakes, or birds' eggs. He would eat anything that would get rid of his hunger pangs.

"I must be careful and not get tangled in any of the floating debris," he thought. He steered closer to the shore, his steering pole working well. Soon he had eaten, so it was back to his raft to continue downwater.

-4-

Quite a way downstream, there were children on the left riverbank. Dreamer couldn't make out what they were doing, but he watched them carefully as he drifted slowly down the Great Father of Waters. He could see they were on the far side of a small creek. They had small pieces of wood laid up in piles. "It must be firewood," he thought to himself.

He had to go right by the children, but they didn't seem to be afraid. There were probably sixteen or twenty of them.. He realized that it was he who should be afraid of such a large group. He had the advantage, though; he was out in deep water and quite far away.

Those who seemed to be the leaders motioned him to come toward shore. They had no weapons, and they were not serious; in fact, they seemed joyful and noisy.

What should he do? Go on by, or point his raft toward the low, muddy bank? They were still motioning him to come in. He was tired and hungry, so he decided to accept their invitation. He steered his raft towards the bank of their small creek. He glided past the gravel bar and was soon alongside the children. He threw them a greenbrier rope, and they pulled him in, even closer to shore. A few rocks rolled under his raft, but he didn't mind.

Dreamer wanted to meet them on his terms, so he held up his right hand, palm out, and in sign language asked who was in charge. It was then that two of the older boys came down the bank to meet Dreamer.

He raised his eagle feather totem high, and they stopped, now cautious. Dreamer invited the taller of the two onto his raft. They could communicate fairly well with signs, and it appeared there would be no trouble.

Dreamer said he had come from far up the Father of Waters. He told them, by sign, he was determined to find out where the water goes.

The taller boy indicated to Dreamer that they were on a firewood-collecting mission. He said firewood was getting scarce at their village, and they now had to go a long way to find it. They were to carry home a supply that would last for a quarter-moon. He pointed to the several piles of wood the troop had collected.

"You cannot take my raft for firewood."

The taller boy again spoke, "We have enough now. You can leave your raft where it is. It will be safe. Now, won't you come to our village? It's almost time for the evening meal."

When he mentioned food, Dreamer felt much more at ease. He secured his raft to the bank by tying it up, both fore and aft, then pushing his steering pole into the mud on the riverside to help hold it in place.

Gathering his belongings and putting them over his shoulder, he followed the children down the path toward the village. He could see smoke at a great distance so he knew they had quite a hike ahead. "Some of them will be tired when they get home, having to carry those big bundles of wood," he thought.

The boy that had helped him with his raft walked by his side, saying he was a friend. He was probably the same age as Dreamer and had no doubt not completed his "man task," either. Dreamer didn't ask. All he cared about was going to their village and food ahead.

Dreamer's new friend said his name was Little Turtle. He was in charge of the group, telling them to rest often; their loads were heavy. Little Turtle and Dreamer had a chance to talk during the eight or nine rests the troop took to get back to the village.

And what a village it was. Many people gathered around little groups of lodges, probably one for each clan of the village. Behind each group of lodges were great mounds of earth. Far to the east, there was the largest mound Dreamer had ever seen. Whose could it be?

Little Turtle said it was the home of The Great Sun, the Chief of the Cahokia Nation, who lived on top of the mound. That was all he would say. He was interested only in getting the firewood home, sitting around the campfire, and eating his evening meal. He asked Dreamer to join him. His parents always provided for visitors to the village, and he knew they would welcome Dreamer.

As Dreamer had guessed, the family was having turtle that evening, cooked in a pot with greens, seeds, and acorn meal. It was delicious. Dreamer had never eaten turtle cooked like that before. He thanked Little Turtle's mother. He was full and satisfied.

"Would you like to spend the night with us in our lodge? There is plenty of room. There are only three of us," Little Turtle's mother said.

How could Dreamer refuse?

"Of course—yes, I'll stay, but I must leave tomorrow, I'm on my way down the Father of Waters to see where the water goes," Dreamer answered gratefully.

By now darkness had settled on the village. The wind had died down, and the smoke from the many campfires was drifting lazily, straight up. The four entered the lodge, and the stories began.

Dreamer explained what had started his quest to find out where the water goes. "It was the little spider on the leaf at my spring, on a cool morning, now almost two moons ago."

They couldn't believe a little spider started such a journey. They had never questioned where the water went, as long as they had enough to drink, cook with, and to catch and raise fish and turtles in.

Dreamer then heard the "Boom, Boom, Boom" of what must be a large log drum. The father said the drumbeats meant they must all turn in, for no one should be out after curfew had sounded. "That's the way it is in our village." he said. "We have so many people that there must be order, and The Great Sun has decreed that we all turn in at the same time. Oh, there are some on watch, but they have been called to do so. As for us, we'll settle in for the night. We can get up at morning light."

. . . .

It was at sunrise when the Second Shaman raised his staff and knocked loudly at the doorway of the lodge of the Turtle family.

Slowly, Little Turtle drew back the deerskin curtain.

"What can I do to help you?"

"I've come for the boy from off the river—the one called Dreamer."

"Why? What for?"

"The Great Sun has requested his presence."

"Oh, —Yes, yes, he's here."

Dreamer hurriedly pulled on his breechcloth, his leggings, then his moccasins and his otter skin vest—the one his mother had given him as he left home. It was the best clothing he had.

"What does the Great Sun want with me?" and before the Second Shaman could answer, he added quickly, "Of course I'll see him, but first, please give me a moment."

Dreamer went to his corner of the Turtle lodge, checked his pack, and pulled out the largest of the brown-green stones and a shiny galena rock. It would be his gift to the Great Sun. Now he was ready to go.

"Follow me," said the Second Shaman.

They climbed the log steps on the east side, up to the first level of the Great Sun Mound; there were two more levels to go.

"Wait here," Dreamer was told.

The Second Shaman climbed to the top level, where the Great Log House, the Great Cedar Palace was located. He knocked on the post adjacent to the door. Slowly the door opened and the First Shaman came into view. "He's here," the Second Shaman said; "He's down on the first level."

"Send him up."

Slowly, Dreamer climbed upward. He was unsure of himself. He had heard the stories of the Great Sun, the ones told last night in the lodge of the Turtle Clan. The Great Sun demanded honor, respect, and obedience, that he knew.

As they entered, The First Shaman said to Dreamer, "Bow to the Great Sun Chief when you are ten paces away from him."

Dreamer did as he was told. Then he said, "Oh Great Sun Chief, how can I be of service to you?" It was said in a low voice, so low that only the Sun Chief could hear.

"Come, sit on the buffalo robe at my feet. I want to hear of your travels. Where did you come from? Where are you going? What are you doing here?"

With all those questions, Dreamer felt more at ease. Sitting, he told the Great Sun of his spider at the spring, of his reoccurring dream, and the challenge to find out for himself just where the water from his spring went. He told the Sun Chief of his father's lessons: how to make a bow, how to hunt, how to find food and fix a meal, and how to understand and use the stars. He told the Sun Chief of his one-day trip to his Rocky River and of the lessons it taught him.

Anxious to please, Dreamer remembered the brown-green stones that Wing Feather had given him. Reaching into the pocket of his vest, he pulled out the large piece of float copper and also the shiny galena rock. Clenched in his right fist, fingers up of course, holding them out he said, "These are my gifts to you, Oh Great Sun Chief."

The Sun Chief motioned the First Shaman to intercede. Stepping forward and between them, the Shaman stretched out an open hand. "Here," he directed.

Dreamer turned over his hand and dropped the two heavy stones into the hand of the First Shaman. Turning the heavy metal pieces over with his finger, and seeing they were harmless, the shaman gave them to the Great Sun Chief.

The Chief looked at them, tossing the stones up and down, and said, "Your gifts I accept. I have similar gifts of this one kind of stone, but not this big and heavy and I've never seen a shiny one like this little one. Thank you."

Dreamer was pleased that the Great Sun had accepted his gifts and that he was smiling. "Put them with the other trade goods," the Great Sun told the First Shaman.

"Now I want to give a gift in return," said the Great Sun. Reaching inside his robe, he retrieved a beautiful, three-notched Cahokia arrow point. "Our best arrowhead-maker made it. Now I give it to you."

The point was pure white, except for a red streak going down one side. It was about as long as Dreamer's little finger. It was perfect, too good to be used where it might be broken.

"I will wear it on my vest as a mark of friendship given to me by the Great Sun Chief," Dreamer said.

The chief smiled. Yes, he had indeed found a friend.

Sitting again, Dreamer continued with his story of his Rocky River Eagle Clan, of the spring where he lived, and of the family to whom he planned to return, after he had completed his journey.

The great wise Sun Chief spoke: "You have a long way to go to find the answer to the question in your dream. I know because I've talked to traders from far down the Father of Waters. The Great River flows on and on. You will be surprised when you reach the end of it."

"Surprised? Does it go into a hole in the ground? Is there danger?"

"You will be surprised, but have no fear. No, I will not tell you what you'll find. It is best you find out for yourself. You will have many dangers along the way; bad people, bad snakes, bad animals, and you must always be on the alert for danger. That is all I will tell you. Be careful and watch your back—and your front too."

The Great Sun Chief cautioned him just as his father had cautioned him as he was leaving home. They were concerned.

"Before you go, I want you to learn more. I want you to live with us for at least five moons, perhaps until the brown harvest moon is full, when the day is as long as the night. You will see. Our Shaman knows the ways of time. I want you to live with a woman who has no children. She will be of great help to you and you will be of great help to her. She is kind person and she will care for you while you stay in our village. Her name is—well, they call her 'The Wild One.' She is not wild; she is just different. She is a fine woman. You will enjoy her companionship. When the days grow shorter, you can be on your way again. I also want you to find out where the water goes—then come back and tell me."

The interview was over.

When Dreamer returned to the Turtle lodge, all the boys gathered around him. They had seen him go up the steps of the Great Mound. They asked what had happened.

Dreamer told them about the interview, especially of his gifts to the Great Chief and of the Chief's gift of the arrowhead. These boys probably would never have such an experience. Dreamer told the boys of the Great Cedar Lodge, about the buffalo robes and how the First Shaman had put the brown-green stone and the galena rock in the treasure chest that held the valuables of the people. Although Dreamer hadn't been able to look inside, he thought it must contain many treasures.

It was time to go inside the Turtle lodge and tell his new friend of his experience with the Great Sun. He thought his friend would be worried because Dreamer had been gone for such a long time. It was almost time for the noon meal. He told Little Turtle he would be staying with The Wild One and that she would be his mother while he stayed in Cahokia.

. . . .

Later that afternoon, the Second Shaman found Dreamer with Little Turtle, at the pond counting turtles.

The Second Shaman had the Sun Totem with him. This meant he was on a mission with orders from The Great Sun. The totem was a long cedarwood pole, the high end covered with small, yellow feathers, too many to be counted. The feathers fluttered in the breeze. The totem was his mark of authority when he was out among the people.

Dreamer asked Little Turtle to leave so that he could talk to the Second Shaman alone.

"Dreamer, the Great Sun said that while you are with us, you will be staying with The Wild One. I will take you to her lodge now."

The two turned their backs on the turtle pond, Dreamer following the Second Shaman, being careful to keep several steps behind him. They walked around some long, narrow, mounds then past a large pond, across a wide, open area and into a small grove of trees.

The Second Shaman pointed toward a fairly large lodge, off by itself. "There is where you will stay," he said.

A small, gray-haired woman was sitting cross-legged in the shade between the lodge and the fire ring.

"Is that The Wild One?"

"Yes."

The Second Shaman held out the totem and moved it up and down. The Wild One stood up. Her hands were on her hips, as if to say, "What do you want with me?"

The Second Shaman motioned to a spot on the ground where Dreamer was to wait.

The Second Shaman now faced The Wild One. Unfortunately, Dreamer was too far away to hear their conversation.

The Wild One smiled as the Second Shaman, turned around and motioned to Dreamer to join them.

It was all arranged. Dreamer would live with The Wild One while he was in the village. The woman, must have seen twice as many summers as his mother. Dreamer wished he could have stayed with Little Turtle and his family, but that was not to be.

The Second Shaman told The Wild One to take care of Dreamer — to treat him as if he were her own son. She was overjoyed to be of service to The Great Sun. "Of course I will do it," she said.

"You have nothing, Boy?" asked his new foster-mother.

"Oh, I do, but it's over at Little Turtle's lodge."

"Well, go get it, and bring it back here with you," she said commandingly. She had not meant to be gruff. She only wanted him to settle in her lodge and hoped he would have clothes and the other necessities a boy would need. She once had a boy of her own. He was young when he left this world for the next—only ten summers old.

Dreamer returned with his pack, his bow and quiver of arrows, and his traveling totem. She looked surprised to see the totem, especially its eagle feathers.

She took him inside her lodge, where many deerskin covers lay. The men of the village had brought them to her. Her job was to tan the deerskins for them, scraping, soaking, and pounding them, before rubbing a deer-brain water solution into them and letting them dry. The agreement was two skins for them, one for her. She had accumulated many deerskins through this hard work.

She put her tanning equipment to one side. Pulling at some of the deerskins, she made three piles, end-to-end, and hung several from the top of the lodge, to make an area Dreamer could call his own. She said she would keep her three dogs out of Dreamer's area.

That evening, she fixed a meal of broiled fish, greens, and some nuts she had shelled that afternoon. They ate, and sat around the fire, not saying much. They were just becoming acquainted, and silence seemed to work best. As darkness came, the pesky mosquitoes started buzzing around their ears.

"Time to go inside," The Wild One said.

In the center of the lodge was a smaller fire with a little smoke-hole above. The Wild One fed handfuls of dry grass to the inside fire, and white smoke billowed out. She fanned the smoke around the lodge, working it higher. Soon the smoke and mosquitoes were carried out through the smoke-hole. Now the two sat in the common area of the lodge and began to talk.

Dreamer told his story again—of the spider, the spring, the brook, his dream, and now his quest. She was quiet, listening and watching his hands describing the leaf with the spider upon it, feeling comfortable as he had opened up to her. Dreamer also felt comfortable. She didn't understand all his words, but she gave him her undivided attention.

Then she told him of herself. She told him she had an occasional "fit." She said she couldn't help it, but her problem made her an outcast. No man would have her. She was a part of the village, all right, and she earned her keep by tanning deerskins, but, still, she lived in solitude.

"I'm really not bad. I'm just different, and I know it. I try to join in, but the other women don't want me near them. The village tolerates me because I make the softest deerskins. I know my place. Perhaps my problem comes from my losses. I lost my only son when he was trying to save one of the family dogs in the flood-swollen Cahokia Creek He had reached out too far, slipped, and had been swept away in the turbulent waters of the bank-high creek."

She told Dreamer that she had also lost her mate in a similar accident, two years earlier, when he was fishing in the high creek water. After losing both her son and her mate she said she had cried herself to sleep for a period of two moons. "I just wasn't the same after losing them. My hair turned gray overnight."

Dreamer didn't know how to respond to such a sad story. He could see nothing wrong with her. He knew he would be using the clothes, table, and bed of The Wild One's son. He would be almost like her own.

"While I'm here, I'll be your son, and you will be my mother. You can take care of me, and I'll take care of you. Together we'll make our place in the village."

. . . .

Maize, squash, nuts, sunflower seeds, and other smaller seeds, as well as fruits and berries and honey when a bee tree could be found, were food items of the village. Venison, bear, raccoon, rabbit, squirrel, and 'possum were also important to their diet . These had to be acquired from afar. Dog was not uncommon, but, it was used only as a last resort, when other meats were not available. Dogs were valuable in many other ways.

Food was a precious commodity. Yellow maize was the most important food, the principle staple of the village. Festivals were held in its honor. Although some years produced more maize than others, there was usually enough grown to last through the lean times, from the Hot Summer Moon until the Brown Harvest Moon, when the new crop would finally be harvested.

The maize was under the care of the Sun Chief's Second Shaman. The Great Sun Chief made him responsible for its collection and distribution. He kept track of the balance, dividing the total maize crop into quarters for storage in the safe houses. When the thaw of late winter came and the honeybees left their winter nests, the Second Shaman knew it was time to start the distribution from the third safe house. Then, as the people were planting their maize seeds, he broke the seal on the fourth safe house. He distributed the food to the village people according to their numbers.

Everyone did his or her share, and everyone was rewarded with a share of the total. If it was a lean year, the shares would be smaller, but the Second Shaman kept track. He used two deerskin tallies containing all the clans' names.

The great clan leaders, with their sub-clan leaders, would go to receive the rations for their people when it was time for distribution. Each sub-clan leader further divided his ration to the local clan leaders. The deerskin tally worked well. If men were hunting afar, their share would be waiting for them when they returned.

By doing good work the Second Shaman kept his position as third in command, and the Sun Chief kept his people fed, satisfied, and under control.

There were some years when there was thievery, but usually the thief was caught. One thief was caught while Dreamer was in the village, at the time of the Green Moon. The Great Sun Chief decreed that the wrongdoer should be tied to four stakes driven in the ground. His arms and legs were stretched wide, and with deer-sinew ropes, he was tied to the four stakes. It was decreed he be left in the sun, on his back for four days. Everyone, except some of the village dogs, which licked his face sympathetically, shunned him. The thief survived his four-day ordeal, but the sun nearly baked him raw. He put water, crushed willow leaves and mud on his burns after they cut him free. He learned a hard lesson at a great price. Watching the thief blister in the sun was a good lesson for others, too, including Dreamer.

Why would anyone want to steal maize? One of the boys told him, that maize was a commodity that could be bartered. A person with a surplus of maize could trade for many things. Dreamer didn't even want to think about it anymore. His parents had taught him, early on, to take only what he worked for and to work hard enough to provide for himself, and later on, for his family

The ground was now warm enough for planting maize. The First Shaman knew the time for planting because he had been keeping little sticks in the ground and watching their shadows. He had been doing this for many years, and today he knew would be planting day—rain, shine, cold, or fog.

For the planting, the First Shaman wore a yellow robe, and carried a yellow rattling totem with flowing yellow feather tails. He had awakened the people with the loud "Boom, Boom, Boom" of the hollow log drum. The Festival of the Planting of the Maize began early, as Father Sun began to show Himself.

The crows, aware of something special, flew in circles above the fields.

The people met on the east side of the Great Mound to wait for the Great Sun Chief. The people said the Great Sun Chief was a "God" and he could do no wrong. As the Son of the Sun he was the supreme leader of the people, their mentor, and their provider; he was their "Father," and they worshiped him.

Today the Great Sun Chief rose early, putting on his finest robe, the one made of yellow feathers, then departed his lodge by the east door. His people were gathered on the east side of the Great Mound, waiting for his command. The Great Sun Chief stood tall, raised his arms above his head, then dropped them quickly. It was the command to start work. The people began planting the maize.

The First Shaman, with his knowledge of the maize, used only the biggest seeds of last year's crop. He had stored away many, many baskets of seed. They were a treasure of the village.

The baskets of maize were placed beside the large, cultivated field. Parallel lines were made in the dirt with marking sticks running the length of the field, about an arm's length apart. Each family had a row for each person in the family. Making small mounds, about an arm's length apart, they poked three holes in the top of each mound, dropped a kernel of maize in each hole, then with their hands, squeezed the black dirt back in over the holes, closing them up. Now the rain would do the rest.

Maize was the main food of the village. Pumpkins, squash, beans, sunflower seeds, and smartweed seeds also provided food, and the plentiful acorns, hickory nuts, and walnuts of the season of no leaves, were also important.

Dreamer was glad he was able to help with the planting. There was very little maize up in his Rocky River valley. What there was, came in very small kernels and on very small cobs.

Dreamer worked side by side with The Wild One until their rows were planted. Dreamer didn't know if he would see his maize grow to maturity; however, he did know that The Wild One must do her share, now, so that she could claim her share later, at harvest time. Father Sun was at overhead before they finished their planting.

The crows were still circling, hoping the people would leave the field.

The planting done, The Wild One and Dreamer went to Cahokia Creek to clean up. They washed the dirt and dust from their hands and arms, also splashing water on one another in playful jest.

Now clean, they returned to The Wild One's lodge to rest, needing a respite from the heat and work of the day. They were each so tired that sleep soon overtook them as they lay on the soft deerskins. They were quiet as if dead—and it was only early afternoon.

. . . .

Several days later, as The Wild One was showing Dreamer around the village, they came upon a group of women making bowls in which to store seeds, cups for drinking, and large flat pans to be used to make salt, from their salt-water spring. They made salt by the evaporation process. The women were also making clay dolls for the children.

The Wild One thought Dreamer would enjoy seeing them form and fire their work.

They used the best clay they could find.

The pot makers of long ago had learned that to make a pot stronger it had to be tempered with sand or crushed river shells. The taller, round pots were made by rolling long thin "ropes" out of the clay. A flat disc of clay was formed for a bottom. Laying their clay rope around the edge, slowly coiling it upward, they could make a pot just the thickness they wanted. Moving the clay rope in or out adjusted the diameter. Along the way the potters would smooth out the sides to make the pots uniform. Together The Wild One and Dreamer watched a woman who had a large ball of clay lying on sticks to keep it clean. They watched her as she coiled the clay ropes to build up her pot. It went up, coil on top of coil, rope on top of rope, until it was as high as she wanted.

Dreamer told The Wild One that the pots reminded him of the ones that he used when he gathered the water at his spring back home.

When a woman had her pot formed and smooth, she used a stick to make a design on it. One woman had already decorated her three pots with the sign of her clan; a bird much like the Piasa bird.

When the women had about 20 pots completed they fired them in a very hot fire to make them dry and hard. These women had learned the firing technique from older women. Dreamer guessed this method had been handed down for generations.

First they put dry grass down, and then laid dry sticks and logs on top. Next came a grid of green sticks. Finally, the potters set their wet clay pots upon this framework with dry wood and sticks surrounding them. They knew the dry wood, encouraged by a little wind, would burn fast and hot.

The women started the fire from both sides at once. The fire was so hot Dreamer jumped back. It almost burned his face. The women had already backed off to a safe distance. They covered their mouths to stop a laugh when they saw Dreamer leap away from the fire.

After the fire had burned to ash and had cooled down, each woman removed her own pottery. It was easy to tell them apart because of their designs. One of the younger women held out a little cup to Dreamer. It had a small lid that fit it perfectly.

"For me?"

"Yes."

"Thank you."

The lesson was over, and with his new cup in hand, Dreamer followed The Wild One home. He decided that pottery-making was not such a hard task.

. . . .

Little Turtle came over early the next morning. With him was his dog, whom he called "Stinky." Dreamer soon realized the reason for such a name. As Little Turtle and Stinky approached The Wild One's lodge, Little Turtle had to put a hand over Stinky's mouth. The dog wanted to bark, but Little Turtle knew better.

The Wild One's three dogs could smell Stinky. They stood facing the lodge entrance flap, the fur on their necks standing straight up.

Little Turtle said, "Sit. Wait." Quieting his dog was probably a good thing. He knocked and came through the door. They were all relieved. There was no problem, but The Wild One's dogs would certainly protect her if she needed them.

Little Turtle's dog would protect him no matter how big the other boy, or how big his dog was. But today, all the boys and their dogs would have fun. They would all go for a swim. Dreamer didn't know how to swim, but he went anyway. Cahokia Creek had a few holes deep enough for swimming, and the boys knew where to find them. They were at the bends in the creek. The boys liked swimming in the deeper water.

Today they would throw sticks in the water, almost across the creek, for the dogs to retrieve. The creek bank was high, and the dogs would run, be in the air for a few moments, then hit the water with a splash.

The dogs swam like fish after a hopper-bug. They would pick up a floating stick in their mouth and soon be back on shore with their master. It was great fun, especially when two dogs went after the same stick. One would try to take it away from the other. The larger dogs usually won, but sometimes both would try to swim back with the same stick.

When Stinky brought a stick back to Little Turtle, he would get a tickle of thanks under his chin. Sometimes Stinky would even get a little pemmican, if there was any left. Dreamer also scratched his dog under its chin. His Little Pup liked that too.

On the way home, the dogs ran on ahead, sniffing here and there, hoping to find something to eat. Once in awhile they would scare up a rabbit or a big whitetail deer. Today a little rabbit ran over the hill. It was quickly down its hole in the gnarled roots of an old oak tree. Both dogs started digging, throwing dirt behind them so fast that it was starting to build up a little mound.

Dreamer and Little Turtle watched as the dogs worked. They were making progress, smelling food just ahead. They could smell him but they couldn't get him. The rabbit was too smart. From behind the tree, the rabbit came out of another hole, his back door, and scampered away. The two boys watched him go, not even sicking the dogs on him. Such a smart rabbit should get away.

On the way to and from the creek, they met other boys with their dogs. It seemed they all wanted to have a fight to see whose dog was the best. Little Turtle refused because his dog had an ear almost torn off in the last fight. It was still healing. In fact, the water had washed it, so now the boys could hardly notice it. Little Turtle knew which dogs his Stinky could fight and win, and which ones he could fight and lose. He was protective of his dog, his best friend, after Dreamer.

He had been a friend with Dreamer now for almost two moons. They did many things together. Little Turtle had shown Dreamer many out-of-the way places in the village. Tomorrow they would go back to the turtle pond.

. . . .

93

Little Turtle had a few duties to take care of first thing this morning. When his mother found out where he was going, she had a request. "Bring a big snapper with you when you come home. Now, watch your fingers and don't let it bite you."

It was a little later when he stopped by The Wild One's lodge. He had his dog with him, as always. Stinky was well fed this morning, so Little Turtle knew he would be no trouble. Together, Little Turtle and Dreamer went around the small grove of trees to reach the turtle pond by the back path. The pond was located just north of the plaza where the people gathered four times a year.

Dreamer thought keeping turtles was a good idea and the way they kept them so they couldn't they crawl out of a pond and waddle away was clever.

Here was the big depression in the ground where turtles were kept. It had taken a long time to build the enclosure around the pond. Little Turtle's clan had built it quite some time ago. Back then, they caught two big snappers under the ice, and in the mud, in this very pond. They ate one on the spot, hoping to keep the other for a later meal, but it wasn't to be done. They laid the turtle on its back, thinking that position would keep it from getting away. No luck. The big snapper flipped itself over quickly. With long legs and a long neck it was easy

They then built a small pen of sticks driven into the ground, side by side to keep the turtle confined. They kept it for several days before eating it.

Little Turtle told Dreamer that was the idea they later expanded upon. It was an easy task to push stakes into the wet mud at the edge of the pond. The men put everyone to work gathering little sticks that would work for the turtle enclosure. It took many sticks to build the enclosure. They were pushed in, side by side, all around the pond.

The boys stepped over the low stick fence onto some dry ground. Little Turtle told Dreamer that turtles didn't stay in the water all the time; they needed some ground on which to rest. There were also a few logs in the water for them to use.

Now inside, and each having a short stick, they were going to catch a turtle. All they had to do was hold the stick in front of a snapper. It would open its mouth wide, hiss a little, and usually bite the stick. It was a safe way to catch snappers.

Little Turtle's mother wanted only one, so Dreamer dropped his turtle—stick and all. The turtle releasing his stick, headed for the safety of deeper water.

Little Turtle lifted his snapper over the stick fence and dropped it. Since turtles don't go fast on dry land, it wouldn't get away.

"Watch how it can right itself," said Little Turtle as he flipped the turtle over on its back. It didn't take long; with a front leg and its long neck the turtle flipped and was right side up again. Little Turtle stepped on its backside to hold it in place. The short stick was still in its mouth, so the turtle was easy to handle. One had to also watch out for the legs with the sharp claws. Little Turtle picked up his prize.

Now they headed back to the lodge, each holding one end of the stick, the turtle in the middle.

Dreamer was invited to stay for the evening meal. The cooked turtle meat and turtle soup were delicious.

"Are all turtles this good? There are painted ones, soft-shelled ones and of course these sharp-mouth snappers. Are they all good?" Dreamer asked Little Turtle's mother.

"Yes, but some are better than others. The soft-shell is hardly worth the fixing. By the time you cut off the tough shell, there's not much left. We just use them for soup and food for dogs and other turtles. Turtles are meat eaters. We must feed our turtles or they won't grow. We feed them fish, too. Fish they like best, since they also come from the water."

"I've learned more about turtles today than I ever thought I would. They are good to eat, and easy to catch, too. I'll probably eat a lot of turtle on my way down the Father of Waters. He will provide for me, I know he will. But, it's getting dark now. I'd better go. The Wild One will be looking for me."

He waved over his shoulder as he departed. It had been quite a day. Soon he was back home, with The Wild One. He told her about his turtle experience.

. . . . .

Today was the day to build the fish trap.

The builders still had many large stones to carry from the ledge where the rocks could easily be broken out. Sometimes it even took two people to carry a big one. This was a project 20 men and boys from two clans of the

Village were working on. When it came time to trap fish, they would also work together and split the catch.

Over 300 rocks were placed in the bottom of Cahokia Creek to make the trap; a simple plan that worked well. The opening was wide, facing downstream, tapering together as it went upstream. The smaller opening was about an arm's length across, opening into a circle of rocks about eight paces wide. The people could make the trap now because the water was relatively low, leaving rocks half-in and half-out of the water. The rocks had to be showing above the water in order for it to work.

After the rocks were in place, the boys were sent downstream. They walked some distance on the bank so they wouldn't scare the fish in the creek. Then, lining up in the creek and walking upstream, they beat the water with their sticks. They also kicked with their feet to make a great turbulence that no fish wanted to go through. The fish swam upstream against the current, ahead of the boys. As they came closer to the opening of the fish trap, the boys on the ends of the line closed in toward the entrance of the trap. The fish were funneled through the large opening, then through the small opening. Before they knew what was happening, the fish were trapped. There was a small way out but most of the fish couldn't find it. They now swam in circles inside the trap.

Because they were taller, the older boys took positions along the circle of stones and with their forked sticks began spearing the fish. Soon they had over 20 large fish. They threw them up on the bank, where they flopped around as life ebbed out of them. It was surprising how long a fish could live out of water. The boys used their sharp flint knives to slit the bellies of the fish, stripping out the guts, which made great turtle food. They must not waste anything useful. Some fish were scaled or skinned.

A lot of the smaller grayfish, the ones with skin and whiskers, were put into baskets and hurried to two fishponds located near the turtle pond. Surprisingly, the boys also caught three turtles for the turtle pond. This day there would be fish for the Beaver Clan and for Dreamer and his Cahokia mother.

· · · · ·

"Dreamer, Dreamer, wake up, wake up! Today is Meeting Day. It is the Festival of the Green Maize. We must go to the Plaza. Today is the beginning of a new year." Wild One was calling him well before dawn.

This was the day Father Sun came up casting the shadow of the due east stick in the due west direction, straight to the center stick. The First Shaman was sitting facing the center stick in the middle of the circle. The circle was small, only six steps across. He would signal over to the Great Sun to begin the festival, but only if the shadow of the due east stick was right.

Without a cloud in the sky, Father Sun peeked above the horizon and the shadow of the due east stick cast its shadow toward the center stick. It was on the mark, so the First Shaman signaled to the Great Sun Chief.

The Great Sun, Chief of all Cahokia Village, was sitting on his throne on the honor terrace of the Great Mound. He was decked out in his yellow cloak of bird feathers. When he saw the First Shaman raise his hand, he knew it was time to start the Festival of the Green Maize. He always addressed his people on this important day. He rose to his feet and placed his arms over his head. The people who were gathered below returned the gesture. Then the Great Sun Chief lowered his arms. The people lowered their arms and became quiet.

The Great Sun began to speak. "My wonderful people. Listen to me, for what I have to tell you is good. Our maize is doing well. It has had rain and it is green and good.

"The First Shaman, who will give us our new sun clock, is this day elevated to the position of 'Prophet.' He will attend to your needs. He is like you, raised up from among the brothers. When he speaks, you will listen. If anyone does not listen to my words the Prophet speaks, woe to him, for the Prophet has authority over you. He is the law, speaking my law, the law under which we all live together in peace and harmony. The Second Shaman is now raised to the rank of First Shaman.

"You have honored me by being here today. You honor me by serving me, as I honor you by serving you.

"Today, the day of equal day and night, is the day we celebrate the Festival of the Green Maize. We must pray to the Great Sun above for rain to water the maize and make it grow even better. Our maize supply is getting low. What we put away in the first three of our safe houses last year is gone. We have already broken the seal on the fourth safe house. We have more people now, so this year we must harvest more maize to feed them. We must all work together to provide for all.

"The Prophet will start to build his new sun clock tomorrow. It will keep the time in days before we begin the harvest."

The Great Sun raised his arms, pausing again for a very long time. Lowering them, he finished his proclamation and set the scene for the rest of the year. "We have all lived well this past year. You have all given of your time and energy. You must continue to give. The hunters have hunted well. The fishermen and the turtlemen have provided well. The traders have traded well. You have all done well, and I thank you for your efforts.

"But wait, I must mention a special person we have with us today. He came down the Father of Waters from his home in the northland. Our young friend, Dreamer, has been in our Village now for two moons' time. He is on a mission to find out where the water of our Father of Waters goes. He is also on his test to become a man of his clan, the Eagle Clan of the Rocky River People.

"Continue to treat him as one of us. Teach him our way. Share with him. Let him work with us and let us work beside him. Teach him our hunting and fishing skills. He comes as a friend, and therefore, I ask that you treat him like a friend. Those are my wishes and my commands.

"I will address you again at the Festival of the Maize Flower. Count the days—one moon's time, then be here for my continuing wisdom." With that, he lowered his arms, took two steps back, and sat on his cedar-wood throne. The First Shaman stepped forward and dismissed the people.

The Wild One looked at Dreamer. She was pleased that he had been singled out as a friendly visitor on a mission. It was a "pass" that would allow him to go anywhere in the village.

The Wild One said the Great Sun Chief was a man of few words, strong words though, and that he treated all of the people of village the same.

"How could he have known I was here today?"

"He knows everything," said The Wild One.

. . . .

The Great Sun Chief decided the Prophet, the wisest man in the village, should start to build his sun clock today. The first post in the ground would be the center, or observation post. This morning The Wild One took Dreamer to see where the tall center post was being installed. Yesterday was the start of the new year, so he had pegged the point were the men would install their first time post, the due east post on the circle.

Earlier, the Prophet had told the Great Sun Chief he wanted to make a very large sun clock to replace his little circle of sticks. How big should it be?

The Great Sun wanted a great circle with a tall, center viewing post. The Prophet figured it would take 48 posts for the great circle. With the center post, the clock would be constructed of 49 posts.

Father Sun rose due east yesterday, and it was the time of equal day and equal night. The Great Sun Chief had decided the clock project should be located to the west of the Great Plaza, and the work should begin quickly; so today, the first post would go in the ground.

When the Prophet first lined up his sticks with Father Sun in the sky, he used only 16 sticks on the circle; the 17th was in the center, the observation stick. It had taken some trial and error to place the circle sticks in the right location, but, being wise, he had figured it out. The shadow went around the center stick—west in the morning, swinging around at midday, then to the east in the afternoon. Father Sun in the sky was regular and predictable, and the Prophet had recorded the days on his deerskin.

Circles, important to the people of the village, were a sign of life. The Great Father Sun in the sky was a circle, and He gave life. He saw to the seasons, to the planting and later to the harvest. He provided for the people.

The time of the four seasons could be counted by the travel of the Great Sun in the sky. The Prophet had kept track of Father Sun's travels. He always came up with the same number of days for a year—365, except for an extra day he had to add every four years to make time work out, exactly.

Over the past twenty summers, the Prophet had recorded the shortest day, the longest day, and the two times of equal days. He marked the number of days over and over on his deerskin.

In preparation for constructing the sun clock, the Prophet had the people of the village clear the area. The product of their monumental effort was to be a monument that would tell time by the days and last forever. No other project like it was known. It would also serve as a meeting place for important events.

The Prophet had sent his scouts, teams of ten men, out to find enough tall, straight trees, all the same size to make the circle. He held his arms in an arc and touched his fingers: "This is how big they must be." He told his men the trees should be as tall as six men lying head to toe. He picked one man from each group who would be responsible to bring back a perfect post. The long needle pine tree, which seemed to grow even in winter, was the tree of choice.

In their hunting experiences, some of the men had seen such tall evergreen trees. Several of the teams went far up the Father of Waters. Two groups even crossed the Father of Waters to get their posts.

Soon the long posts were coming in from all directions. The groups that had crossed the Father of Waters floated theirs back across the Great River. The posts were green and very heavy, so they had to be tied to lighter driftwood. When the men returned the Prophet indicated where each post should go.

The big sun clock was to be in the center of the village. The Prophet had spent a long time planning. He was awake many nights thinking how to set a tall post in the ground. The men couldn't simply push a post up into place. It would be too awkward, and they probably couldn't get it beyond an arm's reach anyway. There must be a better way. Yes, of course, they would use a tripod and ropes.

The men would push the time post as high as possible. Then they would support it with two smaller posts, just under the top end of the time post, these two posts would be tied together near their tops. It would be like the three-legged food storage frame, only it would be on a much larger scale.

The center post, the sighting post, went in easily using the Prophet's method. As the men pushed up the big post, the smaller support posts were nudged upward and inward. The base of the sun post was next to the hole in the ground, the final location, where it would rest when upright. As it was elevated, it would gradually slide into the hole. After it was in its final resting place, the men would use their ropes to pull it straight upright.

To set the post there were four teams of rope workers, one team on each side. After the ropes were taut, the Prophet walked around the post to sight it straight up. When he was satisfied, he gave the signal to fill in the hole. Using short posts with flat ends, the men tamped the soil in, firmly around the upright post.

The Prophet had made another grapevine and greenbrier rope a little over 70 paces long. With the help of many men, he would use it to make the circle. One of the men would hold one end of the rope against the center post. Then the others would hold the rope gently as he walked the outer end around the circle, marking the ground as he went. It was as good a circle as he could make.

On his circle the four main time posts would go in first to divide the circle into quarters. The Prophet knew where the four guideposts would go. One would be lined up at night with the pole star. Another on the circle, through his center sighting post, would be directly opposite the pole star post. The due east post would go in the next day.

Next he had to divide each quadrant into even spaces. On this great circle, he walked ten paces and placed a stick in the ground where a post would be set. It worked well, with only some slight adjustments; he wanted twelve even spaces per quadrant.

For his purpose he actually could have used fewer posts, but that wouldn't have given him a circle. He knew a complete circle of posts would have more meaning to the people. Adding the remaining 44 posts, eleven to a quadrant, would produce a perfect circle, just like Father Sun.

The Prophet planned for the workers to put a post in every two days. He wanted the builders to see how the predictable Father Sun went around the sky during a quarter-year.

The six most important time posts, three on the east and three on the west, would be marked with white clam shells from the river, their white side out. The next most important post, the pole star post, would also be marked, as would its opposite post.

The Prophet was very satisfied with the work. The Great Sun Chief, too, watching the progress, was pleased.

On their way back to the lodge, Dreamer told The Wild One of his star experiences with his father. She, too, liked to watch the stars. He mused, "I wonder which of the posts would line up on my pole star." He thought he would come back after all the posts were set—maybe after curfew, on some dark night when there was no moon to check it out, just to see if it was marked right.

"Unfortunately, I won't see the great sun circle clock completed. But I know I'll come back once I find out where the water goes. On my way home—whenever that may be—perhaps then, all the posts will be in. Dreamer had been in Cahokia Village now for about two moons.

-5-

July 5, 1054

The Prophet was always up early. He would wake the others as usual. But, this morning would be different

When he lifted the flap that covered the door to his lodge and stepped outside, he saw a flash overhead. One of the stars in the sky had exploded. It was a flash brighter than ten stars. He watched in awe, as it grew even brighter. The bright star was a little below and to the right of the crescent Mother Moon.

In the dark this blazing star was something to see. The Prophet stood transfixed.

Would it burn itself out? Would it become another Father Sun? "No," he thought, "It's much too small for that, and it always stays in one place—what is it? It is not a shooting star."

It was an opportunity—the Prophet knew that. He looked around the village. No other person was up; not even the dogs were awake. "Yes, it is an opportunity and I must take advantage of it—I must not miss this chance," he said to himself.

The Prophet's lodge was on the second level of the Great Pyramid. He thought about the bright star for only a short while, and then he climbed up to the top level. The watchers of the Great Sun Chief challenged him until he emerged from the dark to be recognized.

The Prophet used the stick lying next to the opening of the Great Chief's lodge to tap five times on the guard post.

Entering the Great Lodge, he bowed before the Great Sun Chief, who said, "Come, sit beside me. What is the matter? It is early—Father Sun is not up yet. What is the matter?"

"We have a new bright star in our sky. Father Sun has a guardian. He is bright, and stays in one place. He is not like the short-lived shooting stars that flash, streak, and are gone—the ones that tell the story that one of our people has gone to the Great Beyond. No, this new star does not streak; it shines brighter than any other, and it stays in one place. Come outside with me so you can see, and believe."

Outside, the Prophet did not even have to point to this new star. It was ten times brighter than the brightest star, although not as bright as the crescent Mother Moon.

"Well, Great Prophet, you have pegged your sticks and counted the days well. You are the one that watches Father Sun and predicts the days. Why don't you wake our people and show them what you have for them."

"Boom, Boom, Boom." The call of the log drum awakened the people, who came out of their lodges, into the dark, to the Great Plaza, to hear their Great Sun Chief. The throng was large and all were looking and pointing toward the new bright star. The Great Sun Chief and his Prophet went down to the lowest level of the Great Mound. From there most of the people could hear, although they knew the people at the rear would get their message from others who would pass it on.

"My people, look," exclaimed the Great Sun Chief, pointing overhead to the new star. "The Prophet has given us another reason to build our new Sun Clock. He has given us a new bright star."

As daylight beckoned in the east, the crowd grew restless. Now Father Sun peeked over the distant tree line, His rays casting shadows on the ground. Although it was daylight, the new star continued to shine. The people sat down and remained in the plaza all day. Some said the star would go away because a star cannot be seen in the daytime.

Finally, as Father Sun was setting in the west, the Great Sun Chief dismissed the people. It was getting dark, and they were tired from a long day under the hot Father Sun in the Grand Plaza. As they walked away, they watched this new star. As the day grew dark it shone all the brighter. Now that it was dark, the people could see that this new star was going around the pole star, towards the west, like the other stars of the night.

The people of Cahokia Village would never forget this day. They marveled at the star that shone brightly in the daytime for twenty-three more days. They would remember.

. . . .

It was always a treat for the boys of the village to watch the arrowhead-maker, the flint shaper, as he worked. Although he was old and his face was wrinkled, his hands were strong, but gentle, as he held a piece of white flint in one and the stub of a deer antler in the other. A piece of deerskin doubled-up lay across his legs, and a vest of deerskin kept the sharp, flying flakes away from his skin.

His favorite location to work at his trade was with his back to the large cottonwood tree on the bank of Cahokia Creek. He sat on the north side of the tree, the sun shining over his shoulder.

The arrowhead-maker made two types of arrowheads—utility points and ceremonial points. The ceremonial points were long, thin, and quite fragile. They were all sewn to the vestment of the Great Sun Chief, and were his to distribute.

The arrowhead-maker was also known as "Chips." He made more utility points than fancy points because they were used for big game. The hunters needed them for deer, bear, and buffalo. They were allotted only so many points, which were fashioned in the shape of a triangle, small, no notches, and very sharp.

When a hunter returned home with a large animal, such as a deer or a bear, he was given a bonus in arrowheads. Usually five for a deer, ten for a bear, and perhaps fifteen for a buffalo. The hunter also had to give Chips either a deer antler, some bear teeth, or buffalo horns, depending on what he had killed. Bears were scarcer, and they produced more fat, so the bonus of more arrow points was well deserved. The smaller animals, such as the ring-tailed black eyes, and the little gray-hair smooth tail, were worth only one arrow point. Since there were more of the small animals, some of the hunters made as many points by quantity of the smaller ones than they did by the quality of the larger animals.

"So, you're the one from the northland, the one the Great Sun singled out at the Powwow. I was hoping to meet you because I want you to have one of my fancy, three-notch arrowheads." Chips had no idea that he would get something in return; however, Dreamer surprised Chips by giving him five of the beautiful white Black Hawk pre-form flints from up the Great River, from Hawk Eye Creek. Chips put his hand to his mouth, amazed, at the beautiful white flint.

"A fair exchange, don't you think?"

"Yes," was all Chips could say. Actually, it was more than fair.

Dreamer was thrilled with the perfect arrowhead Chips had given him. He thought he had received the best of the trade. It was a long triangle with three notches, one on either side down near the base and one on the bottom, symmetrical in every way. Dreamer understood that the point was too long and fragile to be used as a utility point. He turned it over and over in his hand, admiring its smooth gleam and passing it around for the other boys to see. It was as long as his little finger. It was perfect.

"Thank You," Dreamer said to Chips. "I shall take care of it and try not to break it. I will take it with me to my Happy Hunting Ground in the Great Beyond. I'll use it there."

Dreamer told Chips of the beautiful, three-notched arrowhead the Great Sun Chief had given him, the one with its little red streak on the side.

"Yes, I made that one for him."

The arrowhead-maker had chunks of different types of white flint and gray chert. Many were trade items from faraway places. Some were from the far southwest, a place Chips had never been. The pure white Hawk Eye flint came from up the Father of Waters, found among the limestone bluffs, and it was the best material for making arrowheads.

Dreamer would prize his new arrowhead. He told Chips he would sew it to the front of the otter skin vest, the one his mother had made for him. It would be his mark. He was anxious to show his new treasure to The Wild One.

"You should be proud of such a fine arrow point. Only the chiefs have points with three notches or more, and you have two of them. Take care of them," The Wild One cautioned.

. . . .

It was now afternoon and time for games. Both the men and the boys played "chunky." This game was played in many ways.

Chunky was usually played with six men who gambled mightily. The judge, the man who lost the last game, assisted in the next game by telling who won, eliminating any argument.

Today, the boys would play spear chunky. Four boys lined up, two on each side of the boy who rolled. When he rolled the chunky stone, each of the four threw their spears at the point where they thought the stone would stop. The spears had to be airborne before the round, rolling stone stopped. The judge watched carefully as they threw their spears. He could disqualify anyone who threw his spear late, that is, after the chunky stone had stopped rolling. The one whose spear was the furthest away became the next roller, and he could not bet. The roller moved up to game judge, and the judge moved on to be one of the next spear throwers.

The spears were no more than stout poles with sharp ends. Made of red cedar, the wood of long life; the boy's spears did not have flint tips, however, the back end of the spear had feathers from a red hawk, a white goose, or a blue-and-white duck. The trailing feathers stabilized the spear in flight. To win, the spear must be upright in the ground. Lying flat didn't count. Bets had to be down before the chunky stone was rolled. Whatever the three losers had bet would go to the winner, whose spear stuck in the ground closest to where the chunky stone had stopped.

Usually chunky was played in the spring, on the day after a mild rain, when the ground would be just right for the stone to roll and the spear to stick. The boys had chunky courts that were fairly small. It was on these smaller courts, the boys learned the game, and placed their small bets.

Dreamer had many items with which he could gamble; however, chunky was a game at which he was not very skilled. He knew that if he lost some of his precious trade items, he might lose something he would need later on. Today he did not play, he only watched.

One day Dreamer saw a man from across the river lose everything he brought to gamble—food, furs, arrows, and arrowheads—and he also lost his chunky stones. He had gambled with the best chunky rollers from Cahokia, and he lost. In the final game of that day, the judge drew a line across the court, some twenty paces down. The one who rolled a stone that stopped closest to the line would win both stones. The Cahokian gave the bluff man from across the river the first roll. His chunky stone rolled stopping as close as the spread of his thumb and fingers from the line. The Cahokian, the best roller from the bottoms, stood behind the start line, his arm stretched behind; then, moving forward, he let the stone go. His smooth, tan, chunky stone rolled down the court. It slowly came to a stop and lay over on its side, exactly on top of the line.

The visiting man went into a rage, falling to his knees, and beating the ground with his fists. He was yelling.

The young boys left their small court and went over to the men's court. They listened to the tales of woe of the bluff man. He was supposed to be a good chunky player, but today he had lost everything—even his chunky stones.

One of the boys said to Dreamer, "It's a good thing he didn't bet his canoe, or he would have lost that too; then he would have to swim home. He lives across the Father of Waters, at the village on top of the bluff."

As twilight came, Dreamer and his foster mother were eating their evening meal, he told her of the chunky game he had watched that afternoon. He told her how the traveler from across the river had lost everything he owned except his loincloth and his canoe. And, on the last roll, he had even lost his last stone.

The Wild One told Dreamer that he had learned quite a lesson that afternoon. What was the lesson? She wanted him to repeat it to her.

"Never play chunky with someone who can play better than you can?"

"No."

"What, then?"

She said, "Today, you had a lesson you should never forget. If you gamble, you might lose, so never bet more than you can afford to lose."

"Yes, you're right. That's exactly what I learned."

"There's always someone out there who is better than you, or, sometimes, just luckier than you. Remember that," she said.

Before Dreamer went to sleep that evening, he replayed the events of the day. Never bet more than you can afford to lose. There's always someone out there who is better than you. And finally, even though you think you're good, your luck just might run out. Those were good lessons he had learned this day. Fortunately, he had learned them by watching someone else. He still had his Hawk Eye flint, his last heavy galena cube, his brown-green stones, his fire kit, his arrow kit and his deerskins, He still had his two new

Cahokia arrow points, and his black chunky stone was safe at home. Yes, he considered himself quite lucky.

It was night now, and Mother Moon was shining brightly. It was also very quiet, so he could hear geese above, honking, loudly, as they flew south through the darkness.

"Honk, Honk, Honk," he heard off in the distance, as he was falling asleep.

-6-

The shadows of the clock posts were getting longer. More and more geese also honked overhead. Flying southward, they followed the Great River, and Dreamer, too, was anxious to continue down the river.

"Will you go on your raft?" The Wild One asked.

"That's the way I arrived; I suppose that's the way I'll leave," Dreamer smiled.

He wondered about his raft; he had not been back to see it for some time. Tomorrow he would go back to the Father of Waters to check on it.

Early in the morning he took the path beside Cahokia Creek leading to the Great Father of Waters. Little Turtle, his best friend, was with him. They were first down the path that morning, going through spider webs that had been spun the night before. Many were beautiful, glimmering in the sunlight covered with fine drops of dew. Taking alternate shots, the two boys used their short sticks to knock down the webs.

"My raft should be behind the big sycamore just ahead."

Little Turtle was first down the path.

"Where is it?"

Dreamer put his hand on the sycamore, leaned out and looked down along the water's edge.

"Someone has taken my raft!" he exclaimed, surprised.

Climbing down the bank he saw some of the greenbrier ropes had been cut. Yes, somebody had taken it, but wasn't stealing against the Code? He couldn't believe it was gone. Dreamer had heard the Great Sun Chief tell the people to treat him as an equal, just as if he lived in the village. Who would have taken it?

"I'll bet I know why it was taken," said Little Turtle, "You know, firewood near the village is all gone. The women and children now have to go great distances to find it. Your raft would have been good firewood. I'm sure we'll never find out who took it, and I don't think we should waste time trying. Shall we build another, so you can continue your journey down the Father of Waters?"

"No! Let's just think about it for a while. I might continue my journey by walking. Since there are many people, there are many paths; I'm sure there must be some that follow the river."

When Dreamer and Little Turtle got back to the lodge of The Wild One, they found her busy with her deerskins, but not too busy to hear the story of the lost raft. She sympathized with Dreamer.

"I know you're getting restless to leave. We must find you a raft, or even a canoe; and we must do it quickly."

She went to her clan leader that evening and told him what had happened. The story of the lost raft went up the ladder of authority until it finally reached the Prophet. The Great Sun had said to treat Dreamer as, "one of our own," but, someone had not followed his command.

The following evening the Prophet arrived at the lodge of The Wild One. He had an apology and an offer. He would see that their visiting friend had a means to use the river. He would trade some of the village treasure for a canoe for Dreamer.

The next day, about noon, he showed Dreamer a canoe tied up at the arrowhead-maker's tree, on Cahokia Creek. The dugout made from the log of a cottonwood tree, was small, but it should serve Dreamer well. Dreamer thanked the Prophet, who again said, "The Great Sun is ashamed of his people."

The Wild One knew he had to go. She had sensed the tension of his restless pacing in the day and his continued tossing and turning at night. Wanting to give him a going-away present, she said, "How would you like to take one of my dogs when you leave? You can have any one you like. Your dog can be your friend or you can use it as food."

Dreamer looked over the three and chose the strongest, a small, brown, shaggy dog with a dark mark on her back. She had been his friend. He already called her "Little Pup," "Thank you, my Cahokia mother." he said pleased.

Dreamer put everything together: his pack, his pouch, his bow and quiver of arrows, his pot so recently fired, his deerskin night cover, and, of course, his precious travel totem. The Wild One had made a new deerskin cover for the totem so the black-and-white eagle feathers would be kept clean as he traveled the river. He put all his things just inside the entrance of the lodge. Tomorrow, at the crack of dawn, he would be off, leaving quietly so as not to disturb his foster mother.

"No," The Wild One said, "I want to know when you'll be leaving." She would walk with him to his new canoe, and wave to him as he departed down Cahokia Creek. She would wave until he disappeared around the bend. She had been his mother while he was in the village, and it was her right to give him a good send-off.

Together in the morning mist, they walked to Cahokia Creek. She wanted to walk slowly, but Dreamer was in a hurry, so they compromised. They passed the new Sun Clock which now had three of the big circle time-posts upright, in place.

Where would Dreamer's journey take him now? Although he had intended to stay for only a short time, he had spent over five moons with the friendly people of Cahokia. He would never forget them. His new mother had been very good to him.

Over the bank and down to the creek he went, carrying all his belongings, Little Pup following. Dreamer untied the braided deerskin rope that held his new canoe, looked up at his foster mother, and waved one last time.

He shoved off, making a few backstrokes with his new paddle. The canoe swung around, moving into the current, now heading downstream toward the Great Father of Waters.

The Wild One had collected and saved food for Dreamer. Bartering with the arrowhead-maker she had gotten some utility points which she secretly tucked carefully into his pack. She told him about the food, but the points he would discover later. "He was such a fine boy and no trouble at all. I wonder whether I'll ever see him again?" The Wild One questioned, as she turned up the path toward home.

. . . .

A curiosity that could only be satisfied by his exploration of the river drove Dreamer on. The current carried him along at a good pace. He thought how lucky he had been to be given such a canoe. He hoped someday to return the favor.

Now on both sides of the river, trees, trees, and more trees grew to the water's edge. Sometimes there would be a high bank on one side or the other. It seemed these obstructions always pushed the Father of Waters into a bend the other way.

At regular intervals there would be a little stream flowing into the Great River. Dreamer often stopped at these locations because there was usually a good sand or gravel bar on the upstream side.

After a long time of travel, he guided his canoe toward one of the little sandbars, jumped out, pulled his canoe up on the rocks, and sat down. On the sand bar he felt safe. Little Pup had jumped out first and was on the sand, panting and waiting for her master. She ran up the creek a short way, turned around, and seemed to say, "Come on, let's find out where it goes."

Dreamer was tired. Perhaps he was going too far on his first day out. He did want to find out where the creek went, but not now. He had better things to do. He had to feed Little Pup and himself and he had to find wood for a fire.

"Let's see what The Wild One packed for me."

Sure enough, there was food for three or four days—pemmican, cooked rabbit, and turtle meat—the rabbit and turtle wrapped in moist cattail leaves. He also found a small deerskin pouch of berries and nuts. He would keep the pouch for future use.

He fed Little Pup some of the meat, knowing that dogs didn't like nuts or berries. Dreamer and Little Pup ate well their first meal out. Dreamer decided he would ration his food to last for three days. After that he would have to find food along the way.

"Thank you, my Little Mother."

Putting the food back into his pack, he discovered another folded piece of tan deerskin. Opening the deerskin he found ten of the most perfect, white, triangular utility arrow points he had ever seen, all made from white Hawk Eye flint.

"Mother, Mother—my Cahokia Mother, what have you done. I thank you." He wondered what she had to barter for such a costly gift.

"O.K., time to go, Little Pup." Everything back in the canoe, Dreamer shoved off. Little Pup was up in front again, watching ahead. Going with the current was easy. "Coming back up the river, later, and going against the flow, will be much harder," he thought.

As he continued down the Father of Waters, he was always looking for a safe place to take his canoe out of the water. The safest places, he decided, were on the islands. There were many of them in the river. Each had a sand beach on the downstream end. He could see these islands were continually moving downstream—their fronts getting washed away—their downstream ends always growing. On these islands he could usually find some dry driftwood for his fire. He was pleased.

On this fourth day down the river from Cahokia, he came upon the biggest, highest island he had ever seen. It was composed of white limestone. Yes, it must be an island, for the water went all around it. This island was like a tower in the middle of the river; he decided to call it, "Tower Rock."

Father Sun was not much past overhead, but Dreamer decided he would quit for the day. He used his paddle to steer his canoe to the left, down the narrow passage, and through the chute. It proved to be a good choice. The water was very quiet. There he found a downed tree, bare of leaves, half-in and half-out of the water, a good place to tie up his canoe. He tied his canoe to a big limb, using double knots.

Picking up all his belongings, he balanced on some limbs and carefully made his way to the shore. As usual, Little Pup was ahead of him. He decided to spend the night on top of this Tower Rock. Apparently there had been a path there many years ago, but it had grown over. It was hard climbing. Little Pup had gone on ahead somewhere. Dreamer let her go, because he knew if he wanted her, he would just call or whistle, and she'd return to his side quickly.

As Dreamer climbed the path on the east side of Tower Rock, he came face to face with a black-and-white, bushy-tailed skunk. Both the skunk and Dreamer stopped in their tracks. Who would move first? Dreamer knew what an angry skunk could do and he didn't want any part of it. He froze with one foot in the air. The skunk had quickly raised its bushy tail, but it was still face-to-face with him.

Slowly, Dreamer put his foot back on the ground; backing away, he hummed softly. The skunk stood its ground; it had nothing to lose. Several steps more and Dreamer would be out of range. Another step backwards, then another, then a twig snapped underfoot, causing a twitch in the skunk's tail; the little animal moved one front paw and started its turn.

As Dreamer was bending down, slowly moving backwards, his hand came upon a small, dry stick. Quickly, he underhanded it into a small bush to the right of the skunk. The diversion worked; the skunk did spray, but its aim was towards the noise of the stick in the bush. Now Dreamer could smell the stink, but he was out of harm's way.

"How lucky I am," he said to himself. He knew he could have been the target. Had he been hit, he would have had to get rid of all his clothes, his moccasins, his pack—everything, perhaps even his bowstring. Anything that would have received the spray he would have to discard. Little Pup had also been lucky that she hadn't come this way. Giving the skunk a wide berth, he slowly went around it, and continued up the pathway. Although skunks are only small animals, Dreamer had learned to give them much respect.

Now Dreamer continued looking for a suitable place to spend the night. At the top of Tower Rock there was a little prairie of short grass with yellow and white flowers. It was at the edge of the prairie, at the tree line, Dreamer chose to spend the night. As usual he used the trees when he built his little lean-to, opening to the east, toward the rising Father Sun.

It was at the end of this day that Dreamer and Little Pup finally finished the last of the food The Wild One had put in the pack. Tomorrow, they would have to find themselves something to eat. Dreamer wanted to get an early start. Knowing that drinking a lot of water would wake him early, he went back to the river. Dipping his hands in many times, he drank from the Father of Waters.

Now it was almost dark and time for sleep. Little Pup was at his side. With his eyes closed, but listening intently, he could hear the cries of the wild dogs running along the shore across the river. There must be three or four of them making those awful noises. They would stop for a while, and then they would start crying and howling again. Little Pup's ears were up.

Dreamer was glad he was on the island away from the howling coyotes he called wild dogs. They could not bother him here. Once he had heard of a man from his village who had an accident and was limping home at dusk. A group of wild dogs attacked the lone man out on the prairie. Luckily, the man had fended the wild dogs off with his staff. But it had been a close call.

Now, with Little Pup curled up at his side, Dreamer drifted off to a sound sleep. He didn't worry, because he knew Little Pup would wake him if anything were wrong.

. . . .

Several days after the travelers left Tower Rock, the river turned back on itself as if it wanted to go north, towards the pole star. It was hard to figure out, but Dreamer went with it.

"We'll just go with the current," Dreamer said to Little Pup.

Then, after another sharp bend to the right, he came upon a river, almost as big as his river, joining his Father of Waters from the left,. He wondered, "How will I remember, on my return up the great river, to take the river to the left?"

Then he saw it—a landmark. Yes, he would remember this location because there was a big nest in the top of the dead sycamore tree on the point where the two rivers met. It reminded him of the place his Rocky River, met the Father of Waters.

Two eagles soared overhead, gliding with the ease of a white, fluffy seed upon a light breeze. Not paddling, but trailing his paddle in the water, Dreamer was pulled along by the current. He didn't mind that he wasn't making progress. He watched the pair of majestic eagles in the sky ahead of him, now able to view the giant birds from fairly close range.

Suddenly, one began a wide spiral and swooped lower, toward the surface of the river. Putting its feet out in front, as if to walk on the water, the eagle splashed, and, as if by magic, held a fish tight in its talons. With this heavy load, the eagle, flapping laboriously, gained altitude.

It was headed for the top of the dead sycamore where a bundle of sticks formed a nest, large enough to make a great council fire. Flapping, then on a short upward path, the eagle gently came to rest on the side of the nest. It was holding onto the fish with one leg and onto the nest with the other. Dreamer could see that the Mother Eagle was bringing food to her young. The mother eagle and the young eaglet tore the fish apart noisily.

"That's the way it should be," Dreamer said to Little Pup, "I will take care of you, too, my little friend. "We must all eat," he murmured. Then Dreamer's thoughts drifted back to the camp by the spring where his mother, father, little sister, and brothers lived. His parents provided well for them, just as this Mother Eagle was providing for her young.

"Oh, if I only were an eagle, I'd fly so high that I could see everything below me. I'd fly to the end of this great Father of Waters. Oh, if I were only an eagle . . . it would be easy."

Dreamer steered his canoe close to the shore, as close as he could to the tree with the eagle's nest, but when the other eagle glided down toward his canoe, he knew he had made a big mistake. Dreamer quickly lifted his paddle from the water and held it overhead. The screaming eagle pulled out of its dive just in time to miss the paddle. The hair on the back of Dreamer's neck bristled as the huge bird went by. Protecting mother and child, he

thought; that's what a father should do.

Little Pup sank down in the bottom of the canoe as the big eagle flew by. She didn't want to be scooped up like the fish Mother Eagle had just caught.

Dreamer pointed his trailing paddle toward the water, pushed the blade out ahead, took a bite into the water, and pulled. They started to pick up speed. Soon the tall sycamore with the big nest was behind them, as was their fright. The wide river was now straight for as far as the eye could see, and in order to keep away from any unforeseen danger, he plied the very middle of the great river.

He paddled on and on. One side of the riverbank was a high, wooded bluff; the other was a broad expanse of willows, soft maples, and an occasional sycamore.

The high bluffs intrigued Dreamer. Often, he pulled his canoe up on the rocky shore to look at them, choosing a stream entrance or a big downed tree where he could hide his canoe. He must not lose his canoe. He had started this trip walking, but he had soon tired of that. And although his raft had served him well, it had not been as manageable as his canoe. No, he must never lose his canoe.

Down His River of Dreams ...

Since leaving Cahokia, Dreamer and Little Pup had traveled for what seemed like several moons. In reality it had only been the time of a quarter-moon, and only two full days since they had seen the eagles.

Dreamer guided his canoe in lengthwise, along a fallen log. Little Pup jumped onto the log as soon as it was close. She was tired of riding. Thirsty too, she lapped up river water to quench her thirst. Then she went into the woods and relieved herself. Dreamer covered his canoe with sticks, twigs, and leaves. He hadn't seen anyone for quite a while, but he didn't want to take any chances. Then, almost as a second thought, he took his pack, his fire kit, the empty food pack, and, as always, his bow and quiver of arrows, as he climbed the bluff.

He had his bow strung and an arrow notched and ready, looking for his next meal. He had to be ready for whatever might come along. This time, though, ripe berries and nuts were all he found.

Arriving at the top of the bluff, he looked back to see where he had come from. Looking downstream, he could also see where he was going. Spotting another big island ahead, he thought he might go that far to spend the night. But, enough, "I must be on my way."

He was still hungry. Little Pup was also hungry. They drank some more water before climbing back into the canoe. Near a log Dreamer could see fish splashing, but they were just out of reach, teasing him. He rounded the island and looked downwater. The Great River seemed to go on forever.

Now paddling silently, he guided his canoe into a cove that led to the mouth of a small stream. Here the water was quiet, hardly flowing. Up the stream he paddled, stroke, glide, stroke, glide, steer around a big log—stroke some more. Now the water of the stream was beginning to clear. Leaning he scooped up a refreshing mouthful of water; he could go much longer without food than without water. He splashed some of the clear water on his face, and then, with two hands cupped, he scooped up some more water and wet his hair, hoping it would cool his warm body. As she watched all this, Little Pup turned her head a little to the right, as if to ask, "What are you doing?" Little Pup was thirsty, too, so he cupped his hands, scooped more water, and offered her a drink. She drank and drank. They had now coasted into the shade of a big sycamore tree.

Dreamer paddled upstream until he came to the shallows. "Time to pull my canoe out of the water. Can't go any further, I'm on the rocks." He had found an ideal location to spend the night. But first, food—they must have food.

Dreamer gathered some sticks for a later fire, both to keep the blood-sucking insects away, and to cook their evening meal. But what meal, they had nothing.

Dreamer walked upstream and into the forest, away from the water. Every so often he would return to the water slowly, and quietly. Nothing; nothing that would do for a meal anyway. There were lots of birds, and he did find a second season nest with three small tan eggs. He must have scared the mother bird away, for the nest was unattended. Quickly, he ate the eggs, but he was still hungry.

A tree grew out over the water, and Dreamer climbed on it for a better view of the stream. He lay quietly on the gently sloping tree trunk looking down into the clear water. A movement caught his eye. It was a turtle and a fairly large one, too. Slowly, he lowered himself down, keeping the tree between the turtle and himself. Then, lying on his aching stomach, he edged toward the bank. Out of sight of the turtle, he moved closer to where it lay on the stream bottom, its back extended above the waterline. Suddenly Dreamer raced headlong to catch the frightened turtle before it could hide in the darkness of deeper water. Splash, grab, laugh—"Aha! I've caught my supper," said Dreamer as he lay in the water holding the turtle. Now he had a meal for himself and Little Pup, and maybe some for tomorrow, too. He was happy.

He put the turtle in the canoe. Then, back at his ready-made campfire, with a few twists of the spindle in the bowstring the tinder caught and began to smoke. Blow, blow, blow; white smoke came. Cupping his hands, he blew some more. Flash—an orange flame shot forth. He carefully placed the burning tinder under some of the smaller twigs. They caught immediately. He cooked the turtle whole by holding it over the fire with a green stick—not right in the flame, but in the heat just adjacent to it. It took a little longer that way but, he could wait; he would soon have his meal. He had learned his turtle-cooking lesson back at Cahokia Village.

The meat of the turtle was delicious. Hungry Little Pup watched. Dreamer cut off a hind leg for her. Dreamer ate quite a bit too, but he dared not eat it all. "Save some for tomorrow," he said to himself, setting aside the two front legs and some back meat for the morning meal. There would be more for Little Pup, too.

His hunger now satisfied, he began reviewing the day and thinking about tomorrow. He knew it would be another long day. There had been too many long days. The river seemed to go on forever. He wondered, "Will I ever find the end?" With this question on his mind, the sun already set, and the mosquitoes chased away by the smoke, he lay down on his deerskin cover. Sleep overtook him quickly. Little Pup, at his side, was also sleeping soundly, but of course, as always, with one eye half open and one ear listening.

Early the next morning, he shared some turtle meat with Little Pup. Down the little channel, out of the cove, a gentle right turn into the moving current of the Father of Waters, and he was going downwater again. It was so easy in his canoe. He kept close to the right bank. Sometimes the rock outcrops were intriguing, beckoning him for a closer look, but he kept paddling down the river. He must not become sidetracked from his quest.

This night Dreamer decided he would camp on one of the high bluffs overlooking the Great Father of Waters. He glided his canoe adjacent to some large driftwood trees. There he tied it up and concealed it with sticks and leaves.

Hungry as always, he started looking for food. Finding food was always a problem. In a little backwater pond, he spotted some large green frogs. Fortunately, he had three arrows in his quiver that had no arrowheads on them. One of them he quickly notched, then raised his bow to vertical, took aim, and "zip-thud," the arrow was on the mark. Soon he shot four frogs. He skinned them and saved the hind legs for himself. The rest of the frogs he gave to Little Pup, who was anxiously awaiting her meal. She ate ravenously.

Dreamer picked up his belongings and his frog legs, and zigzagged up the steep bluff to make it an easier climb. The sky to the west was getting darker, the great round clouds towered into giant, ever-changing puffballs and they were moving rapidly toward him. He heard distant thunder—the anger of the gods, so he moved quickly.

At the top of the bluff, he found his campsite for the evening. Then he looked downwater. It seemed the Father of Waters went on forever.

Dreamer wanted to beat the storm, so he started his fire quickly. Two trees nearby would support his lean-to, and he threw it together hastily. He hurriedly cooked his evening meal over the little fire. The white frog legs twitched occasionally as they cooked on the green stick he held in the fire. He savored every bite of his meal, and then finished off with some sweet blackberries and walnuts he had found on his way up the bluff.

The cooling of the air was more noticeable, and the rustle of the leaves became louder. Since his shelter was so rapidly built, he added some more branches. It had to last the night and survive the oncoming storm. He spread one of his deerskin covers over the top and leaned heavy logs on it, adding more leaves and hoping they would help shed the rainwater he knew was coming. Now the clouds were moving very fast.

Now and then, a brittle limb would snap in the wind and fall to the ground close by. Little Pup looked up at Dreamer fearfully, wanting and waiting for an answer to this sudden terrible commotion in the dark night sky.

The stars and the moon were gone, and the lightning was closer. When the time from the lightning to the thunderclap became short, Dreamer knew the storm was almost upon them. The high bluff was not the place to be, but it was too late to move.

As he lay under his deerskin cover, beneath his hastily built lean-to, he feared the coming storm. Suddenly, the rain came down in torrents. He watched as the ground turned into a river of water. Little Pup was close beside him, and he could feel her trembling.

Two nights and two days of steady rain soaked Dreamer and Little Pup. The wind blew and blew, and lightning came down in long, jagged, yellow streaks. Once, during the second night, lightning struck a tree a little higher up on the bluff. The rain quickly put the fire out, but Dreamer could smell the acrid smoke from the burnt tree. He was glad he hadn't chosen that tree for his shelter.

Now he worried about the canoe. When the rain finally began to let up, Dreamer decided to see to its condition. He would leave Little Pup at the lean-to with his belongings.

"Stay, Little Pup, stay and guard."

He knew the water hadn't come up much, but the problem was the wind. It had blown harder than he had ever felt wind blow. Many limbs had been torn from the trees on the high bluff during the past two nights.

Had he tied the canoe well enough? Had he stayed on top of the bluff too long? Anxious thoughts kept running through his mind as he slipped and bumped his rear sliding down the steep, wet hill, on the way back to the canoe.

"There's the tree, but where is the canoe? Is it gone? Oh no, it can't be gone. Now there's a big log in its place. That log must have knocked my canoe loose."

He stood in the tree to which he had tied it. Looking downstream, he spied his canoe in the middle of the river, going down sideways, now tumbling, buffeted by the wind and waves. It was upside down and floating. He felt helpless. "If I had only been here sooner, I might have been able to save my canoe!"

It was another lesson Dreamer learned; in fact it might be a life-threatening lesson. What would he do differently the next time...if there would be a next time? He realized that he should have pulled the canoe completely out of the water, up over the rocks, sand, and mud, and concealed it in the brush on high ground. Next time, he would tie it up from both ends so there would be no chance of losing it. He knew they were in trouble now.

He thought of Little Pup back at the lean-to. He thought about his possessions—his pack and especially his bow and quiver of arrows. He couldn't lose them, too. Why had he left them back at the lean-to?

The rain poured rivulets down the side of the bluff, tumbling piles of last year's leaves along with them. Making his way back up the steep, slippery bluff, Dreamer saw there, shivering under the lean-to, his poor little dog. She looked like a rat-tail musk animal that could swim away at any time. But she was waiting for Dreamer and guarding his possessions with her life. He patted her head and scratched under her chin, thanking her for her faithfulness.

Rain or no rain, food was needed again. The storm was finally about to blow itself out. The sky was becoming lighter in the west, and Dreamer decided it was time to go. Two miserable nights on the bluff were enough. He didn't care if he ever saw this bluff again. With a notched arrow at ready and with all their belongings, Dreamer and Little Pup started making their way down the bluff toward the river.

. . . .

Walking again in the rain. Would the rain ever stop? Dreamer and Little Pup were walking up another bluff, following the path to the top. At the next ravine that cut through the hard, gray stone, he descended to the bottom. He eased himself over the loose, muddy rocks, exhausted. Little Pup followed. They carefully sidestepped big puddles. Dreamer ate berries along the way, but they did not give him the energy he needed. Little Pup chased squirrels she couldn't catch. She dug some small, furry black animals out of the ground and ate each one in a gulp.

Once he spotted a small spring dripping water into a clear pool. Just what they needed! He cupped his hands under the drip and caught some of cool, clear, thirst- quenching water. Little Pup drank from the pool.

They both needed more substantial food. Dreamer had to be careful; being tired and hungry, he could miss a step. A fall from the bluff could be a disaster; he might break a bone, or even die from a fall. His thoughts rambled on. Wolves or coyotes might attack him. He thought of his family back at his camp by the spring. How terrible it would be for his family if they never saw him again, especially if they never knew what became of him.

Dreamer sat down on a log at the edge of the bluff. The rain was only a drizzle. Tired and hungry, he rested there for a long time, gazing at the great valley through which the Father of Waters flowed.

Suddenly he felt a presence nearby, something new, perhaps even dangerous. He looked around and saw two men, perhaps twice his age. They wore no paint, and their only body coverings were their breechcloths and their high moccasins, tied with a thong, which were wet. Dreamer could see their bundle of skins were also wet and heavy because of the rain. They were looking at him and talking to one another.

"How could I ever have let this happen?" he questioned himself.

His backpack with all his belongings and his bow and quiver of arrows were hidden behind the rock. Standing up and facing the two strangers, he signed a greeting by placing his hands out before him, palms out.

What now?

The two laid down their heavy loads and took several steps towards Dreamer, who tried not to panic. Little Pup was now on the rock, and Dreamer had his hand on the dog's neck fur, holding her back.

He again signed to the strangers that he was a friend and added that he was hungry. He decided to meet them halfway and carefully walked toward the two. "Stay," he commanded Little Pup. Both Dreamer and the strangers were cautious.

They stopped when they were about ten paces apart. One of the strangers slowly reached for his pouch under his breechcloth thong. Untying it, he reached in and pulled out several strands of pemmican. He held them out, and, in a language unknown to Dreamer, offering the food to the hungry boy.

In accepting the food, Dreamer knew he would be beholden to the two. They seemed quiet and friendly enough, and he desperately needed their food. Dreamer crossed his arms over his chest and nodded the universal, "thank you." Slowly walking the ten paces between them, he took the pemmican from the outstretched hand, indicating that he wanted to share with Little Pup. That was all right with them.

They motioned around him to the trickling spring. They were thirsty and, he waved them on, holding Little Pup at his side. When they were on their way, up the ravine and out of sight, Dreamer picked up his pack and walked toward the river. He was relieved and quite proud of his composure.

The sky was growing darker, and there was now a mist in the air. The rain had been coming down, off and on, for four days. The raindrops were larger again. The sky was getting darker and more ominous. The lightning and the thunder returned.

7

Dreamer didn't like this new approaching storm. He was already wet, chilled to the bone. Little Pup looked like a drowned muskrat with her tail between her legs.

However, Dreamer and his dog were making progress. Then they came to another small river that had to be crossed. Dreamer pondered, "Shall I cross it now or shall I wait until tomorrow, after the storm has passed and the rain has stopped?"

"It's fairly wide," he said, talking to his dog and trying to overcome a sense of fear. "Maybe we'd better travel a little way up this new river and see if we can find a narrower place." Turning to the right, they began to follow this new river. "Yes, this new river is too wide and too angry to try to cross here," he told Little Pup. As they trudged upstream the rain continued to fall. They hadn't gone far before they came to a large sycamore tree growing at the water's edge. It was under-washed and down in the swirling water, but still anchored firmly to the riverbank. Dreamer thought it might provide the help he would need in crossing this little river.

As luck would have it, on the other side there was also a tree down in the water. There were many trees on the far bank whose roots had been exposed by the swift current during even higher water. If he crossed here, he could use those roots to climb up that far bank. He looked at Little Pup. She was already out on the trunk of the downed tree. He had his answer. "If I wait until tomorrow, this little river may turn into a big river. Maybe I'd better follow Little Pup and cross now," he said to himself.

The giant tree was quivering in the fast current. As Dreamer watched, it seemed as though the water flowed faster and faster. He estimated he would have to float to the willow tree down in the water, a little way downstream. He figured that, even though he couldn't swim, with about five or six fast kicks he could get across and grab the branches of the willow.

"Little Pup," he said, looking down at his wet little dog, "You'll just have to swim for it. You'll be pulled downstream a long way. Come back at the sound of my whistle, for we must stay together. I don't want to lose you, and I know you don't want to lose me." Dreamer could see that his dog was reluctant about crossing; she looked especially alert and was pacing back and forth on the huge tree trunk, waiting to see what Dreamer would do.

Not wanting to lose his moccasins, Dreamer took them off. He wrung them out, knowing it wouldn't do much good. He put his flint knife and moccasins in the arrow kit and the arrow kit into his backpack. He found a short light log to use as a floater, figuring he needed something to help him keep his head above water.

"Go," he said to himself, edging out on the fallen tree. The trunk reached out into the river quite a long way. As Dreamer edged out, he felt the tree shake under him. He knew he would have to take a dunking. When he reached the other side, he would try to find shelter. He would need a place to rest and to dry out his pack.

Dreamer slid into the water on the downstream side and started kicking, pushing his log ahead. Just as he thought, a few quick kicks carried him to the downed willow. Releasing his log, he grabbed a big branch and hung on. Catching his breath, he pulled himself along closer to the riverbank that, just a moment ago had seemed so far away. He had somehow made it to the other side, and was very thankful.

Dreamer walked along the willow trunk to the edge of the stream, then started up the steep bank by stepping on the exposed roots. They were slick and he had to be careful. He felt the roots with his bare feet, his toes gripping them, as he climbed up the slippery bank to higher ground. Careful as he was, his plan met disaster. He slipped and felt his right leg crack as the weight of his wet, heavy backpack forced it into a hole between two of the larger roots.

Looking down he saw a red and white bone protruding through the skin of his leg. He was too stunned to feel any pain.

Tugging to free his leg, he managed to pull himself to the top of the bank, thankful that he had made it across the river. Exhausted, and now beginning to feel a throbbing ache, he lay there, not caring that he was drenched.

The pain soon became unbearable. From early on he had learned not to cry out, but he sobbed, overcome by his unexpected predicament.

Dreamer glanced over to the fallen tree on the far bank and saw that Little Pup was about as far out on a limb as she could go. He could see that she hated to give up the safety of the tree.

"Come," said Dreamer, and he gave a short whistle.

Immediately, brave Little Pup both jumped and slipped into the water. She started paddling. The swift current, pulled her along quickly. Soon she was out of sight. Dreamer felt bad that he had lost Little Pup, but now he was more concerned about his own well-being.

"She can swim. She'll find her way," he said to himself. Dreamer then pulled and crawled to a giant log. Exhausted, he pulled his wet deerskin cover over himself, and then passed out.

. . . .

When he awoke from his faint, Father Sun had finally reappeared, but He was behind the bluffs. He shone on the tops of the trees far across the big river. The sweeping arc of the full rainbow gave Dreamer a sense of calm. He was cold, in pain, feeling lightheaded and very uneasy, but as he looked around, Dreamer saw a dark rock overhang at the foot of a little bluff, a short way from the river. "Can I make it?" he questioned out loud. "I've got to try." He crawled on his hands and his one good leg, dragging his right leg behind. As he slowly made progress, he felt the pain even more.

. He rested on a bed of wet leaves halfway to the rock shelter, the day nearly gone. He crawled the last twenty paces and finally reached the dark, protective, overhanging ledge, thankful he had reached shelter. That gave him a positive feeling, although his leg still hurt.

Dreamer was grateful to have not lost his backpack or his bow and quiver of arrows. He again emptied the wet things from his pack and spread them on some of the damp, flat rocks under the ledge. It would take a long time for his things to dry, even in this newfound shelter. He had no food and everything he owned was wet. Had he lost his dog? He couldn't remember; he hoped not.

Dreamer gave a series of shrill whistles that he hoped Little Pup would hear. Again and again he whistled. Then the sharp pain in his lower right leg hit him again. He leaned back to ease the pain and again lost consciousness.

Some time later, Dreamer felt a warm, moist tongue against his hand, then against his face. He opened his eyes and with great satisfaction said, "Little Pup, Am I ever glad to see you! I thought you were gone forever. I need you to protect me this night, for I have the smell of blood on me. Come close and lie with me. Please be my eyes and ears tonight."

Dreamer covered his broken leg with a wet deerskin cover from his backpack. He then shifted Little Pup to his left side and tried to make this position as comfortable as possible. He tried talking to her, but he was out and asleep before he even got started. He would lie very still until morning. The only disruption to the Indian boy's sleep that damp, dark night was an occasional unconscious jerk caused by the pain in his broken right leg.

The morning dawned bright and clear. The river close by was now bank-full of water from the rain of the past four days, and it was roaring rapidly past. Occasionally an uprooted tree tumbled by.

The noise woke Dreamer out of his deep sleep. He rolled over and the pain from his right leg shot all the way up his back. Little Pup, who had been sleeping beside him, licked his face again.

"Will I die here?" He asked Little Pup, his constant companion through the long night. He didn't want to die here, but how was he to continue? His first concern was his broken leg. He could wash it clean under the little dripping spring over there. Easing his leg over to the spring was no simple task. But before long his leg was clean. He laid it on his wet deerskin cover. Then he rolled over and the wet deerskin covered him to his shoulders. He lay there very still.

Dreamer had water, but he needed food.

"Little Pup, come." Little Pup came over to Dreamer and nuzzled him.

"Go. Find food. Go—go, and bring back some food."

Little Pup understood the predicament they were in—no food and her master in pain and helpless.

She started out down the path along the roaring stream toward the Father of Waters. Then she stopped, came back two steps, and waited.

Dreamer pointed his finger, saying again, "Go—go, find food."

Little Pup seemed to know what was asked of her, so she turned and scampered down the path. She kept to the path, nosing to the right and left as she went along. Then she put her nose up and turned her head to the right and left. She caught a scent of something important. She nosed slowly toward the smell of food, slowly and carefully. It was not raw food she smelled, but food over a fire. Little Pup could see a boy preparing his meal. The boy was wet, too. From her hiding place behind a log, she saw that he was cooking a meal over a small fire. She didn't care what it was; she only knew it smelled good and that was her mission.

The boy cooking the food was leaning back against the canoe he had pulled up to his campsite. He must have slept under it last night and maybe the last three or four nights. He must have kept his firewood under it too. His belongings were spread out beside him, apparently to dry, now that the rain had stopped.

But it was food she was after. The boy had a strip of meat wrapped around the end of a green stick. Little Pup watched as the boy ate the big snake he had cooked. She watched him spit out some of the rib bones he had missed while cleaning it.

Little Pup stealthily came around the end of her protective log. She crawled several steps on her stomach and then lay down, spreading all four paws on the wet ground. She wanted to get the boy's attention, but she didn't want to scare him. Little Pup lay still for some time, waiting.

Now that the boy had finished his meal, his awareness was spreading beyond his fire and his campsite. He stood up and looked around, and then he saw Little Pup. He knew the dog belonged to someone because it was not afraid of him. It was not wild or scared.

The boy walked slowly toward Little Pup. She retreated. The boy came further. Little Pup retreated further. The boy thought it was a game, but Little Pup had a purpose. She wanted the new boy to follow her. She wanted to lead him to her master. She thought this new boy could help.

The game went on. Come forward, retreat. Come forward five steps, retreat ten. Soon Little Pup had the new boy following her. She always kept just enough ahead so he couldn't catch her but not so far ahead that he would lose her. The new boy caught on to her strategy. He followed her along the river path, back to the dark, but fairly dry rock shelter where her master lay.

Little Pup stood motionless at the broad entrance to the shelter. She barked to wake Dreamer. The barking also excited the new boy, and he stopped about twenty paces from the mouth of the rock shelter. Then he saw the head of Dreamer above the deerskin cover. Their eyes met.

"What is that I see? A friend, I hope?" Dreamer said under his breath.

8

"Yes I am a friend, and I need help," Dreamer signed to this new boy," his hands now above his wet deerskin cover.

"Little Pup, come here." He also motioned to Little Pup with his hands.

The faithful companion immediately went to Dreamer, who reached out and stroked the wet shaggy dog under her chin. "Thank-you," was all Dreamer had to give her.

The new boy could see that the person under the deerskin was having trouble. Thinking he could help, he came closer to the entrance of the shelter. Little Pup growled, protectively. "Stay, Little Pup, a new friend has found us and perhaps he will help us."

The new boy signed, "I come in peace," then he reached out and lowered his palm towards Little Pup so she could get his smell and decide for herself whether he was friend or foe. "Sniff, sniff," She decided he was a friend.

Dreamer leaned on his left elbow, holding his right hand to his forehead, as he lowered his head in pain.

The new boy didn't know what to think. He had never been greeted like this before. What was the matter? Then Dreamer showed the boy his leg.

"It is bad," the new boy said in his down-south language. He came closer, looked, then reached out and took the heel of Dreamer's right foot gently in his hand.

"It's very bad," he said. "Friend," and he pointed to himself, "Can I work on it? I know what to do. My father is a shaman. He has fixed many leg breaks, and I have helped him with some. I believe I know how to take care of it."

"Can you make it better?"

"Yes, I believe I can, but first, it will hurt."

"Then do it. It couldn't hurt any more than it does right now."

The new boy went back to his canoe to get his belongings, hiding it again in the brush and covering it well. On his way back, with his flint skinning knife, he cut off some stout willow branches and pulled them behind him. He also found some greenbrier vines to use as cord. He peeled the thorns from the vines and had several long strands with him when he returned.

The new boy then cut the branches into poles and stripped the leaves from them. He had six poles in all, each about half as long as he was tall. Now to work on the leg.

"Ready?" He took Dreamer's broken leg in both hands and pulled as hard as he could. Little Pup growled, not knowing what else to do. Dreamer passed out. The boy pulled a little harder, glad that Dreamer was unconscious. The leg went back together, the bone disappearing beneath the torn skin. He washed the wound again with clear water from the dripping spring.

When Dreamer came to, he complained about the pain. Yes, it hurt even more than when he had first broken it. He fainted again, but woke up moments later.

"Are you sure you know what you're doing?"

"Yes, it's back together, and now it can heal properly."

The new boy did know what he was doing. He had seen his father do it often. He had also seen his father's patients heal up as good as new although it did take a long time.

The new boy now put willow leaves against the wound, wrapping them in long cattail leaves. Next he covered the wound with a piece of deerskin. Then he put the willow poles lengthwise over the deerskin and around the broken leg and tied it all up with the greenbrier vines. It took some maneuvering to keep everything straight, but it was finally done.

"If you want to walk again, then you'll have to leave these poles exactly like they are, and no weight on that leg. The poles will keep your leg straight so it can heal correctly. It will take two moons to heal."

"But how can I? How will I find food? How will I protect myself from the wild animals? How can I?"

His new friend looked Dreamer in the eye, paused, and replied, "I will take care of you until you can walk again. I will bring you food. Your Little dog and I will protect you from the wild animals."

Dreamer couldn't believe what he had heard. "But don't you have to go home? Where were you going, anyway?" The new boy told Dreamer he was on a mission to see where the water in the Great Father of Waters came from.

"I can tell you that," said Dreamer, "Or at least I can tell you what I know of it. I've been on my way down the Father of Waters for more than seven moons. I spent the maize-growing moons at the great Cahokia Village, but now I have been on the river, coming downwater, for more than a moon. I will tell you all I know. I come from far up the river. I live towards the setting Father Sun from the Rocky River, near the ever-flowing spring north of the great oak forest where our Eagle Clan holds its Powwows twice every year.

"Friend, I owe you a great thanks. Oh, ouch, it hurts, but you have saved my life. I know I could not have fixed it myself. You have given me the best gift of all—the gift of healing, and I don't even know your name, or where you come from."

"My people call me 'Morning Boy.' That will be my name until I am a man. I cannot sleep when the sun comes up; that's why they all call me 'Morning Boy.' What is your name?"

Dreamer told Morning Boy about his dream, about the spider, his quest, and the name his little sister had given him.

"'Dreamer?' that's interesting; it fits you like a tight moccasin, and it will until you complete your man task. I can help you complete your task, for I know where the water goes. Yes, I will help you."

"Oh, would you?"

"Yes, but you must heal first."

. . . .

Two moons had passed. Morning Boy had taken care of Dreamer diligently. He caught fish, turtles, frogs and snakes in the river. He brought back watercress from the clear water spring located across the little river. Nuts of various kinds were everywhere, and he cracked great quantities and gave them to Dreamer. He provided well, and together they ate well. Little Pup also shared in the bounty.

Morning Boy counted on his fingers. "Yes, it is now time to walk, but you can only walk a short way on this first day. You must stretch your leg often."

Morning Boy had reinforced the splint several times during the past two moons. During all that time, Dreamer had put no weight on his right leg. During the past several days, he had hopped around a little, with the help of a forked stick under his right arm. Today, he took ten steps, gingerly using both legs.

Morning Boy wanted him to walk a little more each day. "You can't do it all at once, but you can add more steps every day. Soon you can throw that old 'helper-stick' away."

In another five days Dreamer walked the short distance to the Father of Waters. Toward the end it hurt, but now, he could walk. Now it was time to go.

Morning Boy told Dreamer to wait by his canoe. He would go back to the rock shelter and gather all their belongings.

Dreamer looked at the canoe with a careful eye. It was much better than the one they had given him at the send-off from Cahokia, the one he had lost in the flood, now well over two moons ago.

The canoe was small, but one of the boys would be in the front and one in the rear. Their belongings and Little Pup would be in the middle. Being in the canoe on the water would be much easier than walking and much safer too. Little Pup jumped up into the canoe, testing it, then she jumped back out. She liked it.

Morning Boy returned, cleaned the rest of the bushes from around his little craft. He then pulled his canoe to the water's edge and motioned for Dreamer to get up front. This raised the rear of the canoe just enough so Morning Boy could push it further out into the little river. Little Pup jumped in again and sat comfortably on top of the packs in the middle of the canoe.

Now, one foot in the water, Morning Boy lifted the rear of the small canoe and pushed it out into the river. He jumped in himself, grabbing his paddle and, with two strokes, had the little dugout headed downwater.

Dreamer fixed the features of the mouth of this "leg-breaking" river firmly in his memory. He was glad he was finally leaving. On his way back up the Father of Waters, he would steer clear of this awful place.

It was late morning. The three had eaten their morning meal earlier. Now they would be on the river for some time. It was good to be back on the Father of Waters again.

It was a long day, but they made good progress. They stopped and ate their evening meal on a sandy island, sleeping next to the canoe. A fire provided some warmth against the evening chill.

Dreamer slept well. Morning Boy was up first, like always. He looked a long time at the sleeping Dreamer. First a twitch, then a rollover to his left side and finally Dreamer opened his eyes. As he opened his eyes to the clear eastern sky, he could see it was going to be a bright day. Father Sun had already cleared the morning fog; only a trace of it remained.

"Well?"

"I was dreaming how lucky I am that you happened along, found me, then decided to stay and help me and that you knew how to take care of my broken leg. How can I ever repay you?"

"My parents told me, when I was very young, that if I ever found someone in need, I should help them. You needed help, so I did what I could."

Dreamer took a few steps to stretch his leg. It was time to pack their gear and get on the river again.

Morning Boy had made a small paddle and with each stroke Dreamer was getting more used to it. It was not as good as his old Cahokia paddle, but it helped to propel the canoe downstream.

There were also many islands, some merely sandbars in the river. The two paddlers would often beach their canoe on one of the larger sandbars, providing a place for Dreamer to stretch his stiff leg. Dreamer walked better each time he got out; these little hard-packed sand islands were just what he needed. Little Pup also appreciated these stops. When the canoe beached, she hit the sand running, tired of the monotonous motion of the canoe.

On most of these sandy islands there were dry driftwood sticks, and Little Pup was always game to fetch one as the boys pitched it on the sand or away into the river. She always returned to Dreamer and dropped the stick at his feet, looking up at him for a little "thank you" touch under the chin.

Occasionally, Dreamer would throw one of the driftwood sticks upstream. Little Pup had learned to lead it a little; otherwise, it would be gone. It didn't take long for her to master the intercept.

Little Pup always enjoyed the exercise of stick retrieval; however, soon it was becoming work. Dreamer understood her feelings. When she was tired, he would call her to him. He would always stoop down, brush her wet hair, and give her that, tender, affectionate rub under her chin.

After exercising and stretching, and when it was time to shove off, Little Pup would jump back into the canoe. She always sat on Dreamer's pack, where she could see ahead.

Together, Dreamer and Morning Boy paddled down the Father of Waters, snaking around an island on the right and then a bend on the left. The Father of Waters was just like a long snake. Sometimes, it seemed as if the Great River was doubling back on itself, but he always ended up headed south, away from the night pole star.

. . . .

Dreamer was resting with his paddle across the middle of the canoe. Morning Boy was behind him paddling with the current. They were making good time. As he paddled, Morning Boy told Dreamer he had left his home, at the edge of the salty water about four moons ago. He had paddled upstream, against the current, almost every day. It had been hard going because sometimes the wind was in his face; on those days he didn't make much progress.

"On my way upstream, I stayed much in the middle of the river. I figured it would be the safest place. I liked the sandy islands best. They were clean and seemed friendlier. There I spent most of my nights where there were fewer of the blood-sucking insects, and there was always driftwood for my fire. There were turtles and frogs, and occasionally I could spear or trap a fish."

Morning Boy continued, "Sometimes I would come up a chute because the current was lazier there."

"How does your leg feel? Are you all right? Maybe we should have stopped sooner and stretched so you wouldn't feel so stiff now," Morning Boy questioned Dreamer.

"My leg is fine. You did a good job of healing it. You are a 'shaman' for whom I have great respect."

Sometime later, as Father Sun was low on the horizon, Dreamer saw an island ahead. On it grew a thick stand of willows. "Let's stop there for the night," he said, pointing to the patch of green in the distance.

The island's seven, small willow trees growing on the upstream end would provide some cover and shield the light of their night fire.

Morning Boy walked around the small island while Dreamer, working with his fire kit and dry driftwood, soon had a fire going. Morning Boy came back with two small turtles.

"Look, food for tonight."

He used his flint knife to remove the shells. The three of them, enjoyed cooked turtle that evening, Little Pup receiving what the boys didn't want.

Before ending their day, it was time to check their belongings as they did each evening while Father Sun was going down in the west. Bows, quivers and arrows, fire-making kits, bedrolls, and their packs; nothing was missing. Dreamer still had four of his brown-green stones and Morning Boy didn't need to know. They would be Dreamer's secret.

. . . .

After a good night's sleep and a morning meal of nuts and berries and some turtle meat for Little Pup, the three were off again. Dreamer couldn't believe the Father of Waters could go so far. Now rested, their hunger satisfied, and a cloudless day ahead, they would make good time.

Together—pull, break water, forward, splash—then pull, and repeat the process. Their paddles moved efficiently. When it was time to stretch, Morning Boy pointed out a little cove up on the right.

On a worn bank, where many before them had taken their canoes from the water, they would beach their canoe, and stretch. They paddled straight for the narrow cove formed by the end of a slow creek.

Morning Boy's canoe slid into the mud and with a jolt, came to an abrupt stop. Carefully, Dreamer jumped out, making the front lighter. With a few tugs, he had the canoe halfway up the bank.

Although the three travelers didn't realized it, back in the dark forest were two pairs of brothers; eight eyes had been watching every move they made. The wind blew toward the shore, so there was no scent from the four that Little Pup could catch, although she was alert, constantly scanning the shore. She did not bark; all was quiet—everything must be O. K. Absolutely still, the four, back in the shadows, watched intently as the three left the canoe.

"We must find food for the mid-day meal. Let's split up and look around the cove. Turtles, snakes, frogs, nuts—anything will do. Little Pup went with Dreamer and the boys left the canoe unguarded.

Morning Boy fork-stuck a medium-sized snake, held it by the tail, and snapped the life out of it. He had also found a couple of frogs.

Dreamer searched along the bank toward the cove opening back toward the river. He found only one frog. As he made his way across a fallen log in a small brook, he stopped just in time to avoid a large hornet's nest. It was a

136

gray, papery, round object, a little larger than Dreamer's head, longer than it was wide, and head-high. "What if I had bumped it? I would have had to dive into the water to keep those black and yellow flying stingers off me." The nest was low, fairly close to the water, and formed carefully on the end of a small, dead, willow limb. It swayed gently in the breeze. The hornets would land on the side, crawl down to the opening on the bottom, then disappear within.

Suddenly, Dreamer heard a commotion and loud shouting back at the canoe site. Little Pup, barking, ran off in that direction. Morning Boy, returning from his successful hunt, came upon four mischievous local boys. They had his canoe in the water and were just shoving off. He shouted loudly for his friend Dreamer to hear.

Dreamer, too, saw the four as they climbed into the canoe; they used the two paddles to point the canoe toward the opening that would take them to the Father of Waters, but first they would have to come fairly close to Dreamer's side of the cove.

Immediately, Dreamer thought of the hornet's nest. He grabbed a handful of wet leaves, and with the other hand scooped some black mud from the bank of the cove. With no other protection, he went for the hornet's nest. Fortunately, the dead limb on which the nest was built snapped off easily. Hurriedly he packed the leaves into the bottom opening following with the mud. He moved rapidly away from a few flying hornets looking for their nest. He was stung several times. Now the four in the canoe were almost upon him, as he hid in the willows. When they were adjacent, he threw the hornet's nest. It landed directly in the bottom of the canoe and broke open. Now hornets were everywhere.

The boys knew instantly what they must do. "Quick! Underwater! Let's go." So, the four of them, covered with hornets, jumped into the water to get rid of the flying stingers. They swam under water for the far bank, surfacing and gasping for air, then diving underwater again.

The canoe was now empty except for the broken nest and some stingers still flying around it. Dreamer waded into the water and grabbed the deerskin bow rope. Carefully, slowly, he pulled the canoe along behind him as he went back into the cove. He felt a couple more stings as he recovered the canoe.

Next to the bank he saw a long, straight pole. Grabbing it, he speared the hornet's nest and immediately threw it onto the bank. Fortunately, most of the hornets went with it. Now he was pulling the canoe further into the cove, and as he did so, the stingers left, going back to the nest on the bank.

Dreamer raised his head and looked into the canoe. Both packs and both paddles were still there. What luck!

As he pulled the canoe back to the bank where they had originally beached it, he thought, "Never again will we leave our precious canoe unguarded."

Morning Boy still had their noon meal with him. Little Pup was also back at the canoe pull-out site. The three were to-gether, safe, except for the dozen or so welts on Dreamer. He thanked Father Sun for the handy hornet's nest. If it hadn't been there, well, they would all be walking. Yes, he and Little Pup would be walking again.

. . . .

"What an experience we had yesterday."
"Yes, we were lucky to get our canoe back."

"These welts on my face and arms are to prove that I saved the canoe. It's good that our packs were still in it."

They paddled down the middle of the Great Father of Waters. Soon, it was time to look for food. The few nuts left, would not fill their stomachs; it seemed as though food was always a problem.

"What is that dark shape on the high bank ahead?" asked Morning Boy.

"Isn't it a black bear? They can run fast when they want to—when you least expect it. We should stay clear of him."

"Yes, but let's paddle fairly close to the shore, then we can drift by the bear to see what he does. I know he can't swim as fast as we can paddle."

The bear, on all fours, was sniffing first right, then left as it walked along the grassy level above the river. Stopping at a big oak tree and looking up, the bear got on its two hind feet and with a front paw, reached up into a dark hole in the tree. Suddenly, the bear fell back on all four, then to three, using the fourth paw to brush bees away from its eyes. There would be no honey for the bear today. It ran back into the thick forest to escape the swarming bees.

Seeing the bear's bad luck gave Dreamer and Morning Boy an idea. They could use some honey. If they found enough, they could even trade with it. "A little smoke will do," said Dreamer.

They beached their canoe against a fallen tree and covered it carefully with limbs and grass. Hidden at the base of a big hill and across the river from a swampland, the canoe should be safe. "Nobody should bother it here." This time they took their packs with them, concealing them in a little depression behind some evergreen trees about fifty paces from the canoe.

The boys climbed the bluff to the second level, toward the bee tree. Dreamer had his fire-making kit with him. He had gathered honey before. Together, the two of them crept close. On the flat, they gathered dried grass from the clearing. Slowly they approached the tree where the bees were now settling down after the swipe of the bear's paw.

To reach the bee's nest, they needed a big forked stick. With the forked end up, one of the boys could stand in the crotch, reach into the hive and pull out some of the honeycomb.

First, though, they would have to make some smoke brands, so they wrapped the dead grass into a bundle. Then with his fire-making kit, Dreamer quickly had a small fire going. The two had placed the fire where the smoke would float up toward the big oak to the place where the hive was located. They put green grass on the fire to make even more smoke.

"O. K., let's go to work." They lit their smoking firebrands. They soon had lots of honey.

. . . .

Morning Boy and Dreamer continued down the Great Father of Waters, the weather cooling after the passage from full moon to quarter moon. With Little Pup along Dreamer felt more secure. He was always thinking that perhaps the goal of his quest was around the next bend of the Great River. He was anxious as he came around the outside of a bend, always hoping he would find out where the river went.

Now many trees along the Great River were uniform, upright pyramids, with feathery leaves. Some also had gray-green, curly "hair" that seemed to grow on air. These trees also seemed to have "knees" growing next to them along the bank, and some even in the water. The trees themselves grew out in the water, too.

These strange trees did not grow at the Council Grove. Dreamer observed small cone-like fruits on the ground. He wondered if he would take some cones home, plant them, and grow these trees at his spring. "I should take some home with me," Dreamer told Morning Boy.

Dreamer thought often of home and his family's campsite by the spring. He wondered about his mother, father, sister and two young brothers. He wished he knew how they were doing.

The two boys and Little Pup were resting in the canoe, drifting, their paddles lying across in front of them. Morning Boy was also talking more and more about his home in the southland, adjacent to the "Wide Water."

Dreamer asked, "What is the wide water?"

"We'll soon have to carry our canoe across the land," said Morning Boy. He was watching the Father of Waters for the place to take the canoe out. "It's marked with three upright posts on the left. They should be just around the next bend or two."

They paddled on, Morning Boy anxiously watching for the posts

9

The honkers were on their way south, as they usually were about the time the first frost appeared on the cattails and the final green grass of the year. The grass was called, "turkey foot" because its flower and seed head looked exactly like a turkey track in the mud.

Dreamer's mother was a light sleeper. The honkers were low and loud and had awakened her. Getting up, she slowly pushed aside the deerskin flap at the entrance of the little lodge. It was becoming lighter in the eastern sky. The white snow will soon be upon us, she thought. Then, as she had done many times in recent moons, Blue Damsel Fly looked for her son. He had always brought in the water, sometimes even this early in the morning.

"I hope he is careful and safe on his journey as he follows the river. He is so young and has not yet learned all the cares and cautions of life. He is all alone, and I worry about him," thought Dreamer's mother.

She reentered the small, sturdy lodge made of bent sticks, woven grass, and waterproof deer skins that adequately sheltered the family. She placed her hand on her mate's hand and gave it a slight squeeze. He slowly opened one eye at a time, whispering, "What are you doing up so early?"

"I can't sleep. I'm thinking of our son, and I wonder where he is and what he is doing," she said in a low voice so as not to wake the sleeping Otter Tail and her two brothers.

"There's nothing we can do now. He's down the river. He's on his own. He listened at the Powwows, and he sought out good advice from his elders. He will be all right. He will come back home, to our place here at the spring, someday. When he does, he will have stories that will take a moon's time to tell. I worry too, but there is nothing I can do to help him or bring him back. We'll just have to wait until he returns. We did the best we could before we allowed him to go. Now everything is up to him."

Otter Tail stretched under her deerskin covers. She arched her feet and pointed her toes out as far as she could. Her feet slid out from under the deerskin and into the chill of the morning. Feeling the sudden cold, she slipped on her moccasins and pulled and tied the thongs. Pulling the deerskin blanket around her shoulders, she went to the spring with the two clay pots, dutifully filled them, and returned to the gray ash of the nearly dead fire. When she placed a few twigs in the ashes and blew three short breaths, the fire ignited. She placed more sticks on the fire and added a couple of small logs to top it off.

Little Otter Tail had a sparkle in her eye because she had doused her face with cold, fresh water at the spring. "What are you two talking about?"

They said together, "Oh, we're just wondering how our Dreamer is getting along."

Otter Tail replied, "You know, with the chill in the air, the geese flying south and with the first winter snow not too far away, I've been thinking the same thing. I guess when we are worrying about something important; we all do it at the same time. The geese flying south, probably following the

Rocky River, must know something. It's certain they can't live up here when there is so much ice and snow on the ground. Do you suppose they know something we don't? Do you think they're going to a place where it's warmer?"

The five of them sat together around the fire; each had a story to tell about both geese and Dreamer. This day his two little brothers listened and learned much. In fact, they even had a few stories of their own to tell. If only Dreamer could have heard the tales told about him.

10

The three upright posts were in the distance, just as Morning Boy had said they would be. They were about twice the height of a man and easy to see. Dreamer steered the canoe towards the bank where the posts were located. The riverbank was worn from all the canoes that had used it. It looked as though the canoes had been paddled right up and across the mud, but Dreamer quickly discovered that wasn't what would happen.

Pulling the canoe across the dirt trail was a chore. Morning Boy was glad for Dreamer's help. Last time he had had to do it alone, and it had taken him most of a day.

"Where are we going on this land trail?" Dreamer asked. "Are we leaving our Father of Waters?"

"You'll see. I've been here before. There's only one way to go. We follow where others have gone before. We'll make it to the other side before dark and camp next to the lake. Then we'll find some food, light our fire, and settle down for the night."

Little Pup was ahead of them, leading the way. She was out of sight, and then came running back to see if they were still behind her on the path. The landmarks were familiar to Morning Boy. He had carefully recorded them when he came across from the other direction.

It was slow, hard work. The canoe held their heavy backpacks. Last time Morning Boy had made it from the other side without help, but this time, with the added weight, he was glad Dreamer was with him. They rested often. Dreamer, eager to see their destination, walked in front. The path seemed to go on forever. If he meant to come back the same way, he must remember the landmarks. First, the tall dead tree with the big osprey nest at the top, then the two fallen trees, one over the other; next, the small pond on the left. Could he remember it all? Perhaps he should just follow the smooth tracks of the canoe bottoms that had been pulled along the path. That made more sense to him. He wondered if there were also three posts on the other end.

"We should reach the lakeside before Father Sun goes down. There will be more animals out at dusk. That will give us more choice for our evening meal." Morning Boy advised.

Occasionally Little Pup would jump in for a ride as they dragged the canoe. The boys would stop pulling, turn around, and scold her. She would hop out again, enjoying her game, as they made their slow portage.

"How long, how far, do we have to pull the canoe?" Dreamer was getting anxious, but Morning Boy only smiled, knowing they still had quite a way to go. So, pull, pull, pull. Dreamer's leg hurt, but he pulled.

Finally, in the distance Dreamer could see an expanse of water. Was it the lake that Morning Boy had talked about? Morning Boy confirmed that they were almost to their goal for the day and that they would make camp soon.

When they arrived at the lakeshore, they both fell down, exhausted. Now they had to eat. They gathered some dead wood for the campfire, while looking for food. The boys found only three large frogs. It was not much, but they would share with Little Pup.

The campfire was built where the smoke would drift across their sleeping location next to the canoe high up on the bank. The smoke and the breeze from the lake should keep the insects away for the night. Leaning back against the canoe, the boys agreed that they were very tired.

"Watch out for those honeycombs."

As he settled down to sleep, Dreamer reviewed the events of the day, especially the long portage from the three posts on the far side to the three posts on this side. He would remember those landmarks.

. . . .

Dreamer and Morning Boy were off early, the three posts disappearing behind them. They paddled in unison now; Dreamer was in the rear and his new friend in the front. Forward, dip, pull, lift the paddle from the water, swing out wide and forward, then dip. The harder they pulled, the faster they went. Dreamer had been away from his camp at the spring for over ten moons. He thought that he and Morning Boy must be nearing their goal.

They were now crossing the big lake—Lake Poncha, Morning Boy called it. Paddling eastward, they kept the shore on the right in view. After paddling most of the day, they finally came to a point. "Now we'll come to another point on the left and then make our passage out into the Endless Ocean," Morning Boy told Dreamer.

The last bit of land was made up of mossy roots and dark cypress trees, with their long gray-green strands of hanging moss, As they skirted it, Dreamer stood up in the dugout, leaning forward with his hand above his eyes, he said, "There is no other side—it *is* endless." His mouth wide open, he said breathlessly, "So, the water from my spring didn't go down into a hole in the ground; instead, it's trying to fill up an Endless Ocean."

Morning Boy steered their canoe to the far left point where they came close to a small river. "My father calls this little river the Pearl River. He and others of our clan have been here many times. At the outlet, close to the Endless Ocean, are clams with small white pearls, far more than we find in our giant oysters. I've been here twice with my family. The third time I came here I was alone, on my way upriver."

"Later, I'll take you to the exact location where your water ends," Morning Boy told Dreamer, as he pointed off to the southwest.

Dreamer now motioned that he wanted to continue on to the sandy beach. He wanted to step out on the sand and run up to a high spot and look out across the Endless Ocean. They kept to the direction of the curve and

ended up on the sandy beach beyond the Pearl River. In fact, the gentle waves of the Endless Ocean helped them beach the dugout quite high on the wet sand. It was now time to stretch his leg, rest, enjoy the view, and of course to reflect on events of the past several days.

Little Pup was first out of the canoe; dashing down the beach, running on the wet sand, she chased the little sand birds. Dreamer clapped his hands, and she abruptly skidded to a stop. She ran back to her master's side, getting that good scratch under her chin.

Walking higher up the beach to the tangled roots at the edge of the tree line, Dreamer sat down and leaned back. This higher elevation gave him a better view. The sand beach to his left was so long, and it seemed endless, too. "I guess I'll call it Long Beach," he laughed. Morning Boy confirmed that it was the Long Beach, "That's what we called it, but, how did you know?"

In the far distance, over the blue-green Endless Ocean, both left and right, the white, billowing clouds met their reflection in the water—met and touched as one. Dreamer was astonished at the ocean—so wide, so beautiful. So endless.

He closed his eyes, trying to record the beautiful image of what was before him. "I will remember this always," he said to himself.

. . . .

Last night they had camped on the Long Beach. Now, Morning Boy pointed to the east, toward the rising Father Sun. "I live down there. I wish we could be there tonight, but we're still more than a day away from my home. We'll be there tomorrow, but we must get started."

He pulled the canoe toward the water, but it was too heavy and he was too tired. Morning Boy motioned Dreamer to come down off the hummock to help. Dreamer ran down the hard, packed sand. "You sit up front, Dreamer. I'll do the heavy paddling." Little Pup was between them. "It won't be long now." Morning Boy seemed happy.

In the far distance were his home and his family. He wondered if his people had already departed for the island. He was thinking out loud: "We'll find out soon enough, tomorrow afternoon at the latest." Deer Island, their winter home, provided giant oysters from the ocean floor, sea turtles, and the many birds that nested on the island—more food and more eggs than the little clan could use.

The boys paddled straight away from the beach, hitting the swells head-on. Soon they were far out, in smooth water. Morning Boy told Dreamer to hold his paddle in the water on the left side, like a rudder. Several hard sweeps on his left side turned the canoe east, toward home. Now they were traveling parallel to the Long Beach.

Since Morning Boy's home was so close, they had both been paddling a bit harder and they were very tired. They began looking for a place to spend the last night out. Ahead, a small stream cut through the sand of the Long Beach. "That looks good. We'll spend the night there and have plenty of fresh water too," said Morning Boy.

Dreamer didn't understand what Morning Boy had just said. "We've got all the water we want. We can't drink the Endless Ocean dry, can we?"

"No, but we don't drink the ocean water. It has too much salt in it. We drink the water without salt—water from the creeks, brooks, and springs. We could drink from the ocean, once a day, but only if we have to." Dreamer scooped up a handful of ocean water to taste it. Sppputtt—he blew it out in a hurry. "I see what you mean."

Morning Boy would teach Dreamer all about salt, but it would be a lesson for another time. Now, to beach the canoe. They paddled into the little stream and jumped out, Little Pup almost beating them. She took a drink from the Endless Ocean, and she too quickly spit it out. She ran up on the beach, put her head down on the sand, and raked her front right paw over her mouth to get rid of the taste. Dreamer pointed to the stream coming down from the forest. Little Pup went to it and satisfied her thirst.

Morning Boy and Dreamer pulled the canoe up through the little stream and out of sight under the roots of a large oak. They gathered firewood to cook the seven small fish they had trapped in a tidewater pool. They had sloshed them out onto the sand. Fish cooked in seaweed tasted good to the boys and Little Pup that evening.

The breeze from the ocean protected the three of them from pesky mosquitoes. Morning Boy slept soundly in the depression he had made in the sand; it fit him just right. His deerskin cover kept the gritty sand from his skin. Little Pup slept in the canoe. Dreamer was too tired to dream this night. The constant, soothing roar of the ocean swells lulled them quickly into a deep sleep.

Up early and all their belongings packed, the boys slid the canoe down the wet sand of the little stream toward the Endless Ocean. Paddling without let-up until Father Sun was high overhead, Morning Boy saw a familiar shore to the west of his Biloxi Nation. He was nearly home. He knew that his father, Diving Bird, and his mother, Yellow Flower, would be eager to see him. He had been gone for more than five moons. They might even have thought he would never come home.

To his delight, his parents happened to be on the beach when the canoe appeared. When Morning Boy saw them waving, he wondered whether they knew it was him! There were now two in the canoe and a little dog, too.

"Morning Boy, Morning Boy!" they called.

He stood up in the canoe to be recognized. He had indeed returned. Their arms were around each other's shoulders, and they waved a "welcome home" with their free arms.

-11-

"Home at last! It's wonderful!" Morning Boy shouted as he awoke early the next morning.

Yellow Flower looked at her son. "Gone for more than five moons—I thought you might never come home."

Dreamer said, "I've been away from my home at the spring, out west of the Rocky River, for more than ten moons" The three looked at Dreamer. "At home the Harvest Moon has come and gone," he continued. "The maize has all been picked. Now ice and snow probably covers the ground."

"Ice? Snow? What are they?"

"Snow and ice occur when the rain freezes. When it gets very cold, instead of rain we have ice, then snow. Ice clings to the trees, and its weight breaks branches. Snow, on the other hand, is beautiful—cold, but beautiful. Snowflakes that land on the cold leaves, are tiny, white, and with many designs. Each snowflake is different. When many fall, they pile up to form snowdrifts." He gestured to show the family how high snowdrifts could grow. "I have seen snow this high on the ground. When it's that high, most animals stay inside their homes. Well, all except for the deer living under the trees, they are still out. In fact they are the best food in winter, when their meat keeps well. Frozen meat does not spoil. Deer are easy to find, too, because they are dark against the white snow. But enough of my talk, tell me what you do down here?"

"Well, we have to find food, too," answered Diving Bird. "It's our first duty of the day. We eat berries, nuts, rice, and roots, but it's meat, oysters, bird's eggs, and fish that we must have. Later today we'll go out to find some giant oysters. They are plentiful out toward the island. I'll show you shells on the beach on the way, shells that are as beautiful as the snowflakes of your northland. Each shell is different, too, you'll see..."

Down His River of Dreams ...

The ocean was rough today. The waves started to break, eight or nine out. The froth and foam continued to roar in, sometimes the waves crossing one another as they washed up on the beach. The fine, white sand was smooth as it gently swirled with the water. Occasionally, shells washed up on the beach, most of them broken; sometimes, though, a perfect one survived. Dreamer had picked up several perfect halves. "I'll take a few home. They are so much more beautiful and more colorful than our Rocky River clam shells."

At night the little hard-shelled crabs scuttled on the beach. Morning Boy cautioned Dreamer about their pair of legs up front, with large pincers. "Be careful not to let a crab get hold of your finger. They can hurt. I know."

On their walk down the beach, the boys found more seashells than Dreamer could carry. Now he had to choose which ones to keep. The big "ocean flake," the one with five arms, was new to him. Some of the starfish were still alive. Morning Boy told him that when they died, they got hard. "They are really not good for anything—certainly not to eat. Today we must find food; that's our most important task."

. . . .

The boys set out to gather giant oysters from the floor of the Endless Ocean. Morning Boy used a floating log and paddled out toward the island. Then he disappeared underwater. He had a deerskin sash around his waist and he put oysters in it as he found them. He had about ten when he finished. Now he was weighted down. The driftwood log had floated down along the beach for some distance. He hailed Dreamer, who went after the log, floating it back along the beach, then paddling it out to Morning Boy. Together they used it to get back to the beach. In their shells, the oysters were heavy. Together the boys pried them open, wrapping the meat in seaweed to keep it moist and leaving the empty shells behind.

On the way back to the camp, the boys sat down on a big driftwood log that had floated in. They watched the shore birds as they too searched for food. It seemed as though finding food was a constant search for every creature on Mother Earth.

The two birds that interested Dreamer most were the diving bird, the one with the big mouth—the pelican, and the little running bird. It ran so fast that its moving legs were just a blur. These birds, the sanderlings, ran in pairs, right behind the waterline as it moved back down the beach. As another swell pushed in a new waterline, the birds would be right there, looking for food and leaving tiny tracks in the sand. Little Pup liked to chase the sanderlings although she could never catch one.

"Do you eat any of the birds? There are so many different kinds. Some look like they would be good to eat—the ones with the long legs, or the ones with the short wings, the diving ones, the white-and-black ones that drift with the wind." There were just too many birds to describe.

"No, we don't eat many birds. They have to work too hard to find food. To catch and kill a bird is almost not worth the effort. They are almost like snakes—too little meat on their bones. Bird's eggs are more valuable to us as food than the birds themselves. The big duck eggs are the best."

Dreamer told Morning Boy of the big turkeys in the prairies up north. "They are larger than an eagle, and they spend most of their time on the ground. They have plenty of dark meat. One will feed my family for four days. The meat doesn't keep much longer than that during hot weather. In cold weather, however, the meat stays good for a long time. Turkeys also lay big eggs. Sometimes a nest will have as many eggs as you have fingers. They are good too."

Enough of the bird stories. It was time to go.

When they arrived home, Morning Boy's mother cleaned the oysters in the ocean, and then cooked the meat in salt water in a clay pot. It was the best meat Dreamer had ever eaten, and he told Yellow Flower how much he enjoyed it.

. . . .

There were only five families in the Biloxi Clan. They lived on the point of land at the east end of the Long Beach, near the opening of the bay. During the short days of the cooler moons, they went out to Deer Island to live, making their camp in the midst of big piles of oyster shells. The island was long and narrow. Part of it was high ground. A small grove of oak trees and a few pine trees grew there. The children of the clan liked it there, as did their parents, who always knew where to find the little ones. On the island there was no running away down the Long Beach, or going back into the bay.

Morning Boy told Dreamer of a friend who had gone into the back bay one time and never came home. The next morning all the fathers and the older boys went to find him. He had been playing with a little alligator. It had grabbed his foot and bitten him badly. Since he couldn't walk very well, he had climbed a tree for the night. Luckily, he found an oak with many branching trunks—like a hand with outstretched fingers. He spent the night sleeping in this cradle. His mother was very worried, and when he returned, bad foot or not, he was disciplined.

The Island had two long mounds of oyster shells. These mounds ran from one end to the other. The water on both sides of the little island contained excellent beds of the giant oyster. They were good eating, raw or cooked. It seemed that, no matter how many oysters they took, there were always more by the next moon. The shells continued to pile up on the island.

The clan set up their lodges between the mounds of shells and the oak grove. Their homes were built to last, in spite of the sun and the wind. Acorns, brought with them each time the people came to the island, were planted on the high ground to insure that in future years there would always be replacement oaks.

The people stayed on the island for four or five moons each year. Once a day, however, when the weather was calm, one of the elders returned to the spring on the mainland. He had to fill all of the clay pots with fresh water and return with a full canoe. If a storm was coming, he might even go back a second time, to avoid going the next day when he knew the ocean would be rough. When it rained for several days, water was easy to obtain. Each family stretched several deerskins tight to catch the rainwater, sloping the skins so the water would flow down into a large clay pot. Fresh water was important, and it was easy to obtain this way.

The birds were protected from predators by being on the isolated island. Birds' eggs were plentiful. The people didn't harm the birds, and the birds provided food for the people. It was a good relationship.

Deer Island was named long ago, almost before anyone living could remember. Hunters had chased a deer to the mainland point, with the endless ocean on one side and Biloxi Bay on the other. As they were closing in on the deer, instead of crashing through the line of men, it ran down the sandy beach, jumped into the salty water, and swam toward the little island. "As the story goes," Morning Boy related, "The deer made it to the island. That's why it's called Deer Island."

"What happened to the deer of long ago?" Dreamer asked.

"No one remembers. Today, there's very little animal life on the island, except for birds," Morning Boy told Dreamer.

Dreamer and Morning Boy enjoyed their life on the island. They collected shells on the beach, waded in the shallow water, and searched for the giant oysters with their toes. During these oyster hunts, Morning Boy found out that Dreamer couldn't swim.

"You can't? Here many swim before they walk. There's just too much water not to be able to swim. You must learn. I'm going to teach you. We'll start tomorrow."

Father sun was setting far down the beach. When the night meal of birds' eggs and oysters was over, it was time to listen to the elders tell their stories.

Dreamer didn't catch all the words of the stories because he had not yet learned all of the Biloxi words, in spite of Morning Boy's tutoring. What he didn't get, he would ask Morning Boy about later. He didn't interrupt the storyteller. He was respectful—careful to watch the others and respond as they did. He liked the island camp and the story-telling.

. . . .

"Swimming should come naturally. Oh, I know you can't breathe water like a fish, but if you really try, I'll bet you can almost swim like one. When you go after the giant oysters, out in the deep water, you'll have to know how to swim."

Together they went to the lee side of the island. The bottom sloped gradually; it was out of the wind, and there were no high waves to contend with. Together they waded out to where the water was waist-deep. Morning Boy faced Dreamer.

"When you swim, you don't hold your breath like I saw you doing yesterday. You breathe, but you only breathe in when your mouth is out of the water. Watch me."

Morning Boy backed away and took several pulling strokes toward Dreamer. As he turned his head sideways and backward, he took in a breath. "That's how you do it. You can let it out anywhere, anytime as you stroke— but you must take it in when you're almost looking backward, when your mouth is out of the water.

"First of all, get used to floating. Most people who can't swim think they will sink. That's not true. We really do float. Now kick over to me. Hold your breath first, and then just kick and float over to me. It's easier to swim in ocean water than in fresh water. The salt makes floating natural." Morning Boy said.

They practiced this exercise many times. Dreamer was a good follower. He thought maybe he could learn to swim.

"Now, as you float, give your arms a whirling motion—like this. Cup your hands, and pull the water like the canoe paddle. Don't worry about breathing yet—just pull yourself through the water."

"It works. I don't sink. I can move along the top of the water—almost swimming, even without my floating log," Dreamer sputtered excitedly.

"I'll go alongside of you. You watch me as my arms pull and my head moves from side to side. Watch me as I breathe, when my mouth is out of the water.

"Don't work too hard at it. I'll hold you up as you pull and kick and move your head. I'll say, 'breathe,' when you should breathe in. Between those times you'll have to breathe out. You can do it, I know you can."

Dreamer inhaled some water. Coughing and sputtering, he stood up and watched Morning Boy swim by. Dreamer floated again. He floated and worked his arms; then his legs and feet timed in. He moved his head as Morning Boy had said—and it worked, if only for a moment.

"Try, try again." Morning Boy urged. "You're close to swimming. You can go places you never thought you could go. After you learn to swim, well, we'll go hunt the giant oysters out in deep water. They are the biggest and the best. In a couple of days I know you'll be ready to go after the big ones.

"You stay in the quiet shallow water and practice. I'll go and sit on the beach and watch you," Morning Boy was pleased.

All morning Dreamer practiced floating, breathing, arm strokes, and kicking. He was tired, but Morning Boy wanted him to practice a little longer. "Tomorrow we'll come back and practice some more. Soon you won't be practicing; you'll be swimming."

With those words of encouragement, Dreamer floated in, using his arms and kicking with his feet. He also breathed like Morning Boy had told him. Morning Boy shouted to him from the beach, "You're actually swimming! Tomorrow will be even better."

After several days of practice swimming, Dreamer began to feel comfortable. He knew he would not sink, and he was learning to breathe better. Breathing was definitely the most important part of swimming.

Today they would again go to the lee side of the island, where Dreamer would not have to fight the waves. The two boys tied a little willow basket between two floating logs. Morning Boy knew Dreamer would not be as afraid if he had something to float with him, something he could hang onto. It was a good idea, and also a good place to put the oysters.

In the deep water between the island and the point, the boys were in over their heads. Morning Boy watched Dreamer.

"Don't get too far away from the basket. Just do what you feel comfortable with. Nothing bad will happen. Swimming underwater, just hold your breath. When you need air, push off from the bottom and come up to the surface, then take a breath. Now, let's go find some big ones," Morning Boy said.

Working together, they soon had their willow basket full of giant oysters. Of course, Morning Boy found about twice as many as Dreamer, but he didn't brag. Dreamer felt good. He would get better but, today, he knew he could swim.

. . . .

Finding food was important, and boiled crabs were even better than oysters. Traps didn't last long. They needed to be mended, and new ones needed to be built. The big fish would tear them open to get at the blue crabs inside. Morning Boy and Dreamer checked the traps in the early morning, when Father Sun was high overhead, when He was halfway down, and again, just before dark. If there were two or three crabs inside, they were removed as soon as possible. The traps had to be repaired often when sharks were around.

The best trap-maker was Little Bird, Morning Boy's sister. She had been taught the skill of trap-making by her mother. Little Bird used only the smallest and strongest willow branches. She found them growing next to the Ocean Springs, back on the mainland and she cut the branches with the sharp, flint knife, her father had made for her. When she had gathered an armful of sturdy willow branches, she divided them into two piles, weaving the mouth of the circular trap with the shorter ones from the smaller pile. Then, an arm's length away, there would be another opening just large enough for a crab to crawl through. The opening at the front end would be about five times the size of the smaller opening, and this trapping device worked well.

From the mouth of the trap, she wove back over the trap with the larger willow boughs, increasing the size to about twice that of the outside opening, weaving in additional branches as she went. This increased the diameter of the trap. After she reached the middle, she tapered the branches down to where they would all come together at a point. She placed two thick branches across the middle of the trap to make it even stronger. These two branches were important because they would hold the deerskin cords used to hold the trap to the bottom of the bay. A completed trap, standing on end, would be about as tall as Morning Boy.

Little Bird skillfully wove the deerskin cords that were used to tie the three rock weights to the crab traps, one on the end and the other two tied to the middle. She did masterful work.

Swimming to the bottom with a trap, Morning Boy scooped out a little sand and placed the trap opening towards the depression. The rock anchors held the trap down and in place. Several dead fish inside served as the bait.

Morning Boy would set his traps in the water between Deer Island and the mainland. He knew just how deep in the water to set them. They were placed with the opening facing the flow of the receding tide. After the crabs had finished eating the teasing bait tied at the entrance of the trap, they would go after the real bait on the inside. Once they went through the smaller opening, they were trapped inside. Only occasionally, did a crab escape a trap.

Each clan family had its own traps. Floating markers on them identified the traps. Taking another person's trap or taking the crabs from a trap of another was unheard of. No one thought of stealing crabs from others' traps, because stealing was against the "code."

Usually at the first light, since Morning Boy was always up early, he would gently slide his dugout into the bay and make his round of the family traps, collecting the crabs from the traps and putting them into a basket his little sister had made. The lid of the basket in the belly of his canoe was fastened tight. If it weren't securely fastened, the wily little crabs would be out and over the side—gone in the wink of an eye. Today, with luck, delicious Endless Ocean crab would be the noon meal.

The flat-bottomed pots were gurgled with steaming hot water. Morning Boy and Dreamer did not disappoint the family. They brought back crabs equaling the fingers and thumbs on both their hands. Each of the five around the little campfire that day would have four crabs to eat. It was a real feast! Dreamer, of course, shared with Little Pup.

Each family member and Dreamer put their own crabs into the hot water, where they changed to a pale color. The water stayed hot sitting next to red-orange embers of the fire.

After retrieving their cooked crabs with a forked stick, Morning Boy's family and Dreamer cracked them open with their teeth to get at the white meat inside. The meat was delicious, although there was little meat on a blue crab. It was certainly worth making and setting the traps, retrieving the crabs, and finally cooking, peeling and eating them. In order not to deplete the supply of crabs in the bay, the clan ate crab only six times each moon cycle.

Now, with the sun well past overhead, the meal down, everyone satisfied, and the crab shells buried away from the camp, Dreamer, along with Morning Boy and his family, took to the shade for an early afternoon nap. It had been hard, satisfying, work, and they all deserved a rest.

The pelicans, Dreamer's favorite birds were now flying overhead. He especially liked to see the leader of the line dive into the Endless Ocean, hopefully finding a fish that it had seen near the surface. He watched the long line as it glided just above the ocean waves. He could watch these birds all day.

-12-

Father Sun edged above the trees at the horizon, far off to the east. He glistened on the frost of the night that had attached itself to each blade of grass, each twig of shrub and tree, and the rounded shelters of the Eagle Clan at Dreamer's home in the northland.

Even through her eyelids, Otter Tail could tell it was getting light outside. She knew she must open her eyes, stretch, and get up. On these cold mornings, she wished she could stay under her warm deerskin covers forever. The hot rocks she had put inside the rabbit fur pouches last evening were now cold. On days when it was especially cold, after Otter Tail was awake, she would often slip in with her parents, her back to her mother, where she would be warmer.

The small brown grasses, sentinels in the snow, grabbed for the warmth of the sun, carrying that warmth down their frigid stems, where it melted little holes for each of them to stand in. When the sun hit them, a drop or two of water would leak down from the snow clinging to the seed head at the top of the stem.

Outside, the standing snow was nearly up to Otter Tail's knees. No, she didn't want to go out today. She lay there in the brightness of the day as it lit up the inside of the small lodge. The chill penetrated the shelter that had only somewhat protected the family from the ultra-cold of the night.

Ice had formed along the edges of the boulders surrounding the clear water pool at the spring. The spring water had a few white crystals where it tumbled out over the boulders, and farther down the water in the brook was covered with a thin layer of ice.

Otter Tail wondered about Dreamer. Was he warm where he was spending the time of the cold White Moons? Surely he had not taken along enough clothing to protect him from such a cold night. She had three deerskin robes pulled over her, and she was still cold. If there were a wind blowing today, she would only go outside when she had to. She was so very glad she had collected the morning water last evening. It was in the two, brown, clay pots just waiting for her mother to use to make the morning porridge. There was a fire in her parents' lodge, so her mother wouldn't have to go outside to prepare the morning meal. There were still enough hot embers, so all she would have to do would be to place the cooking pot on the foundation stones and add a few dry sticks. Then the fire would restart, and the morning meal would soon be ready.

Last evening's snow on top of Otter Tail's little dwelling actually made it warmer inside, but there would be no fire inside until the snow on top of the lodge had melted or her father had scraped it off. That was one of his rules. No fire until the snow was off the roof, so maybe she'd better do it herself.

"I wonder and I worry about our Dreamer," Otter Tail said to her father, as he was cleaning off the main lodge.

Her father, also concerned, answered, "He'll take care of himself. If he gets cold, he'll hole-up in a shelter, somewhere, or, if none is available, he'll just cut some evergreen boughs and make himself one. He'll keep warm. Don't worry. If he doesn't have enough covers, he will use grass between his deerskins to keep out the cold. He knows what to do. Dreamer will take care of himself, I'm sure of it. When he comes back to our camp at the spring, he'll have many stories to tell, and how he kept warm will be one of them." Her father went back inside to the fire.

Otter Tail was satisfied. It was comforting to know that her father was certain Dreamer would be all right. She gave up her worrying, closing her eyes. She could see Dreamer in a shelter with boughs covering its framework, her brother inside with lots of dry grass spread evenly between his two deerskin covers. "Yes, surely he's warm and safe," she said to herself. "I hope he isn't hungry, though. Oh, well, I know he can hunt and find food even where others have a hard time doing so. But I wish I knew where he is and what he is doing."

Satisfied that her brother was warm, safe and out of harm's way, she went back inside.

Her father piled one of his covers over Otter Tail as he got up to tend the outside fire. The fire had been banked against four, large boulders, and under the gray ash there were still some orange coals remaining. He stirred the fire, adding a few sticks and another couple of logs, then hurriedly went back to the main shelter.

Down His River of Dreams ...

So far, this was the coldest day of the winter. Blue Damsel Fly, too, had decided to stay inside today. Why risk frozen fingers or toes or a frozen nose, if one didn't have to? The family stayed inside for four days. Only Flowing Spring went out to keep the fire going and to bring some logs in for the cooking fire. He also brought the water back, so Otter Tail wouldn't have to. Earlier, Otter Tail and her two brothers, all carrying their sleeping robes, had crept into the large shelter with their parents. Would it ever get warm again?

-13-

The fresh water pot was getting low. "It's time to go back to the spring on the mainland. We'll need some more water before the day is over," Diving Bird said.

Today Morning Boy's father took one canoe, and Morning Boy and Dreamer took another. It didn't take long to cross the passage that separated the island and the mainland. The boys' canoe carried only the pots for the family. The other canoe held pots for the other four families of the clan.

Around the point, into the bay, and soon the two canoes were beached at the smooth, sandy area on the far shore. As always the canoes were pulled up out of the water and secured well. Losing a canoe was like losing an arm or a leg. Dreamer knew that too well.

A walk to the spring bought them to water that was clear and had no salty taste. The boys and Morning Boy's father filled the eight pots and carried them back to the canoes.

Sometimes the people would come upon an alligator at the spring; 'gators liked fresh water too. The people knew to give these fierce creatures a wide berth. The bigger the 'gators, the more distance they gave them. Fortunately, there were no alligators today.

The pots had been filled, a couple of them so large that it took two to carry them. Deerskin covers were wrapped around the tops of the pots, and in the canoes they were secured with ropes. The boys also piled some firewood logs in their canoe to take back to the island. Loaded now, they slid their canoes back into the water, paddled out of the bay into the Endless Ocean, and across to Deer Island.

Now, with fresh water at each lodge, everyone was satisfied. It was the women of the clan who had to see to it that the men went for water and firewood. They were diligent, even demanding in their requests. Firewood was important, but water was vital.

Down His River of Dreams ...

Several days later, on the way to the spring to get water, the men came upon two alligators lounging on the path. The men bided their time. The two 'gators must have been male and female because they were friendly. Fortunately, when the men of the clan went for water, always carried sharp poles, flint knives, ropes, and deerskin capes—prepared for any event.

Although alligators were excellent food, they were dangerous to catch. The men knew they couldn't handle two 'gators, so with great care they chased the larger of the two back into the swamp. They could hear him breaking sticks and splashing water as he retreated.

They thought they could handle the smaller 'gator. Her mouth was open and she was hissing at them, standing firm. Dreamer was worried, but he was confident Diving Bird knew what to do.

Diving Bird estimated the size of the alligator's mouth. Using his sharp flint knife he cut a stick about as thick as two fingers and as long as the distance from his hand to his elbow. He whittled a sharp point on each end. He then stripped bark from some long willow twigs, and using this flexible bark tied the double-pointed stick onto the end of his spear. He tied it on crossways, far out toward the end. Dreamer watched, amazed at how quickly Diving Bird made his weapon.

The men approached the alligator with caution, Diving Bird in the front. He held his spear, with its sharp cross-stick, in front of him. The 'gator hissed again. The men behind the 'gator teased her with sticks. She bent back, almost double, to reach the switches on her back. She snapped her head around again, opening her mouth, then started crawling for Diving Bird. He stood his ground. When the 'gator was a couple of lengths away, she opened her mouth, ready to take a big bite. At that moment Diving Bird shoved the sharp-ended stick into the 'gator's mouth. She clamped down on it. He instantly let go of the spear handle and ducked out of the way. The confused 'gator bit down on it harder, and blood poured out, both from the top and from the bottom of her mouth. The men waited while she struggled. After a long time, she was still.

Dragging the dead alligator back to the canoe was hard work. She was heavy, but the men had their evening meal, a good one—a welcome change from oysters and bird's eggs. Their trip was very worthwhile, indeed. They now had water and meat for many days. They were pleased that none of them had been hurt in the capture. It was a very successful trip.

To thoroughly cook this delicious meal, the people dug a depression in the ground just a little bigger than the 'gator. Then they started a big fire, letting it roar for a long, long time, until it was a bed of coals. On top of the white, dusty coals they placed the whole 'gator, turning it over only once. Then the 'gator was skinned. Dreamer discovered how good cooked alligator was. In fact, he almost ate too much. He was impressed at how cleverly the men had caught the 'gator. It was an event he would never forget.

. . . .

Dreamer had a dream late in the morning, just before he awoke. He was again falling down the riverbank, and again breaking his leg. He was up with a start, and looked down at his right foot. To his amazement he saw one of the large, gray and white, sea gulls tugging at his bare toe, which had slipped out from under the deerskin cover. He was up in an instant, grabbing a handful of sand and throwing at the pesky bird. With all this commotion, the rest of the clan was now awake.

. . . .

Tonight would be the night of a full moon—the story-telling night. It seemed as though every one of the Biloxi Clan had a story to tell.

After hearing about the alligator's capture again, someone asked: "How about you, Dreamer? Tell us a story."

Dreamer told them his story in voice and sign, taking a large part of the evening. More logs were put on the fire to keep the pesky mosquitoes away. He told them of his home by the spring, of his one-day trip to the Rocky River, and of his mother, father, sister, and two brothers, who awaited his return.

Dreamer told them of walking down along the Rocky River, building a raft, traveling the Great Father of Waters, and visiting Chief Hawk Eye of the Black Hawk Nation. The story of his five moons at Cahokia took a long time to tell. The Big Mound, the Great Wise Leader, the Sun Clock, the bright star, his foster mother, the send-off, and the gift of Little Pup—he didn't want to leave anything out. He discovered that they had also seen the bright star.

"You were in the lodge of the Great Sun Chief? We've heard of Cahokia, but none of our people have been there. It's a long way up the Father of Waters. Cahokia has many people. Morning Boy was going there on his man task journey, but he found you with your broken leg," commented Diving Bird.

Dreamer continued, "The Wild One gave me Little Pup when I left. The Prophet also gave me a canoe. It was small, but adequate for my needs. I lost it in a rainstorm. I learned an important lesson."

The clan had heard the story of the two boys coming down the Father of Waters. Their favorite part was the tale of how the two had almost lost Morning Boy's canoe to the ruffians and how Dreamer had recovered it by hurling the hornet's nest.

Diving Bird told his usual story of the biggest windstorm ever, when the Endless Ocean had washed up over the point. In that terrible storm Diving Bird had lost both of his parents, who were swept away by the huge waves. That storm had also downed many trees, providing firewood for years. At least for that, he was grateful.

Diving Bird told of going up the Pearl River on a four-day trip and of the friends he had made along the way. Old Gray Hair told about his trip along the Long Beach. He, too, had been gone a long time. If he remembered right, he had been gone as many days as he had fingers on both hands. He had seen big sea cows in the backwater and a flock of twenty black-and-white eagles eating fish that had washed up on the beach.

Morning Boy's story of finding Dreamer reminded him of another event that had escaped him earlier, so, for the group, the story was new.

It was now late, and the fire was nearly out. On this clear night, the full Mother Moon was so bright that the standing storyteller could see his shadow.

. . . .

Today, the day the day dawned clear. Dreamer had been living with Morning Boy now for over three moons. He had learned to swim. He had learned to dive and find the giant oysters. Morning Boy's father had given Dreamer the four large teeth from the alligator they had cooked in the beach fire. Diving Bird had cut them out and given them to Dreamer before he roasted the 'gator. Dreamer himself had found a triangular shark's tooth that had washed up on the beach. It was as big as his two thumbs placed together. He prized all his possessions and kept them in the little deerskin pouch. He also had a quantity of seashells. Dreamer had only three brown-greenstones left since he had given one to Morning Boy's father. One of his Cahokia arrow points he always wore on his vest. The fragile point he kept protected in a flap of deerskin in his pouch

. . . .

Today the leaders of all the clans of the Biloxi Nation were to meet on the mainland, at the council tree, the big oak on the point. This oak was so old, that it was already tall when Morning Boy's father was a boy. The ten elders met at the oak twice a year to conduct their business. One of the main branches of the old oak had grown along the ground for a short distance; then it grew straight up. That branch, now a trunk, was big enough for the leaders to sit on.

Important business would take place today. Petty arguments would be settled, and stories would be told. Dreamer, carrying his eagle feather totem, would be introduced as a newcomer, a friend and worthy companion for Morning Boy, almost a brother. Once the meeting was underway, the elders honored Dreamer as a new member of the clan. They agreed that Dreamer should be a "brother" of Morning Boy, so they called the two forward.

With Dreamer's sharp Cahokia arrow-point, Morning Boy's father cut a slit on the inside of their wrists. A little blood trickled from each cut. Morning Boy's cut right wrist and Dreamer's cut left wrist were placed together by Diving Bird, who bound them with a small strand of deerskin. Now, they were blood brothers, a relationship no one could ever deny. Each boy's blood flowed in the other's veins.

"You are now flesh of my flesh, bone of my bone, and blood of my blood," Morning Boy said. It gave him a good feeling.

The elders knew Dreamer's man task journey was only half finished. Morning Boy had completed his journey several moons before. Although he hadn't made it all the way to Cahokia, he knew about the village as if he'd been there because Dreamer had shared his experiences with Morning Boy. Finally, the elders stood to vote Morning Boy a man, his father having the privilege of making the motion. Diving Bird called for the vote, which was unanimous, all standing for their vote.

"Morning Boy, you are now a man. You have successfully completed your 'man task.' I now ask that the elders name you 'Morning Dawn,' your new man-name." Again, the vote was unanimous. The man, Morning Dawn, stood and bowed to each elder, pleased to be one of them

-14-

Later Dreamer and Morning Dawn were on the beach reminiscing.

"When I found you with your broken leg, you were in no shape to travel. Fortunately, I knew what to do to get you back to normal. You were on your way down the Great Father of Waters on your man task. Would you like to see where the water from your spring finally ends up?"

"Oh, yes, could I—but the Father of Waters is so far back?" Dreamer questioned.

"We can go along Long Beach, cross over and reach the place where the Great Father of Waters enters the Endless Ocean. We'll eventually get there. It will take four; no, maybe five days for the trip, but the weather must be good. Father said we could use his big canoe."

"Let's do it. When can we start?"

"Early in the morning. We'll follow the Long Beach and Father Sun, camp overnight on the sandy beach at the far point, and spend our second and third nights on Shell Beach."

They started early on a cloudless day. The Endless Ocean was quiet except for the usual small waves that rolled in regularly across the beach and the two boys would soon be out beyond them. They kept the Long Beach in sight as they paddled west, hardly taking a rest all day. Their goal was to arrive at the far point before dark. They were exhausted when they finally reached the sandy point at the end of the day. Just beyond the point was the pass they had used coming out of the big lake—now over three moons ago.

The blazing red Father Sun was just two hands' width above the horizon. They had enough time and daylight to gather driftwood and get a small fire going; not for heat, but to warm some food and keep the pesky little bloodsuckers away.

The two carefully pulled the canoe far up on the beach, well above the high-tide line. Morning Dawn's father had threatened, playfully of course, to cut the little finger from his left hand if the canoe wasn't returned in good condition—all in one piece, and with no new scratches. They spent an uneventful night on the beach, their heads under the partially overturned canoe. It would keep off the morning dew.

Today, instead of entering the pass leading to the big lake, the boys would go out into the Endless Ocean, cross to the far point, and follow the shore to Shell Beach. Morning Dawn had been to Shell Beach many times with his father, so he knew he could get there, even if it looked as though they were headed out into the vast Endless Ocean.

"Are you sure we won't get lost?" Dreamer said, concerned.

"We'll spend the night on Shell Beach, you'll see."

Morning Dawn explained that the many shells on the beach had given it its name.

After the night on Shell Beach, the boys paddled until Father Sun was overhead, making good time going with the wind.

"Now it's time to beach our canoe," said Morning Dawn. They walked down the beach to a little stream flowing into the Endless Ocean. "Taste it," Morning Dawn urged. Dreamer tasted the sweet water as it flowed out of the forest of cypress and live oaks.

Morning Dawn said, "The water from your spring—the water that flows with the Father of Waters along with all of his children—comes out here. Here it reaches the Endless Ocean—now you know."

Dreamer had always known the water from his spring did not go into a hole in the ground. He had seen that his brook became larger as it joined the creek, and that creek became larger as it joined the Rocky River. When his Rocky River met the Father of Waters, it more than quadrupled in size. Now when his Father of Waters met the Endless Ocean, it became part of a vast expanse of water. It was almost beyond belief. Now he knew. Dreamer was satisfied.

"Thank you."

The boys paddled back to Shell Beach where they would spend their third night out. Dead tired from paddling, they were lulled to sleep by the monotonous sound of the waves coming from the Endless Ocean.

In the morning, Father Sun again shone brightly. It looked as if they were going to have five days of clear weather on their trip to the delta. They spent their fourth night on the Long Beach, at the same place where they had spent their first night.

Down His River of Dreams ...

Dreamer felt so lucky that Morning Boy, now Morning Dawn, had befriended him when he was in need of help. "That's the way it should be," he thought, "When someone needs help, one must help."

Returning to Deer Island, they were exhausted, but they could see smoke from the cooking fire. "Mother has food on the fire. I hope it's fish. I've had enough oysters to last for another moon," Morning Dawn said.

As the canoe drifted the last few feet to the beach, Dreamer said seriously, "I thank you for letting me fulfill my dream. Just think, my water—and my spider too—flowed for so many days and nights and then met the Endless Ocean. It might have flowed for as long as four or five moons—who knows?"

They beached the canoe on the lee side of Deer Island, pulling it through the sand and high up into the roots where they tied it tight. The canoe was just as it had been given to them.

Diving Bird was pleased.

. . . .

The semi-annual Council of the Biloxi Nation had been over for almost a moon's time. Morning Dawn and Dreamer were always together. They enjoyed each another's company and always had new stories to tell.

Lately, it seemed that Dreamer's stories were mostly about his camp and family back at the spring. He was getting anxious to head home. The boys had discussed his trip back up the Great Father of Waters many times, and Morning Dawn had convinced his father that a canoe should be made for Dreamer, one he could use on his journey home. It must be small enough for him to handle by himself, only a little over twice as long as Dreamer was tall, with ample room for his belongings and for Little Pup.

Making a canoe required a person in charge who had a lot of patience, and one who had the ability to see the completed canoe in the log from which it was to be made. The wood of the evergreen oak was too heavy. The wood of the sycamore was also too heavy. The canoe would be built from a cypress log.

Morning Dawn's father had convinced the man known as the master canoe-maker that Morning Dawn's new brother should have a canoe, for his trip home, back up the Father of Waters. To seal the bargain, valuables passed between the two, although the boys didn't know it.

The new canoe would be a community project. All of the elders knew of the project, and each went into the forest in search of a tree of the correct diameter, with a ridge on one side. The ridge would form the bottom of the canoe. After several days, the right tree was found quite a distance away— back in the bay. It took six days to down it, and then it was cut again, to the length the canoe would become. The end cuts were tapered to reduce the master canoe-maker's work and time. The men of the Biloxi Nation floated the log to a place adjacent to the canoe-maker's workshop. It was then pulled onto the beach and finally back into the forest shade.

The canoe-maker had sharpened all of his flint tools for the big job. Daily he worked at shaping the canoe. The wood was too green to burn, so it was a cutting job. The canoe needed to be thin enough and light enough for one person to handle.

Dreamer worked every day, following the canoe-maker's directions, Morning Dawn helped too. Eight or nine others also helped; the canoe was truly a community project.

Each night as they left their work, the canoe makers took grass, soaked it in water, and spread it on the log, soon to be a canoe. The canoe-maker put wet deerskins on top of the grass so the log would not dry out and crack. It was a slow process—pound, scrape, cut, peel and scrape some more—all under the watchful eye of the master canoe-maker, who could see a finished canoe in the log that looked more like a canoe every day. It took a long time to remove the wood that would not be part of the canoe. Shaping the inside would be even harder. The canoe-maker would not be satisfied until the canoe was perfect. He was not used to so much help, and using it wisely slowed him down.

The outside work was finished and the log actually looked like a canoe, although a small one. The ridge would be at the very bottom to help stabilize the little craft. The men worked on the emerging canoe downside up. The pointed front end was the smaller end of the log. The finished canoe would go through the water as the tree had been growing, the narrow end up front.

The bottom done, it was now time to turn the log over. The long hard part was about to begin. The men laid the log on the ground and packed wet sand around it to keep it moist and upright. Next, they cut, scraped, and peeled the inside; a process that took days. When a worker became tired and quit, there was always a newcomer to take his place. Both the men and the boys worked on the project. Cut, scrape, peel; the slivers of wood flew. Even with eight or ten working on the log, it was very slow work.

Down His River of Dreams ...

The master canoe-maker knew it would take well over a moon's time to finish the project. The men and boys began their work as soon as there was enough daylight to see and stayed at it diligently, working on into the evening until they could barely see. Dreamer worked as hard and long as any of the men of the Biloxi Clan; he was the example of hard work, never complaining. He, like the master canoe-maker, could visualize the finished product. Cut, pull, scrape, peel—the curls of wood kept coming off, to be burned at the end of each day.

The inside of the new dugout fit Dreamer just right. The canoe-maker marked a small triangle on each side, at the top of the canoe, and told the men to remove that piece of wood. Then he took a small stick, matching each end to the notches in the canoe. He drove the stick in from the side, until it was firmly in place; the ends were then trimmed even, to form a "handle."

Since the first handle had worked out so well, the canoe-maker decided another cross-member should be placed directly behind where Dreamer would kneel, or sit, as he paddled his canoe. These handles would give Dreamer something to lean on and hold onto. He could also tie his pack and his pouch to them so he wouldn't lose his belongings if the canoe capsized.

After about a moon of steady work, the shaping of the canoe was finally finished. Smooth and deep inside, it was wide and stable enough to float well. The little canoe, with its two cross-members, was just right for Dreamer to handle. Raccoon grease was rubbed on the canoe, both inside and outside, and on the paddles to keep the wood from drying out. The men spent one whole day and the grease from two raccoons to finish the project.

Tomorrow the master canoe-maker would launch the beautiful canoe. He would paddle it first, to see if he was satisfied with his work.

One time, many years ago, he had not been satisfied, and he had burned the new canoe on the spot. Not so with Dreamer's, for it was perfect in every respect—a wonderful one-man canoe. Dreamer touched the finished canoe. He was so full of joy that he decided to paddle his canoe all the way around Deer Island. It took him longer than he expected, but he finally beached it on the leeward side, away from the swells. Pulling it up into the forest, he tied it up carefully and proudly.

Diving Bird stood back and watched He was pleased Dreamer was so happy. Dreamer now had a means to get himself back home, to his spring west of his Rocky River—far, far, up the Great Father of Waters.

. . . .

Dreamer was anxious to be on his way back up the Great Father of Waters, to his home. His trip to the Endless Ocean had taken him about three moons' time of actual river travel. He knew his trip back might take even longer, perhaps three or four moons, since he would be paddling against the current, and maybe against some wind, too.

Now it was time to say goodbye and thank all who had been so good to him. He had learned much living on Deer Island. He had a wonderful friend who had fixed his leg and probably saved his life. Dreamer thanked Morning Dawn's parents, who had adopted their son's friend as one of their own and had given him the gift of a magnificent canoe. There were almost no words to convey Dreamer's heartfelt thanks.

"Morning Dawn, I plan to leave tomorrow. Will you see me off? I'm feeling so lucky to have a new canoe to get me home. I will protect it with my life—it really is my life."

Dreamer saved his final "goodbyes" for after the noon meal. Then he would get his things together. He would stow his deerskin bedroll, backpack, the new moccasins Yellow Flower had just made for him, and his little deerskin pouch, which held his prized possessions in his canoe. He hoped Morning Dawn could go part of the way, to give him a good send-off. He needed some words of encouragement. Dreamer sought out the master canoe-maker; clasping his hand, he could hardly speak. With a lump in his throat, he said, "Thank you for what you've done for me. Your wonderful canoe will see me home."

"We all worked on it. You did your share. Morning Dawn's father helped more than you'll ever know," the canoe-maker said modestly.

Dreamer made his rounds to each campsite on the island. It took him most of the afternoon. At the campsites, the women had send-off gifts for him. If it wasn't food, it was a piece of deerskin. He was also given more shells than he could carry. He decided he would make a long string of beads for his mother on the way home,

Dreamer finally came back to Morning Dawn's campsite. He would eat the evening meal with his friends. This evening of the full moon would be his last evening of telling stories around the campfire. He always enjoyed storytelling time.

Morning Dawn's mother checked Dreamer's clothes, finding some needing mending. So, with her sharp spike-needle, she wove a deerskin thread in, patching his worn clothing. She had also been making a breechcloth for him, although he didn't know it. Now she surprised him with it. It was of a size to fit Morning Dawn, so she knew it would fit Dreamer. He gave her a hug of thanks, then put it with his bedroll.

"Dreamer, before you go, can you tell us more of what's up the Great River?" That question really set the scene. Dreamer talked on and on, late into the night. He told them more about the great mounds of Cahokia, of the fish and turtle ponds, and of his foster mother, The Wild One. "She was the kindest, most gentle and loving mother one could have—almost as good as my own mother. I'll be glad to see her again."

He told them again of the chunky games he had watched while he was at Cahokia. They knew what he was talking about, but down here at the Endless Ocean they didn't have the raw material to make the hard, black stones—they had only soft, white stone. He again showed them his two Cahokia arrow points, so sharp, small, beautiful, and so perfect.

It was now pitch-dark because clouds were covering the full Mother Moon. Dreamer took notice. He hoped tomorrow's weather would be good.

Morning Dawn's mother finally spoke, "You'd better get your rest. Tomorrow will be a full day." With that said, they all turned in for the night. Dreamer was restless. He had his recurring dream again; of the spider on the leaf. This time, however, his little spider had reached the Endless Ocean. He awoke with a start.

"Back to sleep, tomorrow will be a busy day, and I want to get away early."

It rained during the night. Dreamer was up with Morning Dawn just as Father Sun should have been rising, but there was no sun today. The clouds were dark and ominous, and the boys could see the rain coming in a dark sheet between the black clouds and the Endless Ocean.

Yellow Flower saw it coming, too. The lodge was already soaked to its willow ribs. With another squall, the rain would be leaking inside, so she took several large deerskin blankets and draped them over the small, wet lodge, hoping to keep out the rain. She put a couple of clay pots at the bottom of the blanket to catch the rainwater.

Dreamer decided not to start his return journey with the wind blowing hard enough to turn over his canoe. "I'll wait another day or two," he told Yellow Flower. "My mother and father and my sister and brothers won't be expecting me at any certain time anyway. They don't know when I'll be home."

-15-

Morning Dawn would spend the first few traveling days with Dreamer, going back along the Long Beach and then into the pass with him, but in his own small canoe. He dreaded coming back to Deer Island alone. He also hated to lose Dreamer, his best friend and blood brother. He would help Dreamer pull his new canoe across the portage before telling him goodbye.

. . . .

This day broke clear and calm. Dreamer and Morning Dawn were up early and had their canoes packed and ready to go. Of course, Dreamer's was full. Morning Dawn had only a deerskin night cover and a small sack of food. Yellow Flower had packed Dreamer a full sack of food containing cooked oysters, some greens, and roots and berries that she had gathered on the mainland, enough for his first three or four days.

The boys shoved off a little after first light, following the same route they had taken when they went west to the delta nearly two moons earlier. The Long Beach seemed even longer this time, although it was just a reversal of their trip of five moons ago. They pulled their canoes up on the beach, secured them, then settled in under the oaks. It was a clear night, lighted by bright stars, and a full Mother Moon, just starting to wane.

Starting a fire to keep the bloodsuckers away, they ate a few roots and berries from their sack, covered themselves with their deerskin covers, and finally went to sleep. They slept late.

The next morning the three were off, down the Long Beach, around the point, then cross Lake Poncha, headed for the portage. Dreamer and Morning Dawn pulled their canoes side by side every so often, to talk. Starting late and with the wind against them, they knew they couldn't make it all the way to the portage before dark.

"Where shall we spend the night? The forest comes right down to the water's edge. We'll soon be out in the middle of Lake Poncha," Dreamer said. There being no beach was a problem, but the larger problem was the many alligators they had seen today on the shore. Remembering the big 'gator Diving Bird had caught and cooked on the beach back on Deer Island, Dreamer reached out and touched his deerskin pouch. He could feel the big alligator teeth inside. That was the only way he wanted to feel alligator teeth.

"We can't stay here where there's no beach. We can't sleep in our canoes because the 'gators will come after us. And we can't make it to the portage before dark. What shall we do?" Morning Dawn questioned.

Dreamer had a thought. "Listen, why don't we sleep in our canoes?"

"What?"

"Wait. Now listen, we can tie one canoe to the other, then one of us can sleep while the other paddles on. It's going to be a quiet night with nearly a full Mother Moon, and there shouldn't be any 'gators way out in the middle of the lake at night. We'll guide by the stars. I know how to do it. I'll show you when it's your turn to paddle. Let me go first. Here, tie my rope to the front of your canoe. I'll pull so you can sleep. Later you can pull and I'll sleep. It'll take longer, but we don't have to reach the portage until tomorrow anyway."

Morning Dawn agreed.

Father Sun sank below the horizon. Mother Moon was so bright they might not be able to see all the stars. The most important star, however, Dreamer already had his eye on—his "pole star." He could always find it although, here in the southland, his pole star was much lower in the sky. Regardless, he would guide by it.

It was slow going, paddling while pulling the other canoe. Fortunately, the wind had died down. Dreamer looked back and saw little ripples reflected in the moonlight, seeming to go on forever, disappearing in the darkness. No alligators would get them tonight. There in the middle of the lake, both Little Pup and Morning Dawn were fast asleep. Dreamer paddled on, always keeping the pole star, his guide star, a little off to the right.

With no clouds it was easy to see his pole star. Dreamer tried to gauge how much of the day it had taken them to get from the portage to the pass leading to the Endless Ocean. Then he figured how fast they were going now: "Maybe a little more than half as fast as I could go if I weren't pulling another canoe." Estimating their speed and the distance, he thought they should arrive at the portage a little past dawn. He hoped he was right.

After paddling for about half the night, he woke Morning Dawn.

"It's your turn now." He showed Morning Dawn the stationary pole star, reminding him that it would not move. "Paddle in this direction. Keep the pole star a little off to the right." He raised his paddle and showed Morning Dawn the angle.

Although Little Pup didn't like the rocking of the canoe, she had lain quiet as a little blacksnake on the whole trip.

Dreamer dozed. When he awoke, Morning Dawn was paddling. A haze covered the big lake, but fortunately, as Father Sun rose, the fog burned off

175

rapidly. The shoreline was far off to the left. Dreamer took back the towing rope. Now each would paddle his own canoe. Figuring the time and distance they had traveled, he knew they should be nearing the portage.

"I hope we haven't passed it," Morning Dawn said doubtfully. When they arrived at the shoreline, they agreed that the posts must be further off to the right.

"It was slow going through the dark last night. Do you think we're near the portage?" asked Morning Dawn.

They paddled directly toward the forest along the edge of the big lake and followed the shore. Soon Morning Dawn pointed out the three posts up ahead. Their direction and their timing had been right on the mark. Morning Dawn and Dreamer were very relieved—and, very proud of themselves.

. . . .

Paddling hard the boys drove their canoes up onto the mud ramp, then they pulled them the rest of the way up to flat ground. Little Pup jumped joyously onto the solid ground, free to relieve herself and to run at last. Exhausted, Dreamer and Morning Dawn lay down and didn't move for several moments until the mosquitoes found them. Using sticks and some dry grass, they started a small fire and got on the smoky side. Now, safe from the little bloodsuckers, the boys ate their morning meal.

"Can you find your way back home?" asked Dreamer.

"Of course," Morning Dawn said. "I know the landmarks. Yes, I can find my way home. But, Dreamer, can you find your way home?"

"You know I can. I'll just go against the current until I reach Cahokia, there I'll spend some time with my old friends. They know I'm on my man task journey and will help me. After that I'll still have a long way to go up the Great Father of Waters, but I'll know when I reach my Rocky River. It will take me nearly a moon's time paddling upriver from Cahokia to arrive there. I remember a wide sand bar, a big log, and two eagles' nests in the trees at the mouth of my river. I have them all marked on my deerskin so that I can remember the landmarks."

Dreamer was excited just talking about reaching home, but Morning Dawn wanted to spend one last night with him before he headed back to the Endless Ocean. Dreamer, too, wanted to prolong the goodbye for as long as possible.

The boys pulled Dreamer's canoe to the other end of the portage. Sharing the load was easier and did not damage the little craft. It had taken them a long time to get it across. On the far side, they concealed it in the brush, and then returned to Lake Poncha.

Dreamer closed his eyes and thought: "Tomorrow I'll be off, back up my River of Dreams, and in my own canoe, too. How lucky I am!" Dreamer and Little Pup would walk the portage in the morning, uncover the canoe, launch it, and be on their way. Morning Dawn planned an early start, too.

As the boys were settling in for the night, Dreamer said, I have three brown-green stones left, and you must have one." He reached inside his deerskin pouch and pulled out one of the stones.

"You shouldn't—you'll need it later," said Morning Dawn.

"Yes, I should. It's yours. It came from the far northland, far north of where I live. There are now two of these stones down here at the Endless Ocean, and you have one of them."

Morning Dawn was pleased. It was a gift from the heart. Maybe he would pound and carve a bird or a fish or maybe even an arrow-point out of it, as Dreamer had said could be done, or maybe he would just keep it as it is and polish it to make it shine. Morning Dawn would never forget how he came to own this precious stone.

The dawn of their departure day broke clear and calm. Morning Dawn was already up. With a couple of small logs, he had restarted the nearly dead fire.

A small black fly landed on Dreamer's nose. He wiggled his nose, opened his left eye, saw the fly, and was up with a start.

Morning Dawn laughed. "What a great way to wake up to a new day."

The two boys went down to the big lake. After splashing a little water on their faces, they were fully awake. Morning Dawn must leave soon; he would have to go across the lake, navigate the pass, and then follow his Long Beach.

His canoe half-in-half-out of the water, he came back up the bank. He and Dreamer clasped hands and looked into each other's eyes. Morning Dawn admonished him: "You must be careful. Don't take a chance. Watch the river. Watch your back. You must reach home safely, with good memories of your many moons in the southland. You are a good brother and a true friend."

Then they parted. Morning Dawn didn't even give Dreamer a chance to say anything. He turned, walked down to his canoe, shoved off, and was gone—out into the big lake. When he was some distance out, he turned and waved a last farewell. Dreamer couldn't see but he had a tear on his cheek.

Dreamer ran most of the way back to the mighty Father of Waters, Little Pup tagging along behind. Clearing the brush from his canoe and sliding it down the muddy ramp and into the water, he jumped in, and he and Little Pup were off. The current was lazy, flowing against his paddle. He and his dog were finally on their way back up his River of Dreams, and he had achieved his goal.

Against the current he paddled, thinking of Morning Dawn, one who would do anything for a friend. Dreamer was sad to think he would never see his friend again.

Paddling upstream, in as much of a straight line as he could. He knew his route home would be shorter that way. But always around each bend was another just like it. He passed the long hours paddling upstream toward home by daydreaming. "I suppose Mother has already gathered the wild strawberries; perhaps now chokecherries are part of the meal. I know she's catching fish from our creek. Soon I'll be there to help her."

He passed many of the rivers feeding the Great Father of Waters: The Black, the Red, the Green, the children of the Father, and he remembered them all. Going upstream was slower, but he didn't mind. He had a goal, and this time he actually knew where it was—it was home, back to his Rocky River Nation.

. . . .

After ten days of steady paddling up the Great Father of Waters, Dreamer sighted a familiar, friendly village ahead. It was Winterville, whose clan had welcomed him warmly. It wasn't often they had a visitor come in off the river. Last time there had been two; this time there would be only one. On the way down the river, more than five Moons ago, both he and Morning Boy had been given the "Key" to the Village, a staff decorated with twenty eagle feathers. He smiled, remembering how pleased and overwhelmed they'd been. Friendship was important so far away from home, and this village was especially friendly. Dreamer wondered if he would receive the friendship staff again.

Dreamer had been seen while he was still quite far down the river. One of the village children climbing a tree saw his canoe when it was nothing more than a spot on the gray water. The child had run to the council ring at the center of the village, pounded on the hollow log drum, and called the clan together. When the shaman came to the drum, the youngster told him what he had seen, pointing down the Great River.

The shaman, wearing his feathered cape, held the eagle feather staff as he stood on top of the big sycamore log to welcome Dreamer. Little Pup gave a bark. Dreamer took his eagle feather totem from its protective cover and held it high in return.

The shaman went to Dreamer and with voice and sign asked, "Where is your friend?"

Dreamer understood and pointed back down the Great Father of Waters and indicated that he was going back up the Great River alone. With his signs he conveyed that his friend had stayed down the river, back at his home. He counted the days he had been gone and told them: "Eighteen days since I have seen my friend."

The shaman took Dreamer to the high chief of the village, parting the crowd as they departed the river.

Dreamer bowed low to greet the chief. The chief seemed pleased to see him again.

Dreamer, by sign, told the chief he had been in the southland for almost six moons. The chief invited Dreamer to spend the night. Dreamer told the chief of the Endless Ocean, which the Chief had never visited. Perhaps a gift from the Endless Ocean was in order, thought Dreamer as he removed one of the giant oyster shells from his pouch. He held it high, in front of the chief; for you, he motioned.

The chief knew what it was, but he had never seen one quite so large. The ones from the river were much smaller.

The shaman took Dreamer to his lodge, where Dreamer would sleep with Little Pup at his feet. Dreamer felt safe among these friendly people. He decided he might even spend a second night here.

. . . .

Dreamer spent two very comfortable nights with the village shaman. He wanted to hear all of Dreamer's interesting stories so much that he suggested that he stay longer. Dreamer, being pretty well exhausted from many strenuous days of paddling, didn't need to be asked twice.

The shaman was amazed as Dreamer described the length of the Great Father of Waters and the size of the Endless Ocean. He could not imagine such a place. He shuddered at Dreamer's description of the big alligators that lived down at the end of the Great River.

On the day of his departure, the people of Winterville came to the river to see Dreamer off. Women pressed food into his hands and into his canoe. The shaman gave Dreamer a clear magic "crystal" as he left. Dreamer in turn gave them a "thank you bow." The village was in the lowland, but it was from the highest hill that the people watched him and waved until he and Little Pup were out of sight around the first bend in the Great River.

Dreamer was alone again. The solitary trip seemed long as he paddled against the current. Occasionally, as he skirted an island, he took the shortcut through the chute. Once a chute was so shallow that he scraped bottom. He was careful after that, deciding to bypass these narrow chutes completely for safety's sake.

He passed the White River, the Wolf River and the Deer River. Many days later, he again came to the big Ohoho River. The sand beach at the point where this new big river met the Great Father of Waters seemed a good place to spend the night. In fact, since he must find some food, he thought he might spend several nights there.

He paddled up beyond the mouth of the Ohoho River, then cut right and went for the sand beach. Pulling his canoe far up on the flat beach, he tied it securely to a big log knowing it would be safe there.

There were large piles of driftwood on this sandy point. He gathered several armloads of smaller sticks, and carried them back to the tree line. He built his fire behind another giant log to shield the flame from strangers.

He didn't have to look far into the dense forest for food. Little Pup ran ahead of him, then stopped and looked back at Dreamer. She had found a large blacksnake, which Dreamer caught easily and killed quickly. Then in the low willows he found some birds' nests full of eggs. He would have snake and eggs for his evening and morning meals.

Dreamer let the fire die down and then put some green leaves on it to provide smoke to keep the mosquitoes away. Against the log he placed his deerskin cover, using his pack for a pillow. Pulling the cover over his head he was soon sound asleep. It had been a long day.

Little Pup slept lightly, always the protector of Dreamer.

. . . .

Upon awaking, Dreamer decided he would explore the big sandy point. He and Little Pup walked up the Ohoho River. As they went around the trees extending out onto the point, they came upon two eagles on the beach, tugging at a dead fish. The two birds didn't seem as though they were fighting, so they must be mates. He knew eagles mated for life and that the smaller one, the one with the faded feather colors, was the female. Dreamer watched quietly, wanting the birds to enjoy their meal. He didn't even need to restrain Little Pup. She didn't want anything to do with the big birds. Soon the pair jumped, spread their wings, swooped towards the river, and flapped away.

"Let's see if they left some for us." Dreamer called to Little Pup as he ran towards the half-devoured fish. He turned it over and found one side was still good. With his flint knife he trimmed it out, right where it lay. Cutting off the head and tail, he gave the insides to Little Pup, who was happy to get them. He took his half fish to the river and washed it clean, then wrapped it in big leaves he found growing in the small pool at the edge the forest.

Upon returning to the campsite, he put some more dry twigs on the fire. They caught quickly. He unwrapped his fish and put it on the hot rock at the edge of the fire. "It's our morning meal, too," he said to Little Pup. She looked at him as if to say, "Thanks, you do take care of me well, although fish isn't my favorite food."

Early the next morning, after another meal of fish, Dreamer and Little Pup shoved off.

Now it would be stroke, stroke, stroke—forward, dip the paddle in, pull, remove, then forward again. All day he paddled, with only one brief stop at a sandy point below a bluff, where he and Little Pup could relieve themselves. He also found some berries and a couple of last year's walnuts that the squirrels had missed. Fish and nuts would do for now. For tonight he would have to find something else.

At the end of the fourth day since leaving the Ohoho, he saw Tower Rock in the distance. "I hope we can make it there before we lose Father Sun," he said to Little Pup.

Father Sun was behind the trees when he pulled his canoe alongside the great island, at the same location where he had stopped on his way downwater. Nothing had changed. He tied his canoe to the same limb, of the same sturdy tree. He felt his canoe would be safe there.

He climbed the path toward the top of the island. This time there was no skunk. He had all his belongings—his bow and quiver of arrows, his deerskin cover, his pouch, and his food sack. In it was another fish wrapped in green-pad leaves. It was late, so he started a fire quickly. His fire burned orange and hot and was soon a bed of coals, where he placed his fish, green-pad leaves and all. After a short while, the leaves became dry and started to burn, so he removed his fish. Although it was not cooked thoroughly, it was good enough to eat. He ate around the edges—the cooked part, the rest he gave to Little Pup.

Vultures liked to fly over the great Tower Rock, floating on the air currents, hardly flapping a wing. Dreamer thought, "How lucky they are— no flapping, no paddling—just gliding up and down the river—so effortlessly; I wish I could do that."

Dreamer was eager to leave the big island. He remembered that it had taken him four days of paddling down the Great Father of Waters from

Cahokia to get there. Paddling up the river, against the current, he figured it should take at least five, maybe even six, to get back to the village. He had been away for such a long time.

Mid-day on his fifth day up the river from Tower Rock, he could see the broad Cahokia valley off to the right. To the left the bluff began to rise; he remembered the bluff and the boys who lived there. Quite a large village was located on the very top of the bluff. He had never been there, but two of the boys who lived there had come to Cahokia to trade for food. They traded a basket of river clams for two baskets of arrowhead root. Dreamer remembered that the two boys had bartered with great skill, receiving twice as much as they should have. He wondered how the trade worked? What he didn't know was that the owner of the arrowhead roots had more than he needed but dearly wanted the clams, as much for their meat as for their shells.

Arriving at Cahokia Creek, Dreamer guided his canoe between the poles, and stopped quickly in the mud. Then he looked up and saw an arm wave to him.

"No, it couldn't be." Yes, it was Little Turtle running down the bank to meet his old friend.

"Look at Little Pup, he exclaimed, "She's a big dog now, at least five hands high. And you, my friend Dreamer, did you ever find the answer to that question in your dream?"

"Oh, yes. I found the answer to many questions in my many dreams; and you wouldn't believe the good times I've had. And you're right, Little Pup has grown to be a big dog, and I didn't have to eat her! She has been my constant companion, looking out for me. Once, she even saved my life."

They pulled Dreamer's canoe high and dry until he needed it again. Unlike his former raft, this canoe would not tempt anyone to use it for firewood. Dreamer's protective eagle totem tied to the two handles should protect it.

Little Turtle and Dreamer walked together toward the village, down the hard-packed path, talking excitedly. Dreamer's first stop must be at his Cahokia mother's lodge, so that's where they headed, both carrying his possessions. He still had the same deerskin cover the Wild One had given him when left the village. He had used it every night, either over him or under him, and he wanted to tell her how soft if was.

The Wild One was sitting in front of her lodge, making rope from several strands of deerskin; busy as usual. Dreamer stopped to watch her.

When she raised her head and focused her eyes on Little Pup and Dreamer, her face lit up. She and Dreamer hurried toward each other, nearly falling together in their excitement.

"Dreamer, Dreamer—you're back!"

"Mother, I'm so glad to see you! I thought I might never see you again. I've missed you."

Little Pup was there too, jumping and barking. It was a grand reunion.

"Tell me, Dreamer, where have you been?" It was a short question, but it needed a long answer.

They went inside the lodge to get away from all the people. Dreamer told her of his trip down the Great Father of Waters, of his broken leg, of Morning Boy, of the healing process, and of the moons spent at the Endless Ocean. Night was upon them. Tomorrow he would tell her more, but now he was dead tired.

Little Pup and Dreamer spent the night with the Wild One.

She couldn't believe the story of the Endless Ocean. How could that be, no other side? Dreamer answered her many questions, and the days of their reunion passed pleasantly. He decided to stay on.

. . . .

One morning the Wild One said to Dreamer, "Tonight is the night of the full moon. You arrived back in time for the Festival of the Maize Harvest. We'll go to the Plaza early in the morning. We want to be a part of it."

To celebrate the Maize Harvest, the leaders of the clans took a wooden staff about the height the tallest could reach. They tied many maize shucks on the top, then put the staff in the ground on a small mound to the west of the big maize field. The elders then danced around the staff, singing the Maize Thank You Song: "Maize, maize, maize; thank you Father Sun for giving us the maize."

The maize harvested would go into the safe houses, to be distributed to the people later. The First Shaman saw to his responsibility with great care.

. . . .

It so happened that one of the chiefs of the Pigeon Clan had died during the night. A graying sixty summers old, he had not been well for several winters, which had made his bones ache. The chief was anxious to go to the

Great Beyond, the beautiful place where everything would be provided. He died quietly. His mate, trying to wake him early in the morning, found him cold. She had known his death was coming, and she was prepared to be alone. Fortunately, her children all lived in Cahokia.

The First Shaman informed the Prophet of the chief's death. The Great Sun decreed it should be a "three staff" burial. Three staffs of the Pigeon Clan would be placed upright in the ground; at the center the chief would be buried. The burial would follow a three-day mourning period.

The death of a Cahokian of status was a time of mourning for all Cahokians. Only necessary talk was allowed, and that only whispered. Quiet indicated respect.

The chief would be buried next to his father, who had passed to the Great Beyond some ten summers earlier. In the after-life it was hoped the two chiefs would walk together, hunt together, and fish together, as they had always done.

On the morning of the third day after his death, six of his family and friends carried him to the burial site. The deerskin bag was heavy, but the weight was distributed evenly among the six.

Now the Cahokia Bird Man danced a silent dance around the body. He danced all day.

The Chief's final resting place, the one in which he would start his life in the Great Beyond, was prepared. A small depression was dug, just large enough for the body.

Finally, the chief was lifted from his temporary wooden cradle and gently placed on the bed of feathers. The women then placed more feathers over the deerskin. Good words were spoken, the Bird Man danced again and the burial ceremony was complete.

The clan believed that in one moon's time his spirit would rise from his mound and walk with the others in the Great Beyond.

All of the clan members helped build the mound. Diggers used flint hoes to fill the baskets with dirt from the bank of Cahokia Creek. Carriers dropped an empty basket and picked up a full one to carry to the mound. Packers walked over the dirt to pack it smooth. Today, Dreamer would be a carrier. He had been asked to help build the mound because he was a friend of Chief Two Pigeons. They had fished together in Cahokia Creek nearly twelve moons ago.

After the mound was finished the family spread seeds of prairie grass over the mound—now it was complete.

Dreamer was glad he had been asked to help. He wondered whether he would be buried this same way. What if he had another accident on his way home and no one found him? Would he be a lost soul?

. . . .

Dreamer told the Wild One that today he would be visiting Chips, the arrowhead-maker. He rose early. With his orangewood bow over his shoulder and his quiver, holding only three arrows and slung over his other shoulder, he was off. He knew the path to Cahokia Creek and to the arrowhead-maker's lodge.

Dreamer could see that the old man had his back to his favorite tree, where he always sat when he made arrowheads. Dreamer sat across from him, scraping a little pile of chips to the side before he sat down. There was no conversation between the two, just the attentive concentration of Dreamer's eyes on the hands of Chips as he crafted a piece of raw, white flint into a symmetrical, white triangle that anyone would wish to own. The arrowhead-maker, with his deerskin protection on his lap and a piece of deer antler in his right hand had just finished making ten small triangular hunting points. Then, to Dreamer's surprise, he held the points out to Dreamer.

"For me?" Dreamer questioned.

"Yes, for you, the arrowhead-maker nodded. You will be leaving soon and I see you need some arrows. You'll need arrows with fine points as you hunt for food and to protect yourself as you go back to your home."

Dreamer thought, "What can I give him? Not the items from the southland. I have plans for them." Then he remembered the two brown-green stones. He would give one to the arrowhead-maker. He got up and ran back to the Wild One's lodge. Soon he was back to sit down across from the arrowhead-maker. Then he held an open palm out to receive the newly made points.

Dreamer extended his other hand—closed into a fist with the brown-green stone inside—and waited. When the arrowhead-maker finally held his hand out, Dreamer dropped the piece of float copper into the waiting palm. There was a silent exchange of thanks between the two as they looked into each other's eyes.

After a long pause, Dreamer said, "Could you make me a little, white, flint alligator?"

"An alligator?" the arrowhead-maker asked.

Dreamer described the fearsome beast, scratching a little likeness in the dirt so the arrowhead-maker knew what Dreamer wanted. It was a fat lizard, with a short tail.

"I'll try," said the old man. "Watch me. Tell me if I get it right, if not, I'll throw it into the creek."

Dreamer had a very profitable morning. In exchange for his next-to-last brown-green stone, he had ten new arrowheads and a little flint alligator.

. . . .

The Sun Clock was now finished and Dreamer was interested in watching the end of the shadow of the center post as it moved across the ground. Day after day, he would peg the end of its shadow. The shadow would move on a slightly different route each day. As it became longer, Dreamer could see that Father Sun was getting a little lower in the sky. It was easy to understand when one worked time with sticks.

The Clock Shaman, the Prophet, worked with it daily. He told Dreamer that on the day of equal light and equal dark the shadow would return to its same location. It would take 182 or 183 days. He said, "Father Sun never fails. He is as regular as water coming from the spring, and right on the mark, too."

As the days grew shorter, the pegs were farther out. Dreamer sensed that he should be concerned. He told the Wild One of his pegging the end of the shadow and the changes it was bringing. "With the days now getting shorter, I must think about going home."

It had been a long time since he had been home, but Dreamer could close his eyes and still see it all. The more he thought about it, the more he wished he were home.

He would gather his possessions, check them all, and secure them in his pouch. His bow and quiver of arrows were in good shape, thanks to the arrowhead-maker. He was very glad he had given chips a personal, "goodbye." Dreamer made some new arrows and now had a full quiver of eight arrows. He also had a small handful of white triangular arrow points in his pouch. He had used and lost most of those that his father had given him so many moons ago. He was now ready to resume his journey.

. . . .

This day The Wild One was up well before dawn.

"Dreamer, Dreamer, wake up, wake up! Today is the Special Day. We must go to the Sun Clock before Father Sun comes up."

Today the day will be as long as the night. Dreamer asked his Cahokia mother how the Prophet knew today would be the day.

"Well, if you had kept track for as many summers as he has, you'd know, too. Father Sun is predictable, like the pole star."

They talked more about the stars, Mother Moon, Father Sun, and the blazing star that Dreamer had seen in the daytime the last time he was in the village.

"That star was really something, wasn't it?" Dreamer had to admit, "I have never seen anything quite like it—and shining in the daytime, too."

"Yes, but now it is only a faint blur in the sky." She pointed high overhead to the Bull Constellation. "It's still dark enough this morning to see it—there—it's quite faint now." the Wild One said, pointing overhead.

Today Father Sun would come up at the due east post and go down at the due west post. This day would be as long as the night. The Prophet sat with his back to the big post in the middle of the Sun Clock Circle. He would signal up to the Great Sun to begin the Festival of the Sun, but only if Father Sun dawned due east to cast its shadow due west.

The Prophet signaled. The Great Sun, who was wearing his cloak of yellow feathers, raised his arms. The people gathered below returned the honor. The Great Sun began to speak: "My wonderful people. Listen to me, for what I have to tell you on this Special Day is good.

"Today we celebrate the day and night of equal time. The maize has been harvested. We have had a good crop."

It was now time to drink the fermented chokecherry juice. This was the time they had been waiting for. The elders held their cups high, towards Father Sun. He had not failed them. He was right on time. Now they touched their cups together. Then all two hundred elders drank the "firewater," the dark red juice, to celebrate this Special Day.

The Great Sun again raised his arms, and then paused for a very long time. He would now finish this Special Day proclamation and set the scene for the time to come.

Before he dismissed his people, the Great Sun said, "I must again mention a special person we have with us today. He came down the Father

188

of Waters from the far northland. He was with us last summer for five moons. He left us and discovered that the water flows into a very large lake—an Endless Ocean. This was his test to become a man of his Eagle Clan of the Rocky River Nation. His name is Dreamer. I command that you treat him well."

"How could he have known I was back here today?"

The Wild One said, "As I have already told you, he knows everything."

. . . .

Dreamer and Little Pup had been back in Cahokia for almost a moon, staying with The Wild One during all that time. Before he left, he planned to repay her generous hospitality.

Before leaving the land down south, Dreamer had collected many Endless Ocean shells. He had watched Morning Dawn's mother make beads, breaking the shells into smaller pieces, and using a flint drill to pierce the center of each piece. After rubbing the rough beads against a piece of stone to make them round, she strung them onto a thin deerskin cord. She made beautiful necklaces.

At his campfires, on his trip up the Great Father of Waters, Dreamer had made beads for his mother. Although his pouch was full of beads, he didn't have enough to make two necklaces, one for his mother and one for the Wild One. He thought about it for a long time.

"I'll make a wristlet for The Wild One," he decided. Earlier he had asked the Wild One for a deerskin string. He then strung thirty beads on the string, each about the size of his thumbnail. Tying a knot at each end of the row of beads, he left tails long enough to tie the bracelet around her wrist. He was pleased with the wristlet.

Last evening, before he went to sleep, Dreamer had checked to see that his belongings were in order. This morning he rolled his deerskin cover tight and tied it with a cord. When he went outside, the Wild One was already there. Dreamer took her hands in his and looking into her brown eyes he bid her farewell. Then he reached into his pouch and retrieved the wristlet he had made for his Cahokia mother.

She couldn't believe the beauty of the thirty, pure-white, matched beads. Dreamer tied the string of beads around her wrist. He stood back with a smile on his face.

"This morning I'll be off, down Cahokia Creek, then up the Father of Waters. Today I will be gone." He told her, "I must return to my home at the spring. I've been away for too long. I give thanks to you, Little Mother, for everything."

He didn't give The Wild One a chance to say anything. He knew she didn't want him to go, but he must.

It was hard on Dreamer, too. During his first stay in the village, and this time, too, he had become attached to his Cahokia mother. She had been good to him, and he would miss her. As a farewell, she handed Dreamer a hurriedly packed deerskin sack of food.

Little Pup and Dreamer were off, down the pathway to Cahokia Creek, to his waiting canoe. Early as it was, Little Turtle was on the path waiting for them. Together, they walked toward the canoe.

. . . .

The Great Sun had heard of Dreamer's pending departure earlier. Little Turtle had told the secret only to the Prophet. Along with the Prophet and the First Shaman, the Great Sun was dressed in his finery, including his headdress of colored eagle feathers and his cape of smaller yellow feathers. The three leaders had hurried to the point on Cahokia Creek where they had been told they would find Dreamer's canoe. Dreamer was surprised, but pleased to see them. Now he was untying his canoe.

The Great Sun Chief congratulated Dreamer and told him how interesting and enlightening his stories of the southland had been. He said that few Cahokians had done what Dreamer had done—gone all the way down the Great Father of Waters to the Endless Ocean. Dreamer had made them more aware of the Great River, both upwater and downwater.

The Great Sun Chief showed Dreamer what the First Shaman had made with the brown-green stone Dreamer had presented to him on his earlier visit. On a cord around his neck was a flat pounded flying bird.

Dreamer said modestly, "I'm glad I gave the stone to you. The six stones I brought with me when I left my spring in the northland some eighteen moons ago have been well spent." He didn't tell the Sun Chief that he still had one left. That would be his secret. He still might need it along the way.

The Prophet, not usually one to be closely involved with the people, rested his hands on Dreamer's shoulders. He told Dreamer that he was a great friend; then reached under his bird feather cape and pulled out a small deerskin pouch. The Prophet poured another ten, perfect, triangular, white arrow points into Dreamer's hand. It was a great send-off gift.

"Thank you," Dreamer said. "I am indebted to you for your kindness. I enjoyed my stay at Cahokia Village. I made many friends. My mother, The Wild One, was as good a mother as a son could have. Thank you for giving her to me."

Dreamer would miss the people of Cahokia. They had all been very good to him.

-17-

Down Cahokia Creek Dreamer paddled. It was so shallow at this time of year that he nearly had to paddle the mud and the sand to make forward progress.

Before long, he reached the Great Father of Waters. The great Muddy River coming in from the west kept him along the eastern shore.

Soon the Great Piasa Bird painted on the high limestone bluff appeared. He wondered again, "How did they do it?" Dreamer wondered how a bird with four legs could fly.

On his second day after leaving Cahokia, he came upon the big river that came in from the north. The current from this river could slow him down, so he headed for the other side where he would make better progress.

After another eight days of all-day paddling Dreamer decided he would put in on the sand beach on the chute side of the next island upstream and spend the night. He was out of food now. He found a big snapper up on the sand and silenced it quickly. A big one had bitten him once, and he knew how painful it could be. He was careful as he used a sharp stick to hold the big turtle upside down and tight to the sandy beach.

Using the glowing red coal his fast-spinning spindle had produced, Dreamer started a fire. He cut a leg from the turtle for Little Pup and cooked the rest over the fire. After he had eaten, he wrapped what was left in a deerskin. It would be his morning meal.

The streams and the rivers he had passed coming down the Great Father of Waters served as landmarks for the homeward journey. He remembered them all. Scratching them on the deerskin map he kept with his bedroll had imprinted them on his memory. He again remarked: "The Father of Waters has so many children."

Soon he would reach the Skunk River, the one he had named after seeing the mother and the little ones playing together. On the sand bar where the Skunk River met the Great Father of Waters, Dreamer would spend his tenth night after leaving Cahokia Village.

Next morning Dreamer finished the last of his turtle meat, but he was still hungry. Then he remembered that less than a day upstream from the Skunk River he would reach the camp of Chief Hawk Eye. "I should be there before Father Sun goes down. It will be good to see Chief Hawk Eye again. He will have something for me to eat."

Surely, they would accept him again. He would tell Little Pup, whom they had not seen, to be friendly to them.

Hawk Eye Creek was on the west side of the river, so he pointed his canoe toward the opening. As before, Chief Hawk Eye and the small Black Hawk Clan were there to welcome him. Dreamer was invited to spend the night.

Later, after an evening meal of fish from the fish trap and nuts from the trees of the grove, Dreamer told stories about the Great Father of Waters, his stay at Cahokia, his trip to the Endless Ocean, and his stay on Deer Island during the short days of the year. He told them he had missed the cold of winter. The people of the Black Hawk Clan didn't understand, for every winter had white snow, as far back as the oldest of the clan could remember. "No," they said. Winter couldn't be warm, it is not possible."

They also couldn't believe the alligator stories, that is, until he showed them the four large teeth.

The people wanted to know where he had found such a friendly dog. He told them about his mother, The Wild One, and that led to more stories that lasted on into the night. He again thanked Chief Hawk Eye for the flint pre-forms. He had used them to great advantage.

Little Pup was growling when Dreamer woke up the next morning. She was not going to let Chief Hawk Eye enter the lodge when her master was still sleeping. Dreamer called, "Little Pup, come here." She quieted down and returned to Dreamer's side. They had both enjoyed a good night's sleep, not having to keep an eye open for trouble. Dreamer spent three, restful nights at Chief Hawk Eye's camp.

Dreamer would thank Chief Hawk Eye with some Endless Ocean beads. He couldn't spare very many, so he chose four beads, and one large shell with two holes in the top. He strung the five on a short cord, with

the shell in the middle, and tied a single knot on each side of the five. It was a sincere token of thanks.

The Chief, especially glad to receive the shell beads from the Endless Ocean, thanked Dreamer. In exchange, he gave Dreamer some maize, jerky, and three more white-flint pre-forms for his thoughtfulness.

. . . .

"In no time I'll be back to my Rocky River. I can see it now: the large cottonwood trees on either side, the giant driftwood log, and, of course, the two eagles' nests. I wonder if the nests will still be there after all this time?" he mused.

Suddenly there they were, the two tall cottonwood trees on each side of his Rocky River and each one still held an eagle's nest at the very top. Dreamer was grateful he had made it this far without a mishap. He paddled toward the trees, coming as close to the east bank of the Father of Waters as he dared. He would never forget how amazed he had been when he saw this new river. He had camped on the north shore of his Rocky River where it met the Great River, now almost nineteen moons ago. He would sleep here again, on the same gravel bar, as he had done those many moons ago.

Camping under the canopy of the giant cottonwood, he would have less dew to contend with the following morning. He could see that one of the eagle's nests was still in use because the mother eagle was resting there. Dreamer and Little Pup were quiet so as not to disturb her.

Near the big log, using the same two trees that had sheltered him before, he made his lean-to. A slight breeze out of the northwest and his deerskin cover protected him from insects, so he slept soundly.

For his morning meal Dreamer went searching for frogs. In the backwater he found three large, dark green ones and two smaller spotted ones. If he wanted to cook his frogs, he must start a fire. His fire-making kit was still in good shape, so he quickly he started his fire, cooked and ate the frog legs, and was on his way. Dreamer gave one last look down the Father of Waters. It had been good to him on his return trip. He was sorry to be leaving the Great River, but glad to be entering his Rocky River, nearly home.

. . . .

Dreamer was now on the last leg of his journey. How many days had it taken him to walk down to this point, so long ago? Was it seven, eight, nine? However long it had taken, he knew that even paddling against the current should take him less time to go up his river. This morning he started out with an air of exuberance.

He was now paddling east, up his Rocky River, almost directly into the morning sun. He looked longingly at the swamplands on the left and on the right, but he didn't want to get involved in any side trips today. This lower part of the Rock River was wide until it began to narrow where the tall evergreens began on either side. He should reach the big double-curve, with the big sandstone bluffs, soon.

He paddled hard towards an opening in the bank of his Rocky River where he could see a little stirring in the backwater. "Yes, Little Pup, we'll have fish for our noon meal."

Quietly, softly, and slowly, he paddled his canoe around the edge of the little cove, letting the wind push him along so he could catch a fish unaware. It worked. Quickly, he drove his sharp forked stick through a good-sized, bigmouth fish.

Starting a new fire, he dressed out the fish, wrapped it in big leaves, and laid it on the fire. It didn't take long to cook. Even after sharing it with Little Pup, he had some fish left over for their evening meal. Soon they were on their way again.

. . . .

Today he could see the tall sandstone bluffs on either side of the "Grand Detour" looming ahead. He had thought a lot about how the water found its way through the sandstone. It had to have started much higher and taken many moons to wear its path through the soft stone.

Two days later they were at the next sandstone bluff on the west side of his Rocky River, the one Wing Feather had traveled to, so many moons ago. He would spend the night here, as he had done almost nineteen moons ago.

Dreamer eased into the one safe landing place, then hid his canoe under the treacherous overhanging roots and tied it securely. He almost sent Little Pup on ahead, but he remembered that if he twisted his ankle or broke his leg in the roots again, he might need her to rescue him. "Little Pup, stay with me," he said.

Up, up, he climbed once again. At the top, with all his belongings and knowing his canoe was secure below, he and Little Pup would settle in for the night.

Here, earlier, on his trip downwater, he had scratched a three-day map on the sandstone wall. He saw that no one had added any scratches to his map. He thought the map was a feeble effort, only a start, now that he had been so far.

That's why at Cahokia he started his first deerskin map. He had scratched the line of the Great Father of Waters on it, adding a little each day. When he reached the Ohoho River, he had already come to the bottom of the deerskin, but he turned it over and continued his river line on the rough side. His map was then on both sides of the deerskin.

After he had reached the Endless Ocean, he had bartered several arrow points for a new deerskin. On this, he reduced the map size even further, with his spring at the top and the Endless Ocean at the bottom. He had put the village of Cahokia about one-third down. There he had made the Sun Clock look like a circle of upright lines. On his good map, he had used the sharp point of the shark's tooth. Later he had rubbed the charcoal stick into the cuts on the deerskin to make them stand out. He was quite satisfied with the finished map. When he unrolled his night cover, he again took out the deerskin map. He scratched another little 'X' on the map at the point of this sandstone bluff. It would further remind him of his earlier effort.

Looking at his old sandstone map on the wall, he saw that it was only a start. With his finger pointing, he said, "Am I really this close to home?"

Dreamer and Little Pup spent the night in the same sandstone bowl on the riverside of the great bluff. They would leave early in the morning, knowing that they would be arriving at his creek in three or four more days. He was anxious to go up his creek, then the brook to his spring. Then he would be home at last!

He paddled hard those last three days. At last he came to a sandy beach he recognized. He had walked on this same beach when he had taken his one-day trip to the Rocky River. The memory of Wing Feather's camp on the bluff remained in his mind. He could never forget the place where his very own little creek met his big Rocky River.

Now Father Sun was nearly down in the west. Wing Feather's camp was only a short way up the little creek. He was nearly home, but he knew he couldn't make it today. He would go up the creek and then hail the camp of Wing Feather, spending his last night with him, just as he had spent his first night there nineteen moons ago. "And, I might even see Bright Spirit, if I'm lucky," he thought to himself.

The people of the Bluff Clan saw Dreamer first and called to him as they came down the steep path to meet him. He was waiting by his canoe, which he had already pulled out of the water and onto the big, flat rock at the bottom of the path. He secured it to a small bush growing out of a crack in the rock. It would be safe.

He had his pack with the night bedroll, his bow and quiver, his pouch with all his precious belongings, and Little Pup at his side. He stood straight waiting for Wing Feather. "Dreamer, Dreamer, you're back—you've grown!" Wing Feather exclaimed.

"Yes, and after nineteen moons away, I have lots of stories to tell, but they must come later. Now I'm hungry and very tired. Can we spend the night with you? Little Pup, my friend, companion and life-saver, will cause no trouble," Dreamer answered.

"Of course. But, do you want me to send a night runner to your family by the spring and tell them you have returned?"

"Oh, no—no, don't do that. After I've eaten and had a good night's sleep, then I'll see them tomorrow. I don't want to tease them by letting them know I'm just a half-a-day away."

Bright Spirit was right behind Wing Feather. She held out her hand to Dreamer. He squeezed it, which no one else could see. She cast a pleasant half-smile at Dreamer. Of course, he returned it.

Questions came at him from all sides, but he told them he would tell of his journey when all were gathered together around the evening campfire, after they had eaten.

"After ten or twelve days down the Rocky River, I came to the Great Father of Waters. I made a raft and floated down the Great River to Cahokia, and that took me almost a moon's time. I stayed there a little over five moons, enjoying every day of it. I continued down the Great Father of Waters, but about a moons' time later, in a great rainstorm, I broke my leg climbing up a riverbank. A boy from the southland found me and took care of me. Two moons later, after my leg had healed, he and I continued down the river in his canoe. We eventually reached the Endless Ocean, a huge, salty lake with no other side. I found out that's where the water from our creek flows. I found the answer to the question in my dream.

Down His River of Dreams ...

"I stayed with my new friend on a little island in the Endless Ocean for another five moons, then came back up the Great River, back to home. Now, I must sleep. I'll tell you more in the morning," yawned Dreamer.

. . . .

"Why did you let me sleep so late? My family must be wondering about me. I want to surprise them by getting home today. I must go."

Dreamer hurried down the steep path that led from the bluff. Untying the rope, he slid his canoe into the water, pausing to thank Wing Feather and Tail Feather for their kindness. Now he saw Bright Spirit and gave her a special look as he waved to the clan. They all waved until he was out of sight.

-18-

Little Pup and Dreamer would be home today. It had been such a long time since he had seen his family, and he had so much to tell them. What if they were away and he came home to an empty camp? Shaking off that worry, he resolutely paddled on.

He passed the big oak trees that grew at the water's edge, then slid his canoe across a couple of downed trees and and pulled it over a new beaver dam that hadn't been there when he left home.

When Dreamer finally reached the brook, he pulled his canoe between two bushes, then walked quickly up the path beside the brook, relieved to see that the path was well worn; his family still lived by the spring. Hurrying anxiously, he came to the small clearing with his spring at the center, just as he remembered it. "Little Pup, I'm finally back home," he whispered.

There beside the spring, he knelt and raised both arms to honor the Great Father Sun above with a prayer: "Thank you, Great Father Sun for seeing me safely home. Thanks for letting me find the answer to the question in my dream. I will give thanks to you often, remembering that you have been good to me."

Little Pup followed her master to the spring, both feet up on a boulder, she lapped up some of the clean, clear, cold spring water.

Dreamer's mother saw him first. "He's back, he's back, Dreamer's home!" she cried loudly. All the family came running. When his sister jumped at Dreamer to embrace him, they both fell down, They both were laughing and talking at the same time, his little brothers watching quietly.

"It is good to be home." Dreamer said happily. "Oh, and yes, you must know, I found the answer to the question in my dream–I know where the water goes."

His mother and father silently embraced their son for a long time, each thanking the Great Father Sun in their own way, for allowing their family to be together again.

They all asked questions at once, but Dreamer said, "Tomorrow morning I'll tell my story. Today I want just to sit and enjoy the camp. I'm home at last and I don't have to rush anymore. Tomorrow we can go over to the Powwow place in the Great Forest at the Council Grove, and I can tell my story to everyone at once.

"Father, can you gather the people of the clans tomorrow? Right now I'm very tired."

Dreamer rested most of the day, then slept deeply that night. Little Pup was at his side. Finally, without keeping one eye open and one ear listening, they slept safe in the family lodge..

. . . .

The next morning, at the Council Grove, Dreamer began: "I have returned the totem. Thank you for letting me take it. It protected me on my journey down the Rocky River, then down the Great Father of Waters, finally to the Endless Ocean. After nineteen moons I am home at last. That is my story."

The crowd buzzed questioningly. Is that all?

After a long pause, Dreamer continued: "The current of the 'Great Father of Waters' carried me to my destiny. Our spring water goes into an endless, salty ocean that has no other side. I know because I saw it with my own eyes."

Dreamer, smiling at his friend, continued, "Little Beaver Tail, I want you to know that the river does not go into a hole in the ground after all. You said that it did. You said I would never return. Well, here I am.

"My father and mother and the elders gave me good advice before I left, so I made the trip without too many problems. I did have one accident along the way, during a rainstorm, when I was careless. During that mighty storm, I was climbing a bank when I slipped and tangled my right leg in some roots and I broke it. I had to crawl to a dry rock shelter and send Little Pup searching for food. She returned with a stranger, a boy who pulled my leg back into position, bound it, and took care of me for two moons while it healed. My new friend rubbed healing herbs on my leg. He found and fixed food for me, and we became good friends—but, wait, that's getting ahead of my story."

Dreamer had been telling his story now for almost half a day, standing on a small mound so he could be seen above the heads of the many people from the outlying clans who had all brought their children to this important event.

Dreamer told the crowd about the Great Star, that shone even in the daylight. They remarked that they had seen it, too. He told them about the clock of wooden posts built by the all-seeing Prophet. "It was comp[leted when I was in Cahokia. All forty-nine posts were upright and casting their shadows–it was quite an impressive structure"

As the long day wore on, there were doubts among some of Dreamer's listeners about his colorful descriptions of the "big lizard." The 'gator, as it was called, wasn't afraid of anyone. It stood its ground and hissed. "Its big mouth could take an arm off with one bite, and it was longer than two men lying head to head." When he showed his listeners, the two pair of long alligator teeth and the large triangular shark's tooth, so sharp it could cut a finger, they had to believe his stories of strange fish and reptiles.

Dreamer told of the long trip down the Rocky River, then the even longer trip down the Father of all Waters, and of his stops and experiences along the way. He told them about Cahokia, about his foster mother, gathering turtles and the turtle pen, the dogs, and the games he played with the other boys. He described his experiences with Chips, the arrowhead-maker. His listeners were spellbound. With Little Pup at his side, he showed his listeners the beautiful Cahokia arrow point that had been given to him by Chips and he also showed them the small, white flint, alligator effigy.

He had a smile on his face when he told of the mischievous boys who had stolen his friend's dugout canoe and how he had retrieved it by throwing the big hornet's nest at them.

The gathered listeners struggled to comprehend that the Endless Ocean had no other side. They could hardly believe the water tasted of salt. Salt to them was hard to acquire; a valuable trade item. He showed the group the giant oyster shell and also told them that he had learned how to swim in the Endless Ocean. He told them how different the ocean fish and the shells were from their Rocky River cousins. When he passed some shells around, they exclaimed that they had never seen shells so beautiful. "And, oh, yes there was no white flint for arrow points down at the Endless Ocean. The people had to trade for their flint from upriver.

"There were big-mouth, large, slow-flying birds, larger than eagles and they called them pelicans. They flew in formation along the beach, the largest usually the leader. The last one in the line was always trying to catch up—they were my very favorite bird. I watched them all day long. Some large birds with long legs and red heads are this tall," he said, holding his hand out. "The doves flew in flocks, that darkened the sky." He described birds with yellow and green heads; white, brown, blue, and black birds, especially the little black coot, with its red head.

The people were puzzled when he described the water and waves of the Endless Ocean: "The waves splashed against my feet and legs. As the larger waves went back out, the water washed the sand from under my feet. I felt as if I were sinking into the beach.

Dreamer told of the long portage, of coming back up the Father of Waters, of the bird with four legs that was painted on the bluff, of the eagles at the mouth of the Rocky River, of seeing familiar landmarks and especially his family's campsite which looked the same as it had the day he left. The warm feeling in his chest when his sister came into view, confirmed that he was really home at last, after nineteen moons away.

. . . .

The lessons dreamer had learned on his long and eventful journey served him well as he grew into his role as a leader. Later at the Powwow the elders unanimously declared him a man of the Nation, renaming him Wise Eagle, at his father's suggestion. His new status as an adult of the Eagle Clan meant that the time had come for Wise Eagle to be given a mate.

He held his breath as his father announced that Bright Spirit had been selected to be his partner for life. Unknown to Wise Eagle, this arrangement had been finalized many moons ago between Flowing Spring, of the Eagle Clan, and Wing Feather, of the Bluff Clan. Wise Eagle was very happy.

Bright Spirit's mother instructed her daughter about becoming Wise Eagle's mate and the mother of his children. The two young people's wrists were tied together with a sinew, the bond to remain for four days, sealing the vows of their fathers. Once the young couple had made the rounds of the camp, thanking all those who had assisted them, they retired to the mating lodge. There they would be granted privacy for one moon. Their guests celebrated late into the night, eating and dancing around the fire, while the young couple slept in each other's arms for the first time.

. . . .

Soon after the ceremony, while Wise Eagle and Bright Spirit were still secluded in their mating lodge, Flowing Spring suddenly became sick, hot with fever and unable to eat. Concerned clan members came to visit him and to offer advice, but soon Flowing Spring was unable to sit by the campfire. In the time of half-a-moon, he was gone, passing peacefully in his sleep. Because his death was not a heroic one—a life lost in battle—his burial was a quiet event. There were few in attendance. Clan members laid Flowing Spring to rest with all the items he would need on his journey through the darkness to the Great Beyond, remembering him generously as they honored him.

When Wise Eagle recovered from the shock of his father's sudden death, he asked Wing Feather, "Who will lead the clan and the Nation now?

The older man confided that, during the young couple's solitude in the mating lodge, Flowing Spring and the elders had discussed the succession. Now they had a proposition for young Wise Eagle.

"Of all the men of the Nation, you have the most experience in the wide world. You have shown wisdom and courage beyond your years. Speaking for all of our clan and the Nation, I have been chosen to tell you that we want you to take your father's position," said Wing Feather.

Wise Eagle was speechless. Finally, recovering enough to ask, "Are you sure? I have so much to learn. I am still very young."

Wing Feather smiled. "You have your father's example before you and you have earned our respect in your own right. We will all support you and help you in any way that we can. What do you think?"

Wise Eagle considered for a moment, took a deep breath, and answered quietly, "In memory of my father and in honor of all our people, I will do my very best to lead the twenty-two clans of the Rocky River Nation." Then he added, "With your help, of course I will accept."

Bright Spirit found events moving very fast, but she supported Wise Eagle as she had been taught to do. Always practical, she busied herself helping her partner to plan and build their own lodge. They built their lodge on a site overlooking the Rocky River, the River of Dreams that was the beginning Wise Eagle's life for nineteen moons. Once the outside fire pit was dug on the riverside, the campsite was finished.

In less than a year Wise Eagle and Bright Spirit had a son whom they named Little Red Feather. Another son and then a daughter followed in quick succession, and their family was complete.

. . . .

In addition to the daily responsibilities of finding food and caring for his family and his regular duties as leader of the Nation, Wise Eagle wished to commemorate his journey downwater. He decided to build a monument to the alligator he had met in the southland. It was one of his most vivid memories of his trip. He would build it on the west bank of his Rocky River.

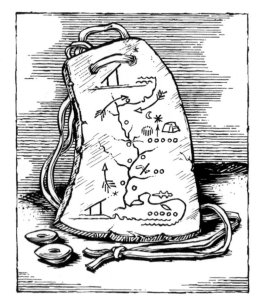

On the first free workday, a large group gathered at the south side of the Hallowed Ground, the site that Wise Eagle had selected for his monument. As he showed them the four long, 'gator teeth, some jumped back. To help them further envision the project, Wise Eagle passed around the little flint alligator. The group enjoyed working together, painstakingly creating the large alligator monument which was to last forever.

In addition to the alligator monument, Wise Eagle eventually found time to transfer the now-faded deerskin map of his journey to a more permanent medium. He used a sharp flint to scratch a small map of the events of his trip onto the large shell fragment he had brought home from

Shell Beach. Sometimes, he found himself gazing into the clouds, remembering the Rocky River passage and his long journey down the Father of Waters. He didn't want to forget anything.

On his shell map he scratched symbols for the bright star, the sun clock, the Sun Chief's mound, his broken leg, the Endless Ocean, and of course, the alligator. Working with his back to the giant oak overlooking the river, he also scratched all nineteen moons on the shell. To finish it off he included the pole star sighting posts, one for a north and one for a south.

When he had finished the shell map to his satisfaction, Wise Eagle drilled two holes in the top for a deerskin thong. "I'll wear my map around my neck," he thought. "It will be my 'mark.' It will remind me to tell my stories correctly. With this amulet, I can carry my journey with me forever."

He was very pleased with himself.

. . . .

For many years, Life was good for Wise Eagle, his family, his clan and the Nation. Now he had now lived as high chief in the lodge on the west bank of the Rock River for seventeen summers.

However, lately there had been little rainfall, and the river was very low. What little rain fell was accompanied by violent lightning, which often started grass fires on the prairies to the west. The alternating drought and fires devastated the wildlife, and food became increasingly scarce.

The neighbors to the west, the Pecatonica Nation, came east looking for food. Their desperation and their search for food in the territory of the Rocky River Nation resulted in a conflict that lasted for twelve moons. The weather gradually righted itself, and all seemed well for a time.

However, Wise Eagle, wounded in the Rocky River battle of early spring, began to suffer increasing pain. Although his older son, Little Red Feather, had tried to remove the arrow lodged in his father's spine, the sharp, fine tip of the arrow had broken off, embedding itself in the bone. Although the wound had healed on the outside, the pain in Wise Eagle's back grew more and more intense. Bright Spirit did her best to keep her mate comfortable, but it was clear that his health was failing.

Wise Eagle sensed that he might not survive his wound. He was determined that he must make a decision about who would follow him as leader of the Nation. After much thought, he selected his son, Little Red Feather, now almost sixteen summers old. From his resting place he spent many hours and most of his energy instructing his son about leadership, just as his own father had taught him.

When the fall Powwow was called, Wise Eagle was too weak to attend. Instead, it was Wing Feather who recommended that Little Red Feather be acknowledged as a man of the nation and renamed accordingly. After much discussion, the elders agreed to name the son after the father: Wise Eagle, in honor of his father's leadership and as a token of support for the new young chief, who would take his father's place.

When the younger Wise Eagle reported these decisions, his father smiled weakly, saying, "My son, I am pleased that you will continue my name, and I believe you are ready to take on the leadership of the Nation. Remember all I have taught you and let Wing Feather and the other wise elders be your constant guides. I know you will make us all proud."

Just days later, Wise Eagle, the father, who had seen thirty summers and many adventures, died peacefully in his sleep. His son and the elders agreed that burial should be near his alligator mound in the Hallowed Ground near the Rocky River, as he had requested.

The people of the clan dug a depression near the riverbank. They lined the burial cavity with blue clay. Bright Spirit had carefully gathered grave goods to be placed with her mate's body. She selected his best orangewood bow and his quiver of arrows, one for each of the years they had been together. Reverently, she and her son positioned the quiver diagonally beneath the body, the arrow notches at his right shoulder, his bow along his left side.

In his Cahokia pot, she put his treasures: the four alligator teeth, the shark's tooth, the beautiful, clear, quartz crystal he had acquired from the White River Clan, and the galena cube his father had given him. The bones of Wise Eagle's beloved Little Pup, who had died some five summers earlier, were placed in a pot near her master's feet. They would be together in the Land Beyond the Clouds.

Finally, items precious to Wise Eagle were ceremoniously placed upon his body. His black chunky stone in its deerskin pouch was placed at his right hip, as was his sharp, flint scout knife; the white shell bead and turquoise pendant necklace that he had given Bright Spirit was draped across his vest; his white, three-notched, Cahokia arrow point and his last piece of copper ore completed the adornment.

As the shadow of the upright post touched the smaller marker post, Wise Eagle the son, stepped before the crowd gathered for the farewell ceremony. Their new young chief eulogized his father by recounting his father's early adventures down the river and back, and his long and successful leadership of their clan and nation. The silent crowd stood mourning their fallen leader.

The last gesture of the son was especially significant, for he gently placed Wise Eagle's pure white shell amulet under his father's folded hands.

Several of the elders then sealed the body with blue clay, and the three children—Wise Eagle, Little Two Feathers, and Little Red Flower—scattered white, blue, red, and yellow wildflowers over the clay. Soil was then spread over the body, the people walking quietly in slow circles, tamping it down until it was smooth. Layer after layer was spread and tamped, the completed mound taller than Wise Eagle, to honor the memorable chief who had become a man by courageously journeying alone, down his River of Dreams, to reach the Endless Ocean. It was there that he found the answer to the question in his dream.

AFTERWORD

Professor Daniel Norman was able to report some good news to his class. His request for a Carbon-14 dating from the University of Chicago had been given top priority. The results were back in time for his summer-session class to review them.

"The results will surprise you," he told them. "They fit into the scheme of time as I hoped they would. In fact, I believe they help confirm what I thought the old Indian was trying to tell us; of course, that is, if he was really trying to tell us anything at all. Perhaps he was just recording important events of his lifetime, ones that had to be recorded so they would not be lost in the retelling of his story over time."

"What do you think he was he trying to tell us?" One of the students asked.

"Well, first of all, let's confirm the time of his death," Dr. Norman said, explaining that Carbon-14, the radioactive isotope of carbon, has a half-life of approximately 5,600 years, meaning that after 5,600 years, there will be only half as much radioactivity left as there was at the beginning. "When an organism is alive, the supply of C-14 remains constant," he told them. "However, when our old Indian died, C-14 ceased to enter his body, and what was in his body began to decay at a steady rate into Carbon 12.

"The scientists have checked the amount of C-14 remaining in the bones of our Beattie Park Indian. Although the test is not perfect, it does allow us to estimate the age of the bones, which in turn allows us to determine when our Indian lived—and, of course, when he died.

"The test shows that he died sometime around 950 years ago, or about 1050 A.D. Since the dating is not perfect, we are in a window of 50 years on either side of that date. I do believe that general date is quite important though, considering the shell amulet we found buried with him. I believe the shell really tells his story—and what a story it is.

"He was, I believe, a traveler beyond all expectations. He was also a story teller who actually recorded his travels. Students, what we have found is quite extraordinary, and almost beyond belief. Each of you should be proud that you were a part of the excavation. I believe the amulet is the recording of a series of events in time. Of course, his amulet only tells us part of the story. I have photographed it, enlarged it, and then made a line drawing of it so that you can see the details clearly." With that, Dr. Norman handed out a drawing of the picture on the amulet.

The professor continued, "Seldom can we date something so old in American prehistory with such pinpoint accuracy, but I believe we can safely say that our Indian was at the Village of Cahokia in the year 1054 A.D."

One of the students questioned, "But, Professor Norman, how can you be so certain? You just told us that Carbon-14 dating only gives a general dating."

"That's correct, but did you look carefully at the scratching, or, perhaps I should say, the 'picture' on the amulet? Our amulet is an enigma. It is both unique—being explanatory—and baffling. It is a record: picture-writing from the eleventh century on part of a salt-water clamshell from the Gulf of Mexico. It is 'written' history, in a time and at a place where no written language existed."

The class was quiet for a long time, looking at the drawing of the amulet. Professor Norman wanted the students to "read" the picture-story themselves.

After a long silence, he dismissed them, instructing them to write the story of the Native American as they read it from the amulet and from the other artifacts found in the mound. They were to bring their versions back to class on Thursday. No, he wouldn't give them any clues today. He wanted them to do some thinking on their own, perhaps some research, and then some writing. "Thursday I want you to tell me the story. Then, I'll tell you the story as I have read it. Maybe with our combined efforts we'll have the exact story of the old Beattie Park Indian, or, at least one as accurate as we can possibly have."

On Thursday all of students arrived early, each with their assignment complete. Most seemed quite satisfied with their effort. After they quieted down, Dr. Norman asked if they had made any discoveries in their research and the interpretation of the amulet. Their Professor was disappointed. Although they all had different stories, every one of them had missed the main clue on the amulet.

Dr. Norman told them what he had gleaned from the amulet found in the burial mound of the old Native American.

"See the crescent moon and the bright star?" Dr Norman asked them.

Down His River of Dreams ...

"Yes. What do they mean?" one of the students in the front row asked.

"I believe they are the most important clues on the amulet," Dr. Norman said. "They set the time of a recorded event in history. If you look closely, you will see the crescent moon and star are next to what looks like an upright circle of sticks and a tall mound, in all probability, Cahokia Woodhenge and Monks Mound, as we call them today. So, we have a time, a place, and an event, and that's quite astounding, coming from a Native American artifact that's almost a thousand years old.

"Of course you know we can date an old Roman coin to the exact year it was made, even if it is over *two* thousand years old, because the Romans had a written language. The Native Americans living in the United States, even half as long ago, were still in the Stone Age. They had no written language. We have to interpret their history as best we can from the articles or artifacts we find."

Continuing, the professor expounded: "The Chinese, like the Romans, also had a written language, and they recorded, in great detail, the observation of a supernova on the other side of the world. It was on July 4, 1054 A.D., that an exploding star, six times brighter than the brightest star, could be seen in the daytime. In fact, they reported that it could be seen for more than 23 days. That same explosion would have been seen on July 5th in Cahokia. When first observed, it was below and a little to the right of the crescent moon, just as the amulet depicts. So, by deduction, and especially since finding the Cahokia arrow point with him, I believe we can safely say that our Native American was in the village of Cahokia in July of the year 1054 A.D."

A murmur came from the class, and one of the students said, "That is amazing, and surely it must be true, for the amulet shows it—proves it."

"That really is amazing," another student whispered.

Dr. Norman further explained that the same supernova scene was depicted on a sandstone wall in Chaco Canyon in New Mexico, probably by an Anasazi Indian artist. There it was a star with 23 rays. Of course, there it couldn't be dated, but logically it had to be the same event witnessed and recorded by another Native American. He told the students that the location of that fading star today is in the constellation Taurus, near the Pleiades, and what remains of that supernova today is a faint smudge, known as the Crab Nebula.

Dr. Norman continued, telling the students, "It takes many disciplines working together to interpret what may seem like a simple detail, but when

210

all the pieces come together, if we are all correct, then we'll have the answer to the scratching on the amulet. Yes, I believe the amulet tells us quite a story."

Reviewing the homework and considering certain details of the twelve students' interpretations of the amulet, the story of the old Indian began to materialize.

Dr. Norman continued, "The amulet is the map of our Indian's journey starting right here in Rockford, Illinois. He went down the Rock River, then down the Mississippi, to the Village of Cahokia. There he spent the summer. That's no doubt where he picked up the fragile Cahokia arrow points. That's also where he saw the bright star, the supernova of 1054. Our Indian then continued down the Father of Waters to the Gulf of Mexico, where he spent a period of five moons. See them on the amulet? Count them.

"How do we know that he was at the Gulf?" Dr. Norman queried the students.

All were quiet, so he answered his own question. "See the two triangles inscribed on the amulet? If we interpret them in their proper context, I believe they give the answer.

"The top triangle is at Rockford on the amulet, and it has an acute angle of about 40 degrees. The angle from the horizon pointing to the North Star today would be the same as it was a thousand years ago. The triangle at the bottom of the amulet gives an angle of about 30 degrees. That's very close to the latitude of the Gulf. Our Native American had to have sighted on the same star, the pole star, when he was at the Gulf. When he was there, of course, it was very dim and much lower, only 30 degrees above the horizon. Also, look at the line of the river on his 'map.' It ends at a wide expanse of water, so it must be the Gulf.

"He also had to have seen alligators when he was at the Gulf because one is shown on his amulet. See, it's down by the Gulf and drawn in a stick form. Also, remember, we found alligator teeth buried with him. Yes, those four large teeth in the little black pot were alligator teeth. A friend of mine at the Chicago Museum of Natural History identified them for us. Of course, they must have come from a more tropical area, for there are no natural alligators in Rockford—not now, nor a thousand years ago.

"The alligator effigy mound in Beattie Park must certainly have been built by our Native American. He must have been inspired and impressed at the sight of so unusual an animal, a creature he could not forget. It's not a lizard mound as we have thought all these years; it's an alligator mound, and our Indian must have built it. I also believe the flint alligator effigy we found in his little pot further reinforces that theory.

"The amulet, though, really tells the story of his journey. It shows that he went down the Rock River to the Mississippi, then down the Mississippi to the Gulf. In all, it shows he spent nineteen moons away from home. See, count them: one to get to Cahokia, five moons at Cahokia, then another four to get to the Gulf. During two of those moons he was recovering from a broken leg. Then he spent five moons at the Gulf. Coming back up the rivers to home, took another four moons and one of those was also spent at Cahokia. Yes, his trip lasted nineteen moons. That would be about 18 months as we tell time today. What a trip it must have been. He must have had a dog with him, too, because the small bones in the pot at his feet contained dog bones.

"Our Native American was the explorer of his time. His amulet proves it. He was a 'North and South,' Lewis and Clark, all wrapped up in one, only 750 years earlier. I can imagine that his senses were acute, his memory never failing and he knew nature like the back of his hand—just like Henry David Thoreau, who followed him some seven centuries later. Yes, he was a dreamer, a scout, a naturalist and a visionary of his time. He started as a boy—a student, and returned as a man—a teacher.

"The rest of the story comes together by adding all the items that we found buried with our Beattie Park Indian. There were so many. Look at the giant oyster shell. We know it came from the Gulf, as did the shark's tooth.

"According to his physical remains, we can also tell that our Indian had an accident on his journey down the river. He had broken his right leg when he was quite young, and it was a bad break, although it healed quite satisfactorily. The amulet shows that he broke his leg somewhere between Cahokia and the Gulf. The Cahokia point from Illinois, the Arkansas quartz crystal, and the shell beads with the small piece of turquoise from the Southwest, the lump of pure copper—probably from northern Minnesota—and the crystal of galena ore, all found with the burial, are indications that he traveled far, or at least, traded wisely. The black chunky stone, and the seventeen hunting points under him must also have significance.

"We can't tell his story exactly, and we don't even know what he looked like. But, from his remains, we do know that he was tall for a man of his time. We know the cause of death, because we found the tip of an arrow point broken off in one of his lumbar vertebra, and the bone showed no signs of healing. From his teeth and bones, we can estimate that he was about 30 years old when he died. He must have been a lad of twelve or thirteen summers when he was in Cahokia, just the age I was when I was in the Boy Scouts. He was probably passing his test to become a man of his nation. From all we have found, we must assume our Indian was a very special Indian, a one of a kind—ahead of his time—and a truly great, wise, traveled individual. I think our Native American could safely be called The First American Boy Scout. He certainly was a wise eagle scout."

. . . .

Professor Daniel Norman, Archaeology Professor at Rockford College, ended the summer session with great satisfaction. He knew that he and his students had made a significant discovery in the mound they had excavated in Beattie Park, along the west bank of the Rock River, in downtown Rockford. He told them that everyone would receive a top grade for the session. He told them that he had kept the modern Nebraska Winnebago informed of progress along the way.

The dig was certainly worthy of reporting in a paper he would present at this winter's Annual Central States Archaeological Conference in Chicago. In fact, Dr. Norman knew it would be the outstanding discovery of the year and certainly the high point of the conference. He already knew it was the zenith of his career.

Professor Norman wished there had been a written language in America back in the eleventh century. He knew there was much more of the story to be told. He was satisfied, however, that the past could be saved. The artifacts must be preserved and the information from the dig must be shared. He planned to preserve the story—and the artifacts, too, if the modern Winnebago would allow it, by depositing them in the Burpee Museum, on the right bank of the Rock River, a short way upstream from Beattie Park. There the story, and the artifacts fifty generations old, would be available for all the generations to come. "We are saving the past for the future," he told the class.

The professional report along with copies of photographs would be given to the Winnebago Native Americans. They had wanted to know what kind of stories the mound of their ancestor could tell: who was he? How long ago was he buried? What was the cause of death? How old was he at the time of death? What grave goods were buried with him? Did he have any health problems? What did he do during his lifetime? Did he travel far?

213

These moderns had allowed a scientific study of the remains. Now Dr. Norman could tell them all about their ancestor.

There were twenty modern Winnebago on the site and the reburial went well. In a solemn ceremony, the old Winnebago Indian, Wise Eagle, who had remained undisturbed for nearly 950 years, was again laid to rest in the "Hallowed Ground" of Mother Earth, alongside his alligator mound, in Beattie Park, along the west bank of his Rock River, in Rockford, Illinois.

This time it would be for good.

Author's Note:

This book was written to let young adults know that almost anything is possible. It is historic fiction, but there is also much reality contained within it.

The story indicates that preparation for a journey is important. One must have a plan—a map—and one must follow that map to the ultimate destination, to the goal. Then, after the journey is complete, with the knowledge learned, one must enlighten others as to the possibilities that lie ahead.

"Down His River of Dreams" is a "must read" for every Boy Scout, and for anyone else, young or old who likes adventure or has a dream to be fulfilled. The book would be a welcome present for any young adult.

Further information on the artist and the book may be obtained from his website: www.danwiemer.com.

This book is available at Trafford's Bookstore at Trafford.com, or through Trafford's toll-free number: 1-888-232-4444.

It is also available by direct purchase from the author: David L. Wiemer—DreamCo, at 733 Canberra Rd, Winter Haven, FL 33884-1210, or toll-free at 1-866-312-2234. Book cost is $19.00. Package, and mailing is an additional $4.00 for the first book and $1.00 for each additional book. FL residents add state tax of $1.00.

DLW

Printed in the United States
By Bookmasters